A MURDER OF CROWS

A
MURDER
OF CROWS

Jan Dunlap

NORTH STAR PRESS OF ST. CLOUD, INC.
Saint Cloud, Minnesota

First Edition: September 2012

Printed in the United States of America

Published by
North Star Press of St. Cloud, Inc.
P.O. Box 451
St. Cloud, Minnesota 56302

www.northstarpress.com

www.northstarpress.com   Facebook - North Star Press

A Murder of Crows

CHAPTER ONE

I HATE SCARECROWS.

They creep me out.

Oddly angled arms, dangling hands, shirts stuffed with straw and stuck up on a pole out in a cornfield. If I were a crow, they'd scare the bejeebers out of me. As it is, being a human, I still wouldn't want to meet one in a dark alley, even though I know they're just lifeless dummies with permanent bad-hair days. Heck, I'd rather not even see them in a cornfield in the bright sunlight.

As far as I'm concerned, scarecrows are second in creepiness only to clowns.

In fact, the worst day of my life was the day my kindergarten class went on a field trip to Emma Krumbee's Apple Orchard just outside of Jordan, Minnesota, to pick apples. The apples were great —believe me, nothing tastes better than fresh apples right off the tree in the crisp days of autumn. But what was not so great was that Emma's had a display of scarecrows for the harvest season, and our teacher, Mrs. Meyers, shepherded us right through the middle of it to get to the apple trees.

Talk about spooky. Not only were there Frankenstein and vampire scarecrows, but straw-filled contorted body shapes wearing doctor and nurse uniforms, complete with scalpels and knee hammers. Throw in a pair of scarecrows dressed in high school letter jackets and it could have passed for the set of a teen slasher movie. The most horrifying moment, though, was when I happened to find myself looking up at a leering clown face painted on a pumpkin head perched atop an over-stuffed tuxedo, and every nightmare I'd ever had of white-faced scary clowns with mops of maniac hair came roaring back at me.

My classmates may never know how close they came to wearing my breakfast of Honey-nut Os and strawberry Pop-tarts.

I clapped a hand over my eyes and grabbed the back of the jacket of the kid in front of me. I was done. No way was I looking at any more scarecrows. I figured my classmate could just tow me blind to the apples, but he ratted me out.

"Bobby White's pulling on my jacket," the rat squealed to Mrs. Meyers. "Make him stop!"

I felt Mrs. Meyers gently prying my fingers off the kid's coat and taking my cold hand in her warm one. I slid a glance at her through my fingers.

"I don't want to see the scarecrows," I whispered, afraid that the clown would overhear and exact a bloody and gruesome vengeance on me. "They look like dead people."

"No, they don't," she assured me.

"Yes, they do," I whispered louder, the fine hairs on the back of my neck prickling as I imagined the clown's gloved hand reaching for me.

Mrs. Meyers smiled her brightest smile and leaned down to give me a hug.

"No, Bobby, they don't," she gently insisted. "But if you're frightened, just stick with me, okay?"

No problem. I stuck to her like super glue all the way to the apples. It's a wonder she could even walk with me wrapped around her left leg.

But now I know for sure that she was wrong.

Scarecrows can not only resemble dead people, but they can look *exactly* like a dead person.

Because I found one scarecrow that was.

A scarecrow that was a dead person, I mean.

Baby Lou was strapped to my chest in the forward-facing carrier thing that Luce and I had given to my sister, Lily, and her husband, Alan, when Lou was born in June. It was a perfect October morning, and since I'd promised to babysit my niece—it's Louise, actually—for the day, I figured it was high time she started her life list of birds, so we'd buckled Lou into her car seat and driven out to the Minnesota Landscape Arboretum in Chanhassen to stroll the trails and see what late migrants we might find.

The fact that it was also a weekend during the Arboretum's annual scarecrow display had, unfortunately, escaped me, but as my lovely wife reminded me, we didn't have to walk where the display was set up around the Visitor Center. Instead, we'd taken Three Mile Drive to a parking area near the restored prairie, and set off on a walk that wound through chest-high golden grasses and into a multi-hued forest of turning leaves.

"She's falling asleep," Luce said, nodding at Baby Lou on my chest.

I glanced down at the fine mop of black hair that crowned my niece's head.

"My fault," I said. "I promised her a rarity to start her list, like that Ferruginous Hawk that was spotted yesterday out in Stevens County, and all we've seen so far are your everyday Canada Geese and Wild Turkeys. I haven't been this bored myself since the back-to-school faculty meeting in August."

"Good morning," Luce said in her greeting-a-stranger voice.

I looked up to see another Arboretum visitor who had appeared a few steps in front of us. He looked about my age, was carrying a thermos mug of coffee, and I guessed he was a regular at the Arb: his dark-green sweatshirt had the Arboretum's logo on it. It reminded me that before we headed back home, I wanted to pick up a similar one in the Visitor Center's gift shop as a birthday gift for my dad.

"Morning," the fellow mumbled, his head down. He hurried past us and continued in the direction from which we'd come.

"I need to stop in at the gift shop before we leave this morning," I told Luce before I forgot. "Dad's birthday is next month, and I want to get him a sweatshirt like that guy had on. Dad loves the Arb."

I glanced back at the man who was disappearing around a bend in the trail. "Geez. He didn't even make eye contact with us."

"Yes, he did," Luce said. "You were too busy staring at Louise and talking about a faculty meeting to notice. We've passed several people this morning, but I don't think they registered on your radar thanks to Baby Lou."

I lightly stroked my niece's soft hair.

"She's pretty enthralling," I admitted, then finished what I was saying about the school meeting. "The only reason I didn't fall asleep during that particular snooze-fest was because Alan and I were trying to guess which of the new teachers is the Bonecrusher."

Not that I'm a big fan of professional wrestling, mind you. I'm a baseball man. I catch a few Twins games every summer at Target Field in Minneapolis and keep a close eye on the season stats for all the major league teams. Every spring, I coach the sophomore girls' softball team at Savage High.

Or, at least, I try to. Believe me, it's much easier said than done.

But when the word spreads that a former world-class professional wrestler joins the faculty at a quiet suburban high school like Savage, it makes you sit up and take notice. That is, you would take notice if you knew who to look at, but so far, no one was admitting to anything. In the effort—which was generally hopeless more often than not—to keep students focused on academics, our assistant principal, Mr. Lenzen, had decreed that the identity of the former wrestling celebrity would be kept secret.

Which, of course, made it the hottest topic of the new school year in both the student cafeteria and the faculty lounge: who, in a previous life, was the Bonecrusher?

"I think you should respect the Bonecrusher's privacy," Luce commented as she led the way along a leaf-strewn trail towards Wood Duck Pond, a small lake that backed up to the marshes behind the Arboretum's Learning Center. "For all you know, it was his idea, not Mr. Lenzen's, to keep his identity secret. Maybe he wants a fresh start without the baggage of his past career. Not everyone enjoys notoriety and being recognized in public."

"But that's exactly the problem," I pointed out. "No one has a clue what his face looks like because he was always masked in his matches. Alan and I looked the Crusher up on the Web, but in every photo, he was always dressed in a full-head mask and bodysuit. For all I know," I said, echoing her words, "Mr. Lenzen could be the Bonecrusher, though I find that highly unlikely since Mr. Lenzen wouldn't be caught dead wearing tights, let alone a full leotard. My bet is on Boo Metternick, our new physics teacher."

"Because he'd look good in a leotard?"

I smiled at my wife. "Because he's built like a tank, and so far, he doesn't talk much. I figure he's trying to keep a low profile."

We followed a curve in the trail, and spotted a late Green Heron wading along the edges of the lake.

"Now that I can recognize," I said. "A Green Heron in Wood Duck Pond. Look Baby Lou," I said, gently lifting her tiny chin up with my finger, "your first Green Heron."

"Bobby, she's asleep," Luce reminded me.

Out of the corner of my eye I caught a glimpse of a contorted form splayed against a thick tree trunk a little ways off the trail. I noted the baggy blue jeans and flannel shirt, the beat-up floppy felt hat and ragged gloved hands of a classic scarecrow. Perched above it in the tree branches was a murder of crows.

It looked like a set for a Halloween movie.

"I thought you said that the display was only set up around the Visitor Center," I said to Luce.

"That's what I read on the map we got at the Arboretum gatehouse," she replied. "I guess they must have decided to stick a few extra ones in near the trails."

I studied the scarecrow from a safe distance.

5

"I hate scarecrows," I said.

"I know," Luce assured me. "At least it's not a clown one."

It definitely was not, but it still gave me the bejeebers. Even from my vantage point on the trail, the proportions of the scarecrow's body held an eerie resemblance to human form. The way the arms hung down from the shoulders looked too real, like there were the weights of a real man's hands in those gloves and not just straw stuffing. The denim-clad legs looked too solid to be packed with old newspapers. I looked up at the head, but the battered old hat hid the scarecrow's face. And then I realized that where there should have been straw sticking out above the collar of the shirt, there wasn't any.

In fact, now that I thought about it, I couldn't see any straw anywhere on this scarecrow.

What scarecrow doesn't have straw?

I moved a foot closer in its direction, and the crows responded with a few harsh calls as they took flight from the tree branches.

I was right.

No straw anywhere.

I lifted a limp Baby Lou out of the carrier on my chest and handed her to Luce.

"Stay here," I told her.

"Arf," she responded.

"Funny," I said, even though "funny" was not the feeling I was getting at the moment.

Try "icy finger on my spine and I'm going to regret it, but I have to do this" feeling, because there was something definitely not good about that scarecrow.

I moved off the trail and stepped through the thick carpet of fallen leaves that littered the forest floor. When I got within four feet of the scarecrow, a startled squirrel leapt from a nearby branch, knocking off the figure's old hat, revealing a thick head of hair.

Human hair.

No wonder the scarecrow looked so life-like.

Because it was.

Or, it had been.

"Oh, crap," I whispered, dropping beside the body and searching for a pulse in its exposed neck.

The skin was cold.

"Double crap," I breathed.

"Bobby, what is it?" Luce called from the path.

"Not what, who," I called back to her. "Call 911, Luce. I think we found a dead man."

I took another look at the corpse's face and felt a wave of nausea rush into my throat.

Triple crap.

This wasn't just any old dead man scarecrow.

This was someone I knew, someone I'd first met eight years ago while looking for a Louisiana Waterthrush in a mosquito-breeding bog outside Minneapolis. Since then, I'd crossed paths with Sonny Delite, one of the state's best known birders, more times than I could count.

I swallowed the bile in my throat and looked in the dead man's face.

"Hey, Sonny," I whispered shakily. "Bad day for birding, huh?"

CHAPTER TWO

"**A**ND I'D BEEN DOING SO GOOD," I complained to my best friend and brother-in-law Alan Thunderhawk. "It's been sixteen months since I last found a body."

Baby Lou sat cradled in her dad's big arms as we waited for lunch at our regular table at Millie's Deli in Chanhassen. After calling the police on her cell phone from the trail where we found Sonny, Luce had called Alan to come get Louise, since we figured we'd be stuck at the scene for a while and didn't want our niece involved in a murder investigation at the ripe old age of four months. Once he'd arrived, though, Alan had insisted on waiting for us to finish with the police, and then he'd insisted we go to Millie's for lunch and tell him everything.

"Just when you thought it was safe to go back in the woods, huh?" Alan tipped up the end of the bottle of formula as Baby Lou sucked it noisily dry. "So when did you last see Sonny? Alive," he added, as if I really needed a reminder that the man I'd found was dead.

"Hey, Bob, you better watch out or Chef Tom's going to talk that wife of yours into coming to cook for him," Red, our waitress, informed me as she slid a hot Reuben sandwich onto the table in front of me. "Luce is back in the kitchen trading recipes with him again."

I shot a glance at the plate that Red left at Luce's place. "Tell her that her Cajun omelet won't wait for her if she doesn't get out here," I said. "I'm hungry enough to eat both of our meals."

"Birds pretty rough on you this morning?"

"Bob's going to be back in the news, again, Red," Alan told her. "He found another body."

"No kidding?" Red grinned. "Man, you birdwatchers have all the fun around here. I'm going to have to give it a try—birding, not body-finding."

"Don't go with Bob, then," Alan warned her. "Those two activities are just about synonymous with him."

I gave him a dirty look as I bit into my grilled sandwich.

"You know, I bet I'd be pretty good at birding," Red continued. "Back in one of my previous lives, I did some tracking when I was in the army."

I swallowed my bite of Reuben. "I didn't know you were a veteran."

Red gave me a sharp salute. "Twenty years, United States Army. That's why I like working here," she added, winking. "Chef Tom's a regular drill sergeant. Makes me feel right at home. Except that the food's a whole lot better here than it was when I was in the service."

Beside me, Luce slid into her chair. "Tom needs you in the kitchen," she told Red. "He says just because you got in late this morning, it doesn't mean you get out of food prep."

"See, what did I tell you?" Red grinned, leaving us to our meals. "Duty calls."

I caught Alan's eye across the table.

"Two or three years," I finally answered him. "The last time I saw Sonny, it was at the public hearing for the proposed power line across the Le Sueur/Henderson Recovery Zone. Sonny spoke rather eloquently on behalf of the eagles and the herons on the Minnesota River Flyway there that would be most negatively impacted by the construction."

"I'd say he spoke very eloquently—and persuasively—since the pro-birding party won that battle," Alan noted. "But we all know that whenever there are winners, that typically means that there are also losers, and sometimes, losers have long memories."

He removed the bottle from Lou's slack mouth and set it on the table next to his plate of old-fashioned meatloaf. My niece's tiny lips pursed in sleep as her dad dug into his lunch with his free hand.

"I also recall that the utilities company that was involved with that project took a pretty public thrashing for its attempt to slide the project into implementation without due process in the surrounding communities first," Alan said. "The company tried to bypass public forums and informational sessions, hoping to avoid the confrontation they knew would result. By the time the conservation advocates rallied their supporters, the press was all over it, and the utilities people took a beating. I don't think that Sonny's group exactly endeared itself to their adversaries, if you catch my drift."

"You mean they made enemies," Luce clarified.

Alan nodded while he took a gulp from his mug of coffee.

"You think Sonny's death has something to do with the Henderson power lines?" Luce asked.

I shook my head in disbelief. "That was years ago, Alan. You're suggesting that someone was not only angry enough with Sonny because of his stance about conservation and his role in stopping the project, but that the same someone would wait three years to get revenge. To kill Sonny. I don't think so."

I popped a French fry into my mouth. Lou threw out a little fist as she stretched in her sleep, and Alan shifted in his chair to keep his daughter's tiny moccasins away from his meatloaf.

"Besides, you're jumping to a big conclusion, here. We don't know that Sonny's death was the result of foul play," I reminded him. "I didn't see any gunshot wounds or blood. Maybe he died from natural causes. A bad heart. Lung disease."

"And so he dressed himself as a scarecrow and conveniently lay down to die off a back path at the Arboretum," Luce observed. "I don't know if you can get any more natural than that, Bobby."

I threw her my evil eye. "Finish your omelet," I told her. "Good wives should be seen, not heard."

"Yeah, right," she said. "Go, Tarzan."

"I'm not suggesting anything," Alan said, loading his fork with more meatloaf. "I'm just saying that events have consequences, and sometimes people do crazy things for crazy reasons. I'm a history teacher, and history is about sequences of events that unfold over time, and some of those sequences begin with the most unlikely scenarios. Not to mention that the economy's bad, and when people lose jobs, which they do when a big construction—make that utility—project gets dumped, tempers flare, and people can get desperate. They look for someone to blame. It's human nature, Bob."

"Yeah, but I don't decide to kill a person if I think he's to blame for something," I pointed out. "I'm a counselor—I believe in negotiation and compromise, resolving issues and moving forward. But even if I didn't, I sure wouldn't have the patience to wait three years to get revenge."

Alan swallowed the last bite of his lunch and washed it down with a slug of coffee. Baby Lou pursed her lips, her eyes still shut. For all she cared about our conversation, Alan might as well have been cradling a sack of potatoes in his arms.

Except that my niece was a whole lot cuter.

And smarter.

Plus, she already had a life list of four birds: Canada Goose, Wild Turkey, Green Heron, and American Crow.

Not bad for a four-month-old.

"Now, see, that's one of the big differences between you and your sister," Alan noted. "If Lily ever decides I'm to blame for something, I'm immediately going into a witness protection program and getting a complete identity change, because she'd kill me in a minute if she thought something was my fault." He smiled broadly. "And that's why I'm perfect. To keep my wife happy, I never make a mistake."

"Yeah, right," I said.

I turned to my own wife beside me who was suddenly choking on her American fries.

11

"That's not what I hear from Lily," she laughed between coughing jags.

I looked back at Alan. "Busted, buddy."

He fluttered his dark eyelashes at me. "I feel so . . . fragile."

I snorted.

"You and the Bonecrusher," I said. "Luce thinks the reason that Mr. Lenzen isn't spilling the beans about our mystery man's true identity is because he's guarding the big guy's privacy or help-ing him hide old baggage. I think Mr. Lenzen just likes that 'I know something you don't know' feeling."

"Wow, is that mature," Luce commented.

"We're talking about a high school assistant principal here," I reminded her. "I think it's in the job description: 'Lofty attitude preferred. Must enjoy taunting colleagues.'"

"I thought that was your job description, Bob," Alan said. "Lenzen's job is to curb enthusiasm and reprimand smart-aleck counselors."

"How's brunch?" Red asked, suddenly appearing at our table with a coffeepot in her hand. "Anybody need a refill? Bob? Alan?"

"I'm good," Alan said. "The meatloaf was great."

Red leaned towards me, her eyes wide. "We just heard a report on the radio in the kitchen," she said, her voice pitched low. "It's about the body you found. You didn't tell me it was Sonny Delite."

I looked at Red in surprise. "You know him?"

She nodded, her eyes still wide. "He and his wife were regulars whenever he was in town. I can't believe it was him you found."

The bell over the deli's front door jingled as another customer walked in, and Red automatically turned her head to smile at the newcomer.

"Oh, my gosh," she breathed, her smile frozen in place as she visibly blanched. "What the heck is she doing here?"

Luce, Alan, and I all turned to see who Red was talking about. A trim blonde woman, probably mid-fifties, stood just inside the door, her face red and blotchy.

"Who is it?" I asked.

Red turned back to me, her eyes wider than ever.

"Prudence," she said. "Mrs. Sonny Delite."

CHAPTER THREE

RED WALKED OVER TO SONNY'S WIFE—widow, I mean—but as soon as she got close to the woman, Mrs. Delite swung her hand back and slapped Red hard across the cheek.

I was on my feet in the next instant, heading to Red's defense.

I couldn't believe it. I was going to have to break up a girl fight, and I wasn't even at work.

"Hey!" I shouted at Mrs. Delite. "What do you think you're doing?"

She took another swing at Red, but this time, our waitress was ready. Red backed away from the punch and caught Mrs. Delite's hand as it swept through the empty air where Red's chin had been. Without missing a beat, Red spun the woman around and leaned her against the wall, her arm twisted behind her back.

"Think about what you're doing," I heard Red hiss into Mrs. Delite's ear. "Put a lid on it, Pru."

Prudence apparently did think about it and decided to comply, because I watched the woman suddenly sag against the wall, all the fight drained out of her.

Wow. I'd always assumed that waitresses knew how to manage surly customers, but this was an eye-opener. I wondered what it would take to get Red to join me on the cafeteria lunch monitor shift at Shakopee. She'd be dynamite to have covering my back during a food fight.

"You need any help, Red?" I asked, even though it was clear she didn't. In fact, judging from the spontaneous demo I'd just witnessed, Red was no shrinking violet when it came to defensive maneuvering, nor was she a slouch in the hand-to-hand combat department, either.

My guess was that her stint with Uncle Sam had taught her more than how to track a few bunny rabbits in the woods.

Memo to me for future reference: don't ever complain about service at Millie's when Red was working.

"She'll be fine, Bob. Thanks," Red replied. "She's just distraught. I happen to know that she doesn't deal with stress very well. Obviously," she added with her trademark grin.

She turned her attention back to Mrs. Delite.

"Okay, Prudence. I'm going to let you go, now. Why don't you just take a table, practice some deep breathing to calm yourself, and I'll bring you a menu."

Over Red's shoulder, I saw Mrs. Delite nod.

Both Red and I stepped back, and Sonny's widow turned to face us, her eyes still filled with desperation.

I took another step back.

Okay, then, I thought. *Crazy woman in first throes of grief. If you don't have a stun gun to protect yourself, back way up and give her some space.*

The bell over Millie's front door jingled again, and I turned to see who it was. Two policemen walked in, one of them holding out a stun gun.

"Smart man," I told him. "You must be with her," I added, pointing at the new widow as Red ushered her across the deli to a table along the back wall.

"You're under arrest," he said to me.

"What?" Alan's deep voice rose behind me as he stood up from his chair at our table.

The patrol officer and I looked at Alan.

He had a burp rag over one shoulder, dark circles under his eyes, and a sleeping Baby Lou in his arms who was drooling creamy formula over his sleeve. He didn't exactly look threatening, unless you were contemplating having children.

In that case, he looked terrifying.

"Sit down, Alan," Luce said to him, directing him back to his seat with her fork. "Bobby can handle this."

Alan dropped carefully back into his chair so as not to disturb his daughter's nap. "Thank goodness Louise is sleeping," he said, "I'd hate for her to see her uncle getting arrested."

"Are you really arresting me?" I asked the officer. I held up my palms in defense. "I didn't even touch anyone. I was just trying to help out."

"And doing a bang-up job at it, too," said a third policeman as he walked into Millie's.

"Hey, Rick!" Luce greeted the newcomer.

The policeman walked past me and over to Luce, where he leaned over to drop a kiss on my lovely wife's cheek.

"It was his idea," the patrolman in front of me said, nodding towards Rick. "Says he's a close personal friend of yours, and that you've always wanted to be arrested."

"You're a jerk, Stud," I said to Savage High School's own Officer Rick Cook, my birding pal and regular pick-up basketball opponent. "Quit hitting on my wife."

He ignored me as he admired Baby Lou and dropped a kiss on her tiny forehead, too.

"And my niece," I added.

"Don't worry, Bob," Alan assured me. "Rick knows that if he messes with my daughter, I'll break every bone in his body."

"Are you kidding me?" Rick asked. "Your wife would take me apart first. By the way, I like the burp rag over the shoulder. It's a good look for you."

I glanced across the diner to the table where Red had seated Mrs. Delite. The woman seemed to have collected herself and was quietly sipping a steaming cup of tea with the two policemen seated across from her.

"What was that all about?" I asked Rick, sitting back down at our table and tipping my head in Mrs. Delite's direction.

"Not sure," he responded. "I heard your name on my scanner this morning, hightailed it out to the Arboretum and got there after you left, about the same time as Mrs. Delite showed up."

He pulled out the fourth chair at our table and sat down.

"She insisted she had to see the man who found her husband, and since you'd told Kurt—he's the silver-haired officer with Mrs. Delite over there—you were heading here, we hopped in the squad car, and here we are."

I thought I had recognized the older policeman from earlier this morning when the local authorities had descended on us at the Arboretum, which was why I didn't think much of it when he said he was going to arrest me. Both Luce and I had given full accounts of finding Sonny's body and confirmed each other's whereabouts for the last twelve hours. If the police had suddenly found evidence that I'd killed Sonny Delite, I was sure curious to hear what it was.

"So you came along for moral support?" I asked Rick. "Or just to play a practical joke on me?"

"A little of both," he replied. "Not much going on in Savage this morning. You're where the action is, Bob. Again. Lenzen is going to love this," he grinned, tipping his chair back on two legs.

"Don't remind me," I told him.

It had been over a year since the last time our assistant principal had threatened me with suspension because of my involvement with murder cases, and I wasn't looking forward to sitting through another lecture from the man.

Yes, I knew that staff being connected with murders in any way at all was frowned upon.

Yes, I knew that staff should always be mindful of public image.

No, I wasn't a serial killer masquerading as a high school counselor.

Although, maybe I could turn that around and use the idea for my costume this year at the annual faculty Halloween party. Usually, I had my costume figured out at least a month early, but this year, I'd been so busy helping students make schedule changes, I hadn't had the time to think about the party. A serial killer costume would be pretty easy to put together, too. I bet I could borrow a hockey mask from our athletic department. Or maybe a buzz saw from the construction trades class.

I realized that Rick was waiting for me to say something else, so I put the serial killer costume idea on the back burner.

For now.

"So Mrs. Delite wants to talk with me," I confirmed with Rick.

He nodded.

"Any guess as to why she slapped Red?"

Rick shrugged. "Beats me. Maybe she didn't like the service the last time she was here."

"She just lost her husband," Luce sympathized. "I think it's safe to say that the woman is extremely distraught."

"Good point," Rick said. He turned to me. "Hey, aren't you a counselor? Maybe you should go counsel, or something."

I opened my mouth to make a smart reply, but Luce cut me off. "You know, that's not a bad idea, Bobby," my wife said. "I'm sure Mrs. Delite could use a comforting word right about now. You're always so good about that kind of thing. I think you should go talk to her."

That was my wife, all right: all heart. I sighed in resignation.

"I'll see what I can do."

I took another look across the room at Mrs. Delite. She sat silently at the table, her eyes gazing vacantly ahead.

"Do you think she's going to slap me?" I asked Luce. "I haven't been trained in defensive moves like Red has."

"Go talk to her," my wife commanded me.

"Arf," I replied.

Luce pushed me out of my chair.

I rehearsed a few opening lines in my head.

"Hello, I'm the man who found your husband. I have to ask, though—who dressed him this morning? He was a dead ringer for a scarecrow. Oops—poor choice of words. Can I suggest the Reuben sandwich for lunch?"

I wound through the four tables between my own and Mrs. Delite's. Millie's isn't a big place, but that's one of the reasons I'd always loved it. Not only is the food delicious, but the whole place has that cozy feel of a small town diner where you know everyone's name, and they know yours. You go there a few times, and Chef Tom and his staff take such good care of you, you'd think they were family.

Only nicer.

In all the years I'd been going to Millie's, Red hadn't kicked me in the shins even once the way my sister routinely did.

Although I bet she could. After watching her handle Prudence Delite, I wondered what other hidden talents our favorite waitress possessed.

I extended my hand to Mrs. Delite.

"I'm Bob White. I'm so sorry for your loss. I knew your husband, and he was a fine man."

She looked blankly at my hand, then lifted her puffy eyes to my face.

"Actually, he wasn't," she corrected me, her voice soft and her eyes teary. "He was a lying, cheating, egotistical excuse for a man. But I loved him. I really did. I would have done anything for him. Anything at all."

I opened my mouth to reply, but nothing came out, so I closed it again.

I glanced at the two policemen, but they both had their eyes glued to the blue-and-white checkered tablecloth.

Smart men.

"So, maybe, condolences are not in order?" I carefully suggested.

What was I supposed to say? Congratulations, the louse is out of your life?

"Oh, Prudence, you don't mean that," Red said, appearing beside me and sliding a plate of eggs and ham in front of Mrs. Delite. "She doesn't know what she's saying, Bob. She adored Sonny. She's clearly in shock." She patted Mrs. Delite's shoulder. "Pru, you eat up, okay? It's all organic, and your morning tea's almost ready."

The new widow obediently picked up her fork and knife . . . and just stared at her platter.

I noticed the two policemen sliding looks at Prudence, and then at each other. Officer Kurt tapped me on the arm.

"That's why we're accompanying her," he explained in a lowered voice. "She was just about hysterical at the Arboretum, and we didn't want her driving herself anywhere, so we offered to bring her over to talk to you. When a woman's that devoted to her husband, we always worry a little about her . . . hurting herself, if you know what I mean."

He looked gratefully at the plate of chocolate chip-banana pancakes that Red laid at his place.

"And I really needed some pancakes," he added.

I looked back at Mrs. Delite to find her staring at me.

"I'm glad you found him," she said, sniffing as she dabbed a tissue at the corners of her eyes. "At least I know where he is, now. That was always so hard on me, when he would be gone for days at a time . . . championing some environmental cause like it was a life-or-death quest. I felt so alone. And now, without him, I just don't . . . ."

"I called him Don Quixote," Red interrupted in a bright voice, clearly trying to divert the conversation and the direction of Prudence's thoughts. "You know, jousting at windmills. That was his latest crusade, in fact: wind turbines. He told me all about it when they were in here for lunch yesterday."

The deli's doorbell chimed, and Red glanced to see who had walked in. She gave a little wave and turned back to me to finish her comment.

"Did you know that wind energy companies have to get environmental approval before they put up wind farms these days? Apparently, if the turbine towers are located near nesting spots or migratory routes, they can kill a lot of birds." She shook her head. "Really, it seems like if it's not one thing, it's another, with alternative energy sources. Maybe we should all just go back to lighting candles, using iceboxes, and staying home."

Sonny's widow threw an anguished look at Red.

"You just hang in there, honey," our waitress consoled Prudence. "We'll get you through this. Remember, you just take one step at a time." She hustled away to help another table of new customers.

Mrs. Delite let out a heavy sigh. "One step at a time," she softly repeated.

"Sonny was working with wind energy?" I asked her, hoping to keep her distracted from more tears.

She nodded and sniffed again.

"That's why we were here in town, Mr. White," she told me. "We were attending the Study of Alternative Sustainable Sources conference at the Arboretum. Sonny was supposed to lead a session," she paused to take a deep shuddering breath, "this afternoon, about the ecological impact of wind energy farms."

She shot another bleak glance at Red as our waitress retreated to the kitchen with a fresh pile of brunch orders. Her gaze lingered on Red's back a moment, and then she took another deep breath, which seemed to help her regain some of her composure.

"The truth," she continued slowly, choosing her words carefully, "is that Sonny made a lot of enemies over the years with his environmental advocacy. And Red made such a big deal about the turbines at lunch yesterday, she might as well have announced it over a public address system that Sonny was going to be . . . personally responsible . . . for the loss of hundreds of jobs in the Minnesota energy industry. As far as I'm concerned, Red painted a target on my husband, and somebody jumped at the opportunity to kill him before he put more people out of work."

I glanced again at the policemen, who were both devouring their weekend specials. Neither one seemed particularly interested in what Mrs. Delite had to say.

"So he was murdered? You know that for a fact?"

"No confirmation on that," Kurt said around a mouthful of his breakfast potatoes. "But Mrs. Delite here says her husband had no pre-existing health issues, so the medical examiner will be doing an autopsy. At this point, all we know for sure is that you found a dead man."

He paused.

"A dead man who was an acquaintance of yours," he added.

"That looks pretty lousy, doesn't it?" I asked, already knowing what he'd say.

Unfortunately, I'd found enough bodies in my life to know that having a relationship with the deceased was definitely not a point in your favor when you were the one to find the body. Maybe I was going to have to make that a condition of acquaintance when I met someone: Hello, I'm Bob White, but I can only become your friend if you promise I won't find you dead.

"Not in your case," Kurt replied, swallowing a mouthful of coffee. "You've got a reputation with the local police departments for being a body-finder. Nobody takes you seriously as a suspect. You're a high school counselor, for crying out loud."

I didn't know if I should be relieved.

Or insulted.

Counseling drama queens may not be the most glamorous job in the world, I know, but I take a lot of pride in what I do. Shepherding kids through the teen years is no piece of cake. I deal with dysfunctional families, suicidal teenagers, bullies, and world-class slackers. At a minimum, I deserve some respect for my dedicated efforts in molding young people into mostly law-abiding, albeit often unemployed, members of society. And combat pay for chaperoning dances wouldn't be completely out of line, either.

"Remind me to call you for a character reference after my boss goes ballistic when he hears about this," I said. "I think he's convinced himself that I'm a walking public relations disaster just waiting to implode at Savage High School."

"What makes you so sure that Lenzen is even going to hear about this little encounter of yours?" Rick asked, coming up behind me and clapping me on the shoulder. "It's not like your name will be released to the media, Bob."

I turned and gave him a glare.

"Who needs the media when I have you?" I said.

He started to protest, but I cut him off.

"Don't even imagine that I don't know that every time I've been connected to a murder case, you've been the one to leak it to Mr. Lenzen, Stud," I said. "I know you. You can't wait to see his reaction, knowing that I'm the one who's going to be bearing the brunt of his righteous mortification, not to mention his tedious and long-winded reprimands."

Rick tried hard to hide his grin.

"Hey, I'm just a humble government employee doing my sworn duty to protect and defend," he insisted. "I figure I'm performing a public service. If Lenzen goes into cardiac arrest at the news, he'll have a first responder right there, and I can save taxpayers the cost of an ambulance."

"You are so full of it," Kurt commented. "You have the biggest mouth on the entire Minnesota police force, Rick."

"Thank you, Officer," I said, giving Kurt a brief nod.

"Not always," Rick amended. He gave me a sly smile. "Case in point: I have yet to divulge to anyone the true identity of Savage High's own Bonecrusher."

I blinked.

"That's right, Bob," he said. "I know something you don't know, and I'm not telling."

Great. Rick and Mr. Lenzen could start a club—Secret Keepers. Maybe they could get a young adult book series out of it, like *The Babysitters*, or *Sweet Valley High*. They could call it *Savage Secrets*.

Although that sounded more like a bodice-ripper. Somehow, I couldn't quite picture Mr. Lenzen bare-chested any more than I could imagine him wrestling in a full leotard as the Bonecrusher. Besides, he'd have to hold a spear or a sword to pose for a romance novel cover, and knowing Mr. Lenzen, he'd probably insist on holding a detention pass.

"You know who the Crusher is?" I asked, stunned. "You scum. You sat right next to me at the back-to-school meeting and listened to me and Alan guess all day long, and you didn't tell us?"

He held up his right hand. "I'm sworn to protect and defend, remember?"

"Protect what? A celebrity's identity? You don't think a professional wrestler can protect or defend himself? Hello, Stud, the guy probably outweighs you by sixty pounds of muscle."

A mental picture of Boo Metternick, Savage High School's new physics teacher and my personal pick for the mysterious Bonecrusher, popped into my head. He had to have at least a half-foot of height over Rick and a good sixty pounds, all of it hard muscle. I knew if I were in the market for a bodyguard, I'd go with Boo long before I'd choose Rick.

Then again, I could be wrong.

Alan was convinced that Paul Brand, our new art teacher, was the former Bonecrusher. Slim and quiet, Paul didn't interact much with the other teachers, so no one knew much about him yet, except that he had been an especially talented hockey player in college. Rumor had it that he had actually played a year or two in the National Hockey League, but quit the ice after getting his nose repeatedly broken. Alan's theory was that Paul put his quick reflexes and lean muscles to work as the Bonecrusher and kept himself masked so his old teammates couldn't recognize him and razz him about defecting to professional wrestling.

Alan was so sure of his theory, he bet me ten dollars that Paul was the Bonecrusher. Given that the remaining five new staff members were either women or men who were too old to be the former wrestler, I'd taken his wager, fairly confident that I had the winner in Boo.

The idea that Rick had known all along, but kept his mouth shut, was not making him my favorite school police officer at the moment.

He held up his hands in defense.

"Truth be told, I didn't know at the faculty meeting," he confessed. "It was only my superior powers of detection that revealed it to me after that point in time."

Officer Kurt gagged on his coffee.

I rolled my eyes.

"All right, all right," Rick surrendered. "I overheard Lenzen on the phone with one of his Missota Conference buddies. They were talking about the high schools hosting wrestling tournaments in the next year, and he let it slip that the Crusher was teaching at Savage."

I gave Rick an expectant look. "And?"

"And what?" He gave me his best imitation of innocence.

I briefly wondered if Officer Kurt would slap the cuffs on me for assaulting a policeman if I smacked Rick up along the side his head. Kurt did have a stun gun with him, after all.

Now there was an idea. Maybe he'd let me borrow it to use on Rick.

"And the real Crusher is . . ." I led, waiting for Rick to follow.

"My lips are sealed," he said, miming zipping his lips shut and tossing away the key.

"For crying out loud," I groaned.

"Although," he said, "I might be persuaded to share that bit of information with you in return for your assistance in finding a certain bird—a Ferruginous Hawk, to be exact—out in Stevens County this Thursday. Since it'll be Fall Break at the high school, we've got the day off, and I figured this would be my best chance to get one for my life list, especially since there have been almost daily postings of people seeing it out there in the last week. What do you say?"

I'd say that it takes a birder to know exactly how to bait another birder, and Rick knew that a Ferruginous Hawk was just about the biggest piece of bait he could offer me this time of the year.

After all, I'd been following those postings as avidly as he had.

Especially since I'd never gotten one of the big hawks on my own life list.

Not that I hadn't tried, but every time I'd heard about a Ferruginous Hawk being spotted, it was long gone by the time I arrived wherever it had been sighted, which was typically in a north-south corridor a little inside the western state line of Minnesota. Stevens County was in the middle of that corridor. The fact that there had been even a handful of reports of the hawk—or was it more than one individual?—in Stevens in the past week was not only a most unusual and irregular occurrence, but it was a clear indication that the raptors were on the move.

The reality was that Ferruginous Hawks, which are more common out west in the Dakotas, make very limited excursions into Minnesota, and even when someone does spot one of the hawks on our side of the border, it never hangs around. That means you can't chase it and re-find it, like you can go after certain warblers or ducks or cranes that might spend a few days in Minnesota during migration. As a result, Ferruginous Hawks are one of the most difficult species to see in the state.

Let me make that an even more accurate statement: while the Ferruginous Hawk is seen in the state each year, it is most often the case that *one bird* is seen by *one observer, once a year*. The thought that several sightings had recently occurred was almost mind-boggling.

Which, of course, only made me more anxious to see one.

If the truth be told, as Rick had just put it, I'd mentioned to Luce on our way to the Arboretum this morning that I was thinking about driving to Stevens on Thursday. She'd be busy all day with an annual banquet event at Maple Leaf, the conference center where she worked, so I'd be flying solo.

Or, at least, that had been the plan.

"I don't know, Rick," I sighed. "Seems to me that if you were really a good friend of mine, you'd have dished up the Crusher's identity without me having to ask. Instead, you're using it as leverage for a birding trip."

"Oh, are you going with Bobby on Thursday?"

My wife's hand slipped into mine as she joined me by the table.

"I always feel bad when I can't go with him," she added, "and I know he really wants that Ferruginous Hawk. He's been checking the list serve first thing when he gets up in the morning, and the last thing before he gets in bed at night."

Rick grinned. "Busted, buddy."

"I was going to ask you along, anyway," I improvised. "You have skills that are crucial to me, Stud: you know where all the speed traps are on Interstate 94."

"That's where they want to put up those wind farms," Red said, returning to the table and catching the last bit of our conversation. "West of 94 towards Morris. Isn't that right, Prudence?"

This time, instead of looking bleak, though, Prudence's face filled with a dark fury.

Uh, oh. Grieving wife goes crazy again. Better have that stun gun ready, Officer Kurt.

"Sonny should still be alive," Prudence said through gritted teeth, her eyes pinned on Red.

"Geez," I whispered to Red. "If looks could kill, you'd be dead on the floor."

"No kidding," she whispered back. "I could be your second body of the day, Bob, and it's not even two o'clock yet. Who would have thought that Sunday brunch could be so dangerous?"

"Not me," I said. "But I never thought birding was dangerous either, and look at me now—I've got a reputation for finding bodies along with birds."

"Lucky you," Rick chimed in.

Yeah, lucky me.

Not.

CHAPTER FOUR

LUCKY, HOWEVER, WAS EXACTLY WHAT I felt when I walked into the counseling department reception area at Savage High School on Monday morning: the line of usual suspects was only two students long, and Mr. Lenzen wasn't bringing up the rear. My weekend escapade was still under wraps . . . for the moment.

"Hey, Sara and Vicky," I greeted the girls waiting beside my office door. "What's up?"

"I've got a kid for the day," Sara Schiller said, pointing her chin at the five-pound sack of flour she cradled in her left arm. "I'm not supposed to leave it unattended for a minute, or I get an F for the assignment. How stupid is that? It's a bag of flour! I can't believe I let you talk me into taking this dumb child development class. The new teacher is a pain in the rear."

"Gee, Sara," I sympathized as I unlocked my office door and flipped on the light switch. "Why don't you tell me how you really feel about this class?"

She gave me a blank look.

"I thought I just did."

Clearly, Sara's ability to discern my incredibly witty sarcasm was not her strong suit.

When it came to insulting her teachers in the middle of lectures and skipping classes, however, she was a virtuoso. Just last Thursday, she'd gotten half-way to Milwaukee before our attendance office ascertained that she was, indeed, missing from school, and the only way we knew for sure she was truant was because I got a call from a Wisconsin state patrolman who had pulled her over for tailgating him.

She may have been a mistress of deception, but no one could accuse Sara Schiller of being the smartest kid on the block, that was for sure.

"I've got one, too," Vicky Coen said, turning her hip towards me.

Sure enough, there was a five-pound bag of flour riding on the low-slung waist of her jeans, protectively secured there by some kind of make-shift sling she'd draped across her chest.

"I named mine," she said. "It's Zoey."

"That is so stupid," Sara told her as the girls followed me into my office. "It's just a bag of flour, Vicky. No joke, Mr. White, I really hate this teacher."

"You mean Ms. Knorsen?" I asked.

Sara rolled her eyes. "Yes, I mean Ms. Knorsen. She's my teacher for the child development class that you forced me to take."

Not surprisingly, Sara's memory wasn't exactly accurate. By the time she came to me to change her class schedule for the third time in the first week of the school year, there were only two courses left that still had open seats: advanced calculus or child development. Suffice it to say that Sara wasn't a math prodigy, which had narrowed her options down to the child development class. I'd felt a little badly about turning Sara loose on a new faculty member, but after getting to know Gina Knorsen during our back-to-school workshop, I was pretty confident that if anyone could handle Sara Schiller, it would be our newest Family and Consumer Science teacher. With five years of inner-city classroom experience behind her, Ms. Knorsen knew all the tricks in a delinquent's book, which meant she was going to be the one teacher Sara couldn't manipulate.

I could hardly wait for their first classroom confrontation. The very thought of it gave me goosebumps of anticipation.

"So you have to do me this favor, Mr. White," Sara continued. "I have to meet with Officer Cook about my truancy last week, and no way am I walking into his office with a bag of flour. Vicky can't help me because she's already got her own baby to take care of. So you have to watch my sack of flour while I talk to Officer Cook because you're the reason I'm in this stupid class."

I dropped my briefcase behind my desk and looked from Sara to Vicky.

"You can't handle twins?"

"Ms. Knorsen said we can't babysit for each other," Sara informed me. "Please, Mr. White, I really don't want an F in this class."

That was a first. From what I'd seen of Sara in the last two years, she always wanted an F in class. Maybe Ms. Knorsen was already working a little turn-around magic on my perennial problem child.

Given my own less-than-stellar track record with straightening Sara out, it would be awfully nice if someone could.

But babysitting a bag of flour?

As I studied the girls' earnest faces, I had a sudden recall of Baby Lou's soft weight in my arms at the Arboretum. I had to admit that there was something infinitely sweet about a little person tucked so trustingly against your body. Granted, Sara was talking about a bag of flour, but nevertheless, I could feel my tender new-uncle feelings beginning to kick in.

"I just have to keep it with me, right?"

Yes, it was true. If I hadn't already been the biggest sap in the world, I sure was now.

Sara's face lit up.

"Oh, Mr. White, thank you, thank you! Now I don't have to feel so dumb when I talk to Officer Cook. I promise I'll do everything he says and get back here as soon as I can. Thank you!"

She dumped the bag unceremoniously on one of my two visitor chairs, grabbed Vicky's arm and disappeared out the door.

I realized I didn't know what time she had her appointment with Rick.

I looked at the bag of flour on the chair and sat down behind my desk.

"I think I'm an idiot," I told my new baby.

"I know you're an idiot," Rick said from where he was leaning into my open doorway.

"Please tell me you have a meeting with Sara Schiller first thing this morning," I said to him.

"Sorry, buddy. No can do. Why would I be talking to Sara Schiller?"

I dropped my head to my desk.

The Mistress of Deception had struck again.

"Hey, you've got somebody's baby in here," Rick said.

I lifted my head and saw him picking up the bag of flour.

"Gina told me about this assignment last week," Rick told me. "She said I could be the child protection officer, and if I see any abandoned babies, I should pick them up and bring them to her right away. I was kind of hoping I'd find one at the end of the day, though, so I could take it over to her townhouse to return it to her."

"Her townhouse?"

"Absolutely," he replied. "She's got an awesome deck with a fire pit out back. There were some beautiful nights this weekend, let me tell you. Gina must know the names of every constellation in the sky."

"Wait a minute. Are you telling me you're dating Gina Knorsen? When did this happen?"

He dropped into the chair and set the bag of flour on the front edge of my desk.

"When I asked her out two weekends ago. You were out of town. You and Luce went to that bed-and-breakfast place in Stillwater for your anniversary, and I took Gina out to dinner."

He rubbed the diamond stud in his ear, his mouth curling into a smile.

"We really hit it off," he added. "I just didn't want to tell you about it yet. You know . . . I didn't want to jinx it."

"Afraid I'd tell her about your sordid past and all your serious character flaws?"

"Something like that. I don't know, I've just got a feeling about Gina."

"I hate to remind you, Stud, but I've heard the 'I've just got a feeling' speech from you before," I pointed out. "Several times, in fact."

I glanced meaningfully at the diamond in his earlobe. Rick had come home with it after a vacation cruise with his then-girl-friend. Four years later, the stud was still there, but the woman was long gone.

"Yeah, well, we all make mistakes," Rick chuckled. "At least I didn't go for the nipple ring."

"I don't want to know," I assured him.

He pointed at the flour on my desk. "So where did you find this?"

"I didn't," I said. "Sara Schiller asked me to babysit."

"Did you agree?"

"Well, yeah," I conceded. "But that's because she said she had an appointment to talk to you about her truancy last week, and she was too embarrassed to be carrying in the flour. Plus, she said that she didn't want an F in the class. I thought that alone was significant progress as far as Sara is concerned, so I said I'd take the baby for her."

Rick steepled his fingers and considered the flour.

"So, technically, Sara did not leave her child unattended," Rick concluded. "Though she lied to do so, she did obtain care for her baby."

I dropped my head on my desk again. "Yes."

"That's awfully generous of you, Counselor."

"Don't remind me."

"I'm not turning Miss Schiller in, then. I am, however, returning the baby to your custody."

He stood up, lifted the bag of flour, and carefully laid it back on the visitor chair.

"What time do you want to leave on Thursday for Morris?" he asked.

"I don't know. If Sara doesn't come back and get her baby by then, I might be busy babysitting. By Thursday, that girl could drive all the way to Florida."

A buzzing sound filled my little office. Rick pulled out his cell phone and answered the call.

"No kidding?" Rick asked whoever was on the other end of the connection. "My, my. That does change things, doesn't it?"

His eyes met mine, and he smiled. "Thanks, Kurt. I'll be in touch."

He returned his cell to his pants pocket.

"Looks like the widow was right: somebody wasn't delighted with Mr. Delite," Rick reported. "Kurt just saw a preliminary report from the medical examiner. Unless Sonny D was pulling a Socrates, it looks like somebody else did the honors."

"Socrates?" I said, just before I realized what Rick meant.

Socrates, one of the founding fathers of Western philosophy, was sentenced to death with a cup of poison hemlock.

"Sonny was poisoned?"

"Give the man a cigar," Rick said. "According to Kurt, the examiner initially thought the cause of death was respiratory paralysis, but then a sample of the stomach contents—"

I held up my hands to make him stop. "Whoa. Too much information, buddy."

"Wuss," Rick said.

"Okay, I'm a wuss," I readily agreed. "Just spare me the gory gastric details."

"They think they found traces of hemlock in the stomach. It'll take a little time to confirm it, but as of right now, Sonny D's untimely demise is looking pretty suspicious."

Rick sighed.

"Put a new notch on your binoculars, Bob," he told me. "I think you found another murder victim."

CHAPTER FIVE

"**H**ONEY, I'M HOME!" I CALLED as I walked into the house just after four o'clock. I dropped my briefcase by the front door and set Sara's bag of flour down next to it.

"Sleep tight, Goldie," I told the flour. "We'll find your mommy in the morning. I promise. And then we'll make sure she spends lots of time with you—in detention."

Yes, I was still the designated sitter because Sara had—no surprise!—gone AWOL from school for the entire day. By ten o'clock in the morning, I stopped kicking myself in the head for falling for her empty pledge to reform, and, instead, committed myself to setting an example of trustworthiness for every student at Savage High School. I christened the bag Goldie in honor of the yellow medal emblazoned on the face of the sack and dutifully carried it with me all day long. When I ran into Gina Knorsen in the cafeteria at lunch, I caught her smiling even as she shook her head in disapproval.

"I keep my promise, even if a student doesn't," I'd told her. "Honor is my middle name."

"Mine's Patience," she'd replied. "But your Sara Schiller is sure testing it."

"Is that a tongue-twister?" I asked.

"No," Gina said. "It's the truth."

I walked through the living room and headed for the kitchen.

Luce wasn't home yet, but thanks to her new schedule at Maple Leaf, I could now look forward to a leisurely dinner with my wife every night. Aligning our work days had taken us almost a year of marriage. After an initial couple of months of strained nuptial bliss due to her long evening hours as executive chef, Luce had switched to the early morning catering shift at the conference center, which, unfortunately, wasn't much better in allowing us newlywed, let alone birding, time thanks to her pre-dawn departures and seven o'clock bedtimes. Finally, she'd hit on the current solution: she was the noon banquet and pastry chef. The result was two-fold: for the first time in our lives, we had similar working hours, and for the first time in my life, I had all the desserts I could eat.

I knew there was a good reason for marrying her.

I took a turtle éclair out of the refrigerator and walked out to the deck to check on my birdfeeders. Just last evening I'd seen a river of Red-winged Blackbirds heading south. I must have watched for a good five minutes as thousands of the birds streamed through the sky. Thankfully, they hadn't needed to make a refueling stop at my feeders, so I figured what I had left in my bag of sunflower seeds would probably last till the end of the month. After that, I was going to switch over to suet blocks to keep all the woodpeckers happy. Humans weren't the only species that enjoyed having a full belly.

As long as it wasn't a belly full of hemlock.

I leaned on the porch railing and ate my pastry.

Sonny Delite was a skilled birder, a man totally at home in the natural world. Often, when we birded together, he pointed out dozens of plants to me and recited both their common and scientific names. To think that a man like that could mistakenly ingest poisonous hemlock was nothing short of an unbelievably long stretch.

But that only left two equally disturbing possibilities: Sonny either committed suicide or was murdered. His wife had jumped without hesitation to the second option yesterday at Millie's, and, I supposed, without any suicide note or other mental distress indications, the police had to take her allegations seriously.

So who would be mad enough at Sonny Delite to feed him a toxic plant? And who would have the opportunity to do that at a public place like the Minnesota Landscape Arboretum on an early Sunday morning?

If you listened to Prudence Delite's accusations, I guess you'd have to look for someone who might have held a grudge—and a murderous one, at that—against Sonny because of his opposition to utility projects that impacted the environment. Considering that there was a conference about energy sources underway at the Arboretum, it wouldn't be surprising if a lot of the folks in attendance knew Sonny from past projects. Determining whether those people were his friends or foes would take some legwork, but unless I missed my guess, the police were already sifting through the conference rosters looking for anyone who might have had some past history with the newly deceased. Then, if the police could place any of those people at Millie's during lunch the previous day when Red had made a scene with Sonny, they'd have a head start on investigating suspects.

Piece of cake, I thought. Make a list, check it twice, narrow it down to naughty and nice. Pick a killer, and you're done.

Except then you had to find the evidence to prove that your designated killer did it.

Which meant you also had to identify the motive.

And pin down the opportunity.

I swallowed the last bite of my éclair, licking some wayward cream filling off my fingers.

Man, I loved éclairs. They were definitely not any old piece of cake.

But neither was solving a murder.

A Downy Woodpecker flew in from the woods and perched on the porch railing a few feet away from me. He gave me the once-over and then took off. I guessed that since I wasn't a block of suet, he didn't have much use for me at the moment.

Sort of like Officer Kurt at Millie's yesterday.

Not that he was looking for a block of suet, but he could have been a little more generous with his evaluation of my usefulness to a murder investigation that I had unwittingly and unwillingly initiated.

Oh, that's right—I was only a high school counselor, *for crying out loud*. Heaven forbid that I tread on the sacred territory of local law enforcement, despite the fact that I'd made significant contributions to solving three Minnesota murders last year.

Granted, I didn't set out to become an amateur sleuth, and much of what I had contributed, I discovered through blind luck, but what could I say? When it came to birding or solving murders —if you've got it, you've got it.

And if you've got it, you might as well use it.

Or lose it.

And I had no intention of losing my birding skills at the ripe old age of thirty-six.

"Honey, I'm home!"

I turned in time to see Luce stepping out onto the deck.

"Red's in the hospital," she announced. "I stopped by Millie's Deli on my way home to drop off a sample of my new quiche recipe for Chef Tom, and he told me that Red went to the emergency room right after we left yesterday."

"For what?"

My wife gave me a kiss.

"For a concussion," she said. "Red fell down the steps to the deli's basement storage area, and hit her head. She doesn't even know her own name. Tom said he overheard Red and Prudence arguing when they went to the basement, and the next thing he knew, Prudence was yelling for someone to call 911."

"Prudence Delite?"

"Yes, Prudence Delite," Luce repeated. "Red asked her to help her bring up some supplies. I gather they're old friends, from what Tom said."

Red's comment that Sonny and his wife had been regular customers at Millie's came back to me. I'd assumed that was the extent of the women's acquaintance. Although, now that I reconsidered what I'd seen of their interaction at Millie's, I'd thought the whole girl-slap thing had been way out of line for a server-customer relationship. And the way Red had handled it also seemed like she was pretty familiar with Prudence's behavior. What had Red said?

"Think about what you're doing." And *"Put a lid on it, Pru."*

That sounded like a lot more than a passing acquaintance, I'd say.

That sounded like some kind of warning.

About what, though?

If I had to guess, it might have been that Red was reminding Prudence about her martial arts superiority so Sonny's widow wouldn't find herself laid out on the floor of the deli. I doubted, however, that Chef Tom would be pleased with that kind of customer service from his employees. It was one thing to knock your customers out with great food, but literally landing them between the tables was a culinary approach I wasn't familiar with.

At the same time, if Red's military experience was common knowledge among Millie's regular clientele—did that make me "irregular" since I hadn't heard about it?—Mrs. Delite should certainly have known better than to launch an assault on a trained combatant. Last I heard, attacking a skilled fighter was rarely a good idea, unless you were equally skilled. I knew that I, for one, was going to be especially diligent at work about not angering the Bonecrusher, once I knew who he was. And until I did, I was going to be sure I didn't antagonize anyone . . . just to be safe.

But if Prudence and Red were old friends, as Luce had learned from Chef Tom, then Red must have been warning Sonny's widow about something else.

Making a scene in a public place?

Could be. But if that was the case, Red was too late. According to Officer Kurt, Prudence had already done that at the Landscape Arboretum.

Yet I could still hear the particular register of the tone in Red's whisper, and it had sounded urgent. It had reminded me more of a Killdeer's cry as it protected its young, rather than a Blue Jay calling to stake out its territory in defense.

Okay, that's weird—trying to interpret human behavior through bird calls, but what can I say? Given the choice between figuring out birds or humans, I think birds are a whole lot easier. With birds, what you see—and hear—is what you get, which is definitely not the case with a lot of humans.

Trust me. I was the one who'd been suckered by the faked sincerity of a habitual reprobate into babysitting a bag of flour for a day.

Two American Crows flew across the yard, followed by a pair of Blue Jays.

So, had Red been trying to protect Prudence from something else, or was she just reminding her friend of her physical prowess? Did it even matter? As Luce had reminded me, Prudence had just learned that her husband was dead. Of course, she was out of control. As a counselor who dealt with students and their families, I'd seen the whole gamut of reactions to stress and crisis. In fact, Red gave Prudence the same advice I offered in those situations: take it one step at a time.

And Prudence had immediately responded, which, I had to say, wasn't always the case with my students. Gee, maybe I should ask my favorite waitress for some pointers in that department the next time I saw her.

Assuming that Red had her memory back by then, that is. Until that happened, no one would be asking Red much of anything, I guessed.

Including the police trying to place suspects at Millie's Deli on Saturday.

Ouch. Bad timing for a concussion.

I watched two dull-colored American Goldfinches fly in and land on the feeder's perches. Without the usual collection of summer birds around, they had the feeder all to themselves for the moment. I wondered if they would stick around for the winter or fly south before the end of fall.

Talk about timing.

"Salmon or tilapia?" Luce asked.

"Salmon," I said, "with that really tasty glaze you put on it."

She lifted a shapely blonde eyebrow at me.

"And which glaze would that be? I've only tried about six different ones in the last month, and as best as I can recall, you said they were all very tasty."

I gave her beautiful lips a big smacking kiss.

"They were," I agreed. "But the one I'm thinking of had a half-cup of teriyaki base, a pinch of ginger, a tablespoon of rice wine vinegar, a clove of garlic, and, I believe, one-third cup of oyster sauce."

Luce laughed. "If I had your memory for details, I'd never have to write down another recipe."

"Speaking of memory," I said, "don't you think it's a little odd that Red just happened to fall down the stairs and lose her memory on the same day that Sonny Delite was murdered, especially when the police might need to question her about who was in the deli the day before?"

She pulled the clip that had held her hair back during her work day at Maple Leaf and shook it loose down her back. "Are you suggesting that Red knocked herself out on purpose?"

"No," I replied.

At least, that hadn't been my first idea.

My first idea was that Prudence had attacked Red in another surge of crazed fury over Sonny's death and sent her tumbling down the stairs. My second idea was that Prudence did it deliberately to keep Red from talking to the police about Sonny, the husband she adored, but also claimed was a liar and a cheat. If Red and Prudence were such good friends, it certainly was possible that

Red would have information about Sonny that the police might be interested to learn. Prudence had, after all, told me she would have done anything for Sonny. Could that include guaranteeing that nobody spoke ill of him, especially to the police investigating his unexpected demise?

I mean, his murder?

Now that Luce had proposed another way of looking at Red's fall, though, I couldn't help but wonder if my wife might have a point. Maybe it wasn't Prudence who wanted to keep the police from questioning Red.

Maybe Red didn't want the police to question Red.

And why would that be?

"You're such a suspicious man, Bobby," Luce said, demonstrating once again her eerie talent of reading my thoughts. "I'm going inside to start dinner. Let me know when you solve the case, Sherlock."

A lone House Finch landed on one of the feeder's perches and gave me the once over.

"So I'm not Sherlock Holmes," I told the bird. "Doesn't mean I can't play detective, does it?"

The finch cocked its head.

"I know, I know. I'm just a high school counselor, *for crying out loud*. Geez, everybody's a critic."

From inside the house, I could hear the crinkling noise of butcher paper being unwrapped from what would soon become our dinner. My mouth began to water in response. Just the thought of Luce's fresh salmon had me salivating like one of Pavlov's dogs. I followed my wife inside to where she was standing by the counter, already measuring ingredients into a bowl for home-made biscuits.

"Why in the world would Red want to hurt herself?" Luce posed the question when she saw me.

She'd been thinking it over, too, which didn't surprise me in the least. In the year since our wedding, I'd learned a secret about my bride. Luce was as stubborn as I was when it came to solving a puzzle. If I was a Sherlock Holmes, she was my Dr. Watson.

"Because she wanted more days off than Chef Tom would give her," I said in exasperation. "I have no idea! I just think it's too co-incidental that the one time Red might have key information for a murder investigation, she's suddenly memory-less."

Luce stopped blending milk into the mixture.

"It's a murder now?"

I'd forgotten she didn't know.

"Rick was in my office this morning when he got a call," I explained. "Sonny was poisoned. The medical examiner found traces of hemlock in his stomach. In lieu of any evidence that he committed suicide, they're treating it as a homicide."

"Oh, my," she breathed, staring into the bowl of dough. "What about an accidental death? Maybe Sonny mistakenly ate . . . no," she declared, affirming my own opinion. "No way. Sonny was an expert woodsman. He couldn't have mistakenly ingested hemlock."

She went back to stirring the biscuits, but I could tell from the tilt of her head that she was still mulling it over. I may not be a mind-reader like Luce, but I do know body language, and body language doesn't lie.

Sure enough, a moment later, she added, "Wild ginseng does look an awful lot like water hemlock. If you were harvesting your own ingredients for brewing a natural tea, I guess it could be possible that . . ."

"You'd pick poisonous water hemlock by mistake? Remind me not to drink any loose leaf ginseng tea the next time someone offers it to me," I told her. "For that matter, I don't think I want to drink any more ginseng tea, period."

Luce dumped the dough onto the floured kitchen counter and patted it out with her fingers into an oval shape.

"I'm just saying it could happen," she insisted. "I know Sonny was into natural foods. Maybe he routinely harvested his own tea leaves. Lots of people hunt for edible mushrooms and roots these days to use in their diets."

I suddenly remembered Red reassuring Mrs. Delite that her meal was all organic. Maybe Luce was onto something here. Maybe Sonny's death was just a terrible mistake—he'd taken an early morning stroll, picked some leaves and thrown them into his morning cup of tea, thinking he was going to savor some wild ginseng.

"But what about the scarecrow get-up he was wearing?" I wondered aloud. "You're the one who thought that was a clear indicator of foul play," I reminded her.

She looked me up and down.

"Maybe I spoke out of turn," she said.

I glanced down at my weathered blue jeans and my favorite flannel shirt that I'd worn to work. Stick an old hat on me, and I could be Sonny's fashion double.

"Okay, so maybe the clothes aren't a dead giveaway."

Luce groaned.

"Sorry. I didn't mean that intentionally," I tried to apologize. "It was a slip of the tongue. Bad Bob! Bad Bob!" I reprimanded myself.

Luce laughed and cut the dough into biscuits.

I watched my wife's expert chef's hands smoothly transfer the biscuits onto a waiting cookie sheet. She could probably do it in her sleep, I realized. Had Sonny likewise been on automatic early Sunday as he strolled the Arboretum and unthinkingly tossed in a deadly leaf to steep in his morning tea?

Stranger things had happened, I supposed, though at the moment I honestly couldn't think of any.

"I think you should call Rick and tell him about the ginseng," I told Luce. "You might be able to save the local detectives a lot of trouble for nothing." I watched her pop the tray of biscuits into the oven. "And maybe you're right—I am too suspicious."

Luce cleaned her work area and put away the bag of flour. "By the way, thanks for picking up flour. I forgot to put it on the grocery list when I shopped yesterday afternoon, and I know how you love those buttermilk biscuits with salmon."

"What flour?" I asked.

"The bag of flour I found in the front hallway when I came in. To be honest, I was surprised you'd thought to stop at the store and pick it up. I didn't know you were aware we were out of it."

The bag of flour.

Goldie.

Oh, crap.

I looked into the oven where the biscuits were already rising into fluffy magnificence.

"That's somebody's baby in there," I said, not sure if I should laugh out loud or pound my head against the kitchen wall.

"Say again?" Luce asked.

I pointed at the oven, a smile pulling at the corners of my mouth.

"That bag of flour was Sara Schiller's child development class 'baby.' I was babysitting it for her today, and I had to bring it home overnight."

Luce looked from me to the oven, then back to me.

"Well, that settles that question," she said. "Once we have kids, I'm sure not leaving them alone with you at home."

CHAPTER SIX

I MADE A QUICK DETOUR on my way into work on Tuesday morning and pulled into the Stop 'n' Go gas station two blocks from the high school. I grabbed the first bag of flour I could find and went to pay at the register.

"Morning, Bob," said a voice behind me.

I turned to find Paul Brand, our new art teacher, holding a steaming cup of coffee in one hand as he dug in his pocket with the other.

"Hi, Paul," I replied. I nodded at his large cup. "You're a wise man. The java here is far superior to what we get in the teacher's lounge."

I paid the young man behind the cash register, and waited for Paul to do likewise.

"So how are you adjusting to life at Savage High?" I asked him. "Are the students treating you okay?"

"They're good kids," he said, taking a sip of his coffee.

I waited a beat for him to say something more, but he didn't. I fished through my memory to see what tidbit I could retrieve about him to continue the conversation, but came up empty. I really didn't know anything about him, other than he was our new art teacher and had played hockey.

And Alan thought he was the Bonecrusher.

I studied Paul while he dropped his change in his pocket. Only an inch or two shorter than I was, he was broader through the shoulders and slimmer at his waist. I tried to visualize him in a black mask and leotard, which was a little tough at the moment, since he was wearing a mustard-colored cotton V-necked sweater over an open collared shirt, his sleeves rolled neatly up to his elbows. Even though I could see the definition of muscles in his biceps, with his wavy jet black hair and chiseled cheekbones, he looked more like a GQ model than a former wrestling star.

Except for his broken nose. That was definitely not GQ.

I propped my bag of flour against my hip and abruptly realized that I was staring at Paul's crooked nose.

"It looks a lot better now than it did when it happened," he informed me. "Fortunately, I have a very high pain threshold."

"Sorry," I apologized. "I didn't mean to stare. Still, that must have hurt," I added. "Hockey?"

"State tournament, my senior year of high school," he said. "My mother cried all the way to the emergency room. I figured I was just paying my dues as a hockey player. Believe me, I've taken worse hits."

The way he said it made me think about Alan's insistence that Paul was the Most Likely Faculty Member to Be the Bonecrusher in our bet. Did Alan know more about Paul than he had shared with me? I always made a point of being on good terms with all of the teachers at Savage, but that didn't necessarily mean I had access to the same grapevine of information that teachers seemed to share amongst themselves. Before I could ask Paul to elaborate, though, he abruptly changed the subject.

"You're the counselor for students in the last part of the alphabet, right?"

"I am."

"I've got some real issues with a student named Sara Schiller," he said. "She's cutting my class on a regular basis. Last week we started a scrapbooking project, and she has yet to even get started."

"Scrapbooking? You mean like photo albums?"

"It's a lot more than that," he corrected me. "It's actually an art form that goes back to the fifteenth century in England. It's the creative selection and preservation of personal and family history through the use of photographs, literature and artwork. Most of the students really enjoy the embellishment techniques I teach them."

Embellishment?

Embellishment?

Heck, I was still grappling with the photo album as art concept.

Paul checked the time on his watch. "I've got to go," he said. "Would you talk with Sara, please?"

"I will," I assured him, following him out the door to where I had parked in front of the store. I shifted my newly-purchased bag of flour into the crook of my arm and watched him walk towards the rows of gas pumps. While he wasn't the biggest guy I'd ever seen, he carried himself with a certain swagger that reminded me of my brother-in-law, back when Alan and I were in college together. Alan had been, and still was, a talented athlete. Judging from his easy gait, it looked like Paul was in that same club.

Savage's new art teacher also carried something else, I noticed.

Slung over Paul's left shoulder was a satchel bursting at the seams with art equipment. I could see the tips of paintbrushes and the edges of drawing pads poking out . . . just above the silhouette of what looked suspiciously like two Greco-Roman wrestlers silkscreened on the satchel.

Paul Brand had an interest in wrestling.

Shoot. Had I bet on the wrong teacher?

Could the intimidating Bonecrusher have turned into a scrapbooking art teacher?

Not in my universe.

Then again, I was a birder who found dead bodies.

Go figure.

I popped the lock on my SUV and laid the bag of flour on the back seat. Whether he was the Bonecrusher or not, I was glad I'd run into Paul and that he'd given me the heads-up about Sara's absences. As soon as I saw my favorite delinquent, she was going to not only get her baby back, but she was also going to get another lecture about skipping school.

Not that I had any illusions that one more lecture would make a difference. Sara was a habitual truant. With two workaholic parents who seemed to show little interest in her, I was fairly certain that her school-skipping behavior was a desperate plea for attention. In that sense, Sara was a wild success, because she got my attention all the time.

Unfortunately, it didn't do jack for her visibility with her parents—from what I could tell, they hardly noticed they even had a child, which just encouraged Sara's own irresponsibility and acting out even more. From years of being a school counselor, I knew that I could talk until I was all shades of blue in the face, but if a kid wanted to keep doing something, she'd do it . . . until the stakes got high enough to make her pause and hopefully make changes.

In my experience, that frequently meant that the stakes had to entail a close encounter with either the police or the Grim Reaper, or in some cases, both.

Seeing as Sara had already added the Wisconsin highway patrol to her list of acquaintances, I wondered what kind of near-death experience it would take to make her change her delinquent ways.

A vision of Sonny Delite, sprawled dead in the woods, popped into my head.

Yup. That would certainly cause a change in a person's behavior—being dead. The downside was that it would also change everything else about the person. Permanently.

I thought again about Luce's theory. Could Sonny's death have been the result of a fatal mistake in a natural diet? The absence of any suicide evidence had caused the police to label it murder, but I seriously doubted that organic tea fans routinely left notes stating that in case they were found dead, the investigators should know they had picked their own tea leaves that morning.

My, what a pleasant way to start another day of counseling high school students. Some people repeated affirmations or listened to music. I pictured dead bodies.

I pulled into my usual parking space behind the gym and turned off the engine. As I opened the car door and stepped out, a perfect V of Canada Geese flew overhead, heading south.

In another month, we could be looking at highs in the teens for temperatures. We'd already had one hard freeze, and the *Farmers' Almanac* was predicting another long, frigid winter. Last week, Mr. Lenzen had even posted his annual ridiculous list of energy-saving tips in the teachers' lounge in hopes of miraculously lowering the school's heating bills.

Somehow I doubted that putting up posters of tropical destinations was really going to make a difference in how students and teachers perceived the chill factor in a freezing classroom. I knew from my own cubbyhole-of-an-office experience that when your fingers got too cold to feel a pen in their grip, not even the memory of a hundred-degree day in July was enough to get the blood pumping again. If Mr. Lenzen was really serious about reducing energy bills, he should have pushed harder to get one of those wind turbines that the Savage school district installed last spring near the middle school.

I'd forgotten about the wind turbines.

A year ago, the School Board had asked for input from the schools in the district about where the turbines should go. It was part of a project with the local utilities company, as I recalled—something about ensuring compliance with the Minnesota state law that required electrical utilities to provide twenty-five percent of their total electricity sales from renewable sources by the year 2025. I think there had been some debate about the turbines functioning in sub-zero weather, but the turbine manufacturer assured everyone it wasn't an issue and swore that the schools wouldn't get stuck without power in the middle of winter.

Of course, if I was representing a multimillion-dollar project that was dependent on turbines, I'd probably say the same thing, especially if I was staring at a government deadline for developing alternative sources. What utility company wouldn't be eager to tap into wind power first and then work out the kinks in the technology as it developed? Being the first kid on the block—or in this case, the first turbine on the block—could only be good for business.

Which would also make it understandable that those same energy companies wouldn't appreciate Sonny's vehement protests against their wind farm plans in Stevens County.

Renewable sources versus conservation.

Weren't those two supposed to be on the same side?

I wanted to believe that, but anyone who read the news in Minnesota would find out differently.

The LeSuer/Henderson Recovery Zone utility battle had ended years ago, but another environmental debate was now raging in Goodhue County, east of Savage, between a proposed wind farm project and federal and state wildlife officials, not to mention local residents and conservation advocates. The issue was what would happen to the eagles—nesting and migrating Bald Eagles, as well as visiting Golden Eagles—that used the proposed site, once the wind farm was up and running. With fifty turbines planned for the farm, everyone knew that some eagles would be killed by the big blades of the wind towers—eagles that were protected by federal law.

Consequently, every interest group involved was trying to come up with a way to combine land use and energy development with environmental responsibility, but, as usual, sometimes the strategies got ugly. I'd even heard that the wind company was accusing local residents of deliberately luring more eagles into the area to pad the numbers of potential bird deaths from the turbines. At the same time, the developer's plans to remove nearby habitat in order to keep the birds and other wildlife away from the deadly turbines was getting a thumbs-down from state and federal officials. While putting distance between the towers and nests would save some birds, land-clearing would only displace the other critters in the area.

Basically, what used to be simple utilitarian decisions about land use had become intricate balancing acts of a multitude of interest groups and subgroups. Depending on where in the state a piece of property was located, a real estate transaction could come under the scrutiny of a dozen agencies, not to mention public discussion and debate.

And Sonny Delite had often been smack in the middle of a lot of those discussions, according to his wife, verbally slugging it out with the opposition, giving utility groups and project developers a painful, and often embarrassing, black eye.

If Sonny was repeatedly going to step into the ring with big bucks energy providers, maybe he should have taken a page from the Bonecrusher's book by wearing a mask and remaining anonymous. That way, if someone had decided to go after Sonny looking for payback, he'd still be looking.

And Sonny wouldn't be dead.

In that case, I'd say anonymity was a huge advantage.

"Mr. White!"

Sadly enough, I wasn't acquainted with that particular advantage in my own line of work. I turned to find Sara Schiller, Goldie's missing mom, weaving her way through a row of parked cars towards me.

"Where's my baby?" she asked.

I pointed at the bag of flour laying on the back seat. Sara peered through the car window.

"That's not safe," she informed me. "You have to use a carseat with a baby. Just like you have to plug your electric outlets with covers and make sure kids don't eat poisonous plants at the playground. We had a whole unit on child safety last week. It's a good thing you don't have any kids, Mr. White. Ms. Knorsen would flunk you in a minute for not using a carseat."

"I'm not taking the class, Sara," I reminded her. "You are. Supposedly."

"What do you mean, 'supposedly'?" she argued. "I show up . . . sometimes. It's a stupid class. Ms. Knorsen just keeps harping about how important it is for parents to spend time with their kids. That's ridiculous. My parents never spend time with me—my mom's too busy with work and her club, and my dad's always traveling for his job. I don't need to spend time with them."

And I was pretty sure that was exactly why Sara didn't like Gina's class. As her counselor who was aware of her family situation, I could just imagine that every time Gina started discussing healthy family relationships, Sara immediately tuned her out. Not having experienced a nurturing bond with her own parents, Sara wasn't interested in hearing about others'. Along with her truancy problems, Sara's disciplinary issues in the classroom were directly related to her feeling that no one cared about her. To cope with that void in her life, she'd perfected deceiving her teachers—and her counselor—to an art.

Which reminded me about the conversation I'd had earlier with possible-Crusher Paul Brand.

"What about art, Sara?" I asked. "Mr. Brand told me you've been skipping his class. Is that a stupid class, too?"

"Yes," she snipped. "He wants us to scrapbook."

Well, okay, maybe she had a point there. Personally, I was still pretty much lost about that whole scrapbook thing, let alone it being high school art class material. To be honest with you, it sort of reminded me of trying to braid leather strips into key chains when I was in Cub Scouts.

Time-consuming, yes.

Artistic? I don't think so.

In its great institutional wisdom, however, the school district of Savage High didn't pay me to question the curriculum. My job—

a fairly large part of it, as it turned out—was making sure that students parked their little cabooses in their classroom seats at the designated times.

Whether or not they were going to be scrapbooking in those seats.

"Sara, you have to attend classes," I told her. "That's how school works. You go to class, you do the work, you get a grade, you graduate . . . hopefully. Eventually."

I reached into the back seat and grabbed Goldie.

"You're welcome," I said to Sara, plopping the flour into her arms.

She looked down at the sack and frowned.

"This isn't my baby."

"Sara, it's your baby."

"No, it's not."

"Yes, it is."

"No, it's not," she insisted. "My bag of flour had a picture of a gold medallion on it, and this one has Robin Hood."

I looked at the bag she held up in front of my face.

Sure enough, Robin was there. He even had a green cap with a feather in it.

"What did you do to my baby?"

I could have sworn she actually sounded upset. Sara Schiller, world-class truant and absent pretend-parent, was distraught over a bag of flour she hadn't wanted in the first place.

"Your baby turned into some excellent buttermilk biscuits," I informed her. "They were great with the salmon. I tell you what. Just take old Robin here and wrap him up in a baby blanket. Ms. Knorsen will never know the difference."

Sara gave me a glower. "Yes, she will. I will never trust you again, Mr. White. That's the last time I ever ask you for help."

She tucked Robin under her arm and stomped off into the building.

That went well, I decided. Now I didn't have to lug Goldie—or Robin, as it turned out—around for the morning, and, with any luck, Sara would park her little caboose in front of the other counselors for a while whenever she got in trouble with teachers.

Not bad for a Tuesday morning, and I hadn't even stepped into my office yet.

More geese honked in the sky as I walked into the building and hung a right to detour by Alan's classroom. As the faculty's local news junkie, he might be able to fill me in on any other controversies that could be cooking with turbines in Minnesota.

Not that I intended to do any extracurricular sleuthing for the police, mind you. I was, after all, a high school counselor, as I'd been so recently reminded.

Although, if I did uncover an important clue to Sonny's untimely demise, I might consider sharing it with Rick.

If, in return, he would tell me which teacher was the Crusher.

True, I already had a deal with Rick for that information if I helped him find the Ferruginous Hawk in Morris later this week, but since the MOU-net had been silent about the bird yesterday, I was beginning to lose hope. Fall migration had a way of becoming unpredictable with some species. A sudden cold front could push migrating birds through the state much faster than expected, while a lingering spell of warm weather could entice other species to stick around their summer haunts longer than normal. Either way, the hawk's absence from any sightings on Monday didn't bode well for finding it Thursday.

Then again, when it came to birding, you just never knew what you'd find until you looked.

Kind of like my weekend walk at the Arb.

"Look! Here's a late Green Heron."

"Look! Here's a dead man dressed like a scarecrow."

I leaned into Alan's classroom and spotted him back in the corner, his head down on his desk top and his eyes closed.

"Rough night, huh?" I said.

He opened one eye.

"Parenting is not for the timid," he informed me, "or for those who want to sleep at night."

I walked to the back of the room and sat down in a student's desk across from my brother-in-law.

"Are you finding fault with my niece?"

"Not at all. Louise is perfectly incredible," he insisted. "It's the rest of the world that has its nights and days mixed up."

"What do you know about turbines in Stevens County?"

"Frankly, very little," he replied. "I'm lucky if I even know what day it is. I figure I'll have time to catch up on state news again when Louise is—oh, I don't know—seventeen?"

"Months?" I asked.

Alan closed his eye and sighed.

"Years."

"How the mighty Hawk has succumbed to such a tiny child," I observed.

Both of Alan's eyes flew open and fixed on me.

"I'm not the one who carried a sack of flour around school all day yesterday," he reminded me. "At least my baby smiles and drools."

"But mine made good biscuits," I said. On second thought, I added, "Forget I said that."

"I'm not even asking," Alan assured me. He yawned, lifting his head from the desk and stretching his arms toward the ceiling. On their way back down, his hands smoothed over the crown of his head as my brother-in-law shook away his tiredness.

"But back to the turbines," he continued. "As luck—and the lovely wide-awake Louise—would have it, I did happen to catch a program on public radio late last night that featured a panel discussing wind energy. Apparently, when it comes to reducing bird mortality, fewer and taller turbine towers are turning out to be a big piece of the solution out in Altamont Pass in California."

I knew about Altamont. Set atop a ridge in central California, the Altamont Pass Wind Farm was constructed back in the 1970s as one of the first wind farms in the country in hopes of developing alternative sources of energy for a nation dependent on Mideast oil. At its peak, the farm had almost 6000 turbines in operation, making it the largest concentration of turbines in the world.

Unfortunately, its location, prime for catching electricity-generating winds from the Pacific Ocean, also was a critical corridor for raptor migration and overwintering, especially as the Golden Eagle population rebounded thanks to those same federal protection statutes that were now such an obstacle for the proposed farm in our neighboring Goodhue County. By the turn of the new century, experts around Altamont were counting 2,000 raptor deaths every year from bird-turbine collisions, in addition to some 8,000 other bird and bat victims. As a result of the carnage, alternative energy proponents and the local Audubon Society chapters determined to find a compromise that would permit wind generation with reduced avian fatalities. Last I'd heard about it, part of that compromise included replacing the old turbines with an improved design that made wind harvesting more efficient . . . and less deadly.

"I can understand how fewer turbines to fly into would certainly help," I said to Alan, "but how do taller ones make a difference?"

My brother-in-law yawned again and leaned back in his chair. I thought I spotted a small dribble of dried formula on his shoulder.

"Taller towers are the reason they can go with fewer turbines," he explained. "When the turbines are up higher where the wind is naturally faster, you don't need as many turbines to produce the same amount of energy. For the hawks, eagles, and owls, though, taller towers are especially good news: the blades are much higher off the ground, well out of the zone where the birds fly to hunt their prey."

"So the hawk doesn't run into a blade that will slice him in half just as he's diving for some dinner," I said.

"Exactly. They've already seen a big drop in avian mortality at Altamont. If I'm remembering this correctly, they're hoping for an eighty-percent decrease in bird deaths."

The familiar sound of slamming locker doors began to echo in the school hallway. I stood up to go.

"So you're saying that the turbine manufacturers have already been working with conservationists to come up with more bird-friendly wind farms."

Alan nodded. "And if Sonny Delite was as sharp an advocate as you say he was, he'd know about those turbine improvements, just like the utility company would. If birds colliding with towers was the problem, Altamont's taller towers are the solution."

I stood to the side of the doorway as two students sauntered in.

"Which means that there had to be some other reason Sonny was opposing the construction in Stevens County," I concluded.

"Who says he was opposing it?"

I looked at Alan suspiciously. "Red did. She said he was Don Quixote jousting at windmills. Alan, do you know something I don't?"

Alan laughed. "I always know something you don't know, White-man."

"Such as?" I gestured for him to elaborate.

"Oh, let's see . . . I could tell you about the formation of the Italian city states prior to the Renaissance and how their political structures—"

"Alan." I stopped him before he got to full lecture mode. "What do you know about Sonny and the wind farm plans for Stevens County?"

He got up out of his chair and walked across the room to join me at the doorway.

"According to a news article I dug up last night—or was it this morning?—on the Internet, Sonny Delite didn't want to take any windmills down in Stevens County, Bob."

He gave me a soft punch in my right shoulder.

"He was on the team wanting to put them up."

CHAPTER SEVEN

It WAS ALMOST THE END of the school day, and I sat in the back row of the Savage High School auditorium watching Mr. Wist the Amazing Hypnotist up on the stage telling eight students they were now chickens in a farmyard.

"This should be good," Boo Metternick, our new physics teacher, whispered next to me. "Was this assembly your brainstorm, Bob, or did the whole counseling department come up with it?"

I assured him that my colleagues and I shared the credit for the day's special activity.

"We wanted to make sure students took advantage of our break this week to attend some college open houses," I explained. "Mr. Wist came highly recommended. At the end of his show, he does some trick that really motivates students to think about life after high school."

"That would take a magician, not a hypnotist," Boo pointed out. "The last thing high school students think about is life after high school."

I threw a quick look at Boo. "Are you sure you weren't a high school counselor in another life?"

Boo shook his head and lapsed back into silence beside me.

Shoot. Even if I had tried, I couldn't have come up with a better opening line than that for my new colleague to tell me he was the Bonecrusher.

Me: "Are you sure you weren't a high school counselor in another life?"

Boo: "A high school counselor? No way. I don't pretend to have even half of your brilliance and insight, Bob. But I was a famous wrestling celebrity once. They called me the Bonecrusher. Melodramatic, I know, but hey, it was a paycheck."

Instead, Boo continued to sit in silence in the next chair.

I mentally reviewed the latest I'd heard through the faculty grapevine about him, which wasn't much at all. He was single, he was new to the Twin Cities, and he'd only been teaching for three years, the last two in a rural school district in northern New Mexico. What he'd done prior to that, no one seemed to know. But he had dropped in to play some pickup basketball with me and Rick last Wednesday morning before school, and I could personally attest to the man's strength and agility in an athletic contest.

Oh, and there was one more thing I knew about Boo Metternick: his middle name was Charles, giving him the initials of B.C.

Bonecrusher.

Maybe I'd spend the ten dollars that Alan was going to owe me on something cute for Baby Lou.

The sound of a rooster crowing filled the auditorium, pulling my attention back to the students on stage, who were now diligently pecking at invisible grain and flapping their imaginary wings. The rooster cry was coming from a short freckled boy who had jumped up on a chair and was currently stretching his neck as far upwards as humanly possible.

"The farmer's wife is coming to gather eggs," Mr. Wist announced to his subjects, who began to scurry around the stage, clucking and bumping into each other. The rooster-boy crowed even louder.

"It looks like the hallway outside my classroom when the first bell rings for class," Boo said. "Do you think we could get this guy to hypnotize my students to study more?"

Before I could answer him, a loud crash came from the stage, followed by a cacophony of chicken noises. The rooster picked himself up from the floor, crowing repeatedly in agitation as he shook out his arms.

Mr. Wist, now laying beneath the rooster's overturned perch, was out cold.

The other seven students continued to squawk in confusion, then abruptly leapt from the stage and fled out the auditorium doors.

"Is this part of the act?" Boo asked.

Up on the stage, Mr. Lenzen made a beeline for the prone hypnotist. In the packed audience, students shifted uneasily in their chairs, while faculty members asked them to remain seated. From outside the auditorium, I could hear wild clucking. I turned to Boo.

"How are you at rounding up chickens?" I asked. "Unless I'm mistaken, until Mr. Wist gives them the release word, those kids are going to think they're hens in a barnyard."

"I grew up on a farm," Boo said, already moving toward the closest exit. "If I can wrestle steers, I can catch a few student-sized chickens."

Wrestle . . . steers?

I followed him out the door and spotted three of the hypnotized students making a turn into the girls' locker room down the corridor.

"You take them," Boo said, pointing at the disappearing students. "I saw the other kids head towards the cafeteria." He took off in that direction at a run, his arms pumping smoothly like big pistons.

Boo Metternick, Savage's own steer wrestler, catcher of hypnotized chickens, and physics teacher.

Aka . . . the Bonecrusher.

"Yup. You're the man, all right," I said under my breath to his retreating form. "I am so going to get you on my lunchroom shift."

I turned and jogged down the hall to the locker room door.

Seeing the word "Girls" stenciled on the door gave me only a moment of hesitation. It wouldn't be the first time I'd had to enter the girls' facilities at Savage High in the course of my counseling duties, but it still tugged a tiny bit at my sense of propriety. Call me old-fashioned, but I didn't think men belonged in the girls' locker room.

At the moment, though, I supposed I could consider it less a girls' locker room and more a chicken coop.

A henhouse?

Talk about politically incorrect. Our female coaching staff would tar and feather me if I ever let that one slip. And then Mr. Lenzen would get into the act. He'd probably suspend my coffee machine privileges.

Ouch. A day without school coffee was a day without . . . school coffee.

Something to think about there . . .

A loud cackle came from the other side of the door, focusing my attention back to the problem at hand. There were really big chickens in the locker room.

"It's Mr. White, and I'm coming in," I called out before I pushed on the door to open it.

It wouldn't budge.

From the other side came the sounds of shrill squawking.

I put my shoulder against the door and pushed.

Again, it wouldn't budge.

Again, more squawking. Louder this time.

Great. I was probably the first counselor in Savage High School history to be stymied by students who thought they were chickens barricading a door.

I needed another tactic.

"Oh, my," I said loudly, hoping that the power of suggestion would work as well for me as it had for our ill-fated hypnotist. "What do I have here? Grain, and lots of it. I bet hungry chickens would just love to eat this grain."

The squawking stopped. I pressed my advantage.

"Especially hungry chickens at the end of a very long school day," I called through the door. "I wonder if there are some really hungry chickens in this locker room? If they would just open the door, those really hungry chickens could have some of this wonderful feed."

I silently counted to ten, wondering if the ploy would work, and what else I could try to dislodge the hypnotized students if it didn't. The idea of climbing into the girls' locker room through a back window wasn't on my list of things I wanted to accomplish in my counseling career, and I certainly didn't want to imagine what kind of punishment Mr. Lenzen would dream up for me for that particularly egregious transgression.

But it popped into my head anyway: lunch room duty twice a week for the rest of the year.

Over my dead body.

I pounded on the locker room door.

"I'm going to wring your scrawny necks if you don't open this door and do it now! I feel like chicken tonight!"

From the other side of the door I could hear a frantic rustling sound of bodies moving around the room. The squawking became a soft clucking.

I put my hand on the door and slowly pushed it open.

Thankfully, no crazed hens came flying at me to scratch my eyes out. I peered around the door.

One student perched quietly on a bench, arms folded along his sides, his nose bobbing rhythmically towards his shoulder. On the floor, the remaining two students were sitting on top of basketballs.

"Nice eggs," I commented to the two girls on the balls.

"Cluck," one replied, giving me a suspicious frown.

"Tell you what," I told the hypnotized students. "I'll carry the eggs very carefully and you can follow me back to the barnyard and sit on them there. And then you can eat the grain. Yum, yum."

The boy on the bench cocked his head at me.

"Hey," I told him, "cut me a little slack, will you? We never covered talking to hypnotized students, or chickens either, in my graduate counseling program. I am truly winging it, here."

"Are you in there, Bob?" Boo called from the hallway.

"Yup. It's just us chickens," I replied.

Boo's big body almost filled the doorframe to the locker room.

"We're putting the kids in the nurse's office until the hypnotist can release them," he informed me. He looked at the two girls on the basketballs.

"Nice eggs," he said.

"Extra large," I added.

"Clearly," he commented. "That's going to be one heck of an omelet."

He began to flap his own arms at the students.

"Shoo!" he cried, expertly herding them out the door in practiced moves. Cackling all the way, the students scattered out of the locker room with Boo close on their heels.

I wished I had my camera with me. I could see the headline now in the supermarket tabloid: "Former wrestling star pursues students in high school locker room."

Ha. Take that, Mr. Lenzen. I'm not your only public relations nightmare.

I caught up with Boo and the students as he funneled them into the office of our school nurse, Katy the Trauma Queen.

"Thanks, you two," Katy greeted us, her perennial smile cranked up to its usual megawatt force.

She indicated the row of seven students now happily squished next to each other on the single cot in the office.

"Aren't they just the cutest things you've ever seen?" she said. She picked up the candy jar from her desk and poured out a handful of little Tootsie Rolls, which she then passed out to the students.

"This room usually smells like sweat and vomit when I have this many kids in here at once," Katy continued, "but I swear these

kids smell more like a barnyard. Horse manure and chicken drop-
pings. I wonder if that hypnotist gave us all some subliminal sug-
gestions while we were watching the show? Wouldn't that be a
kick?"

"Speaking of the Amazing Mr. Wist, where is he?" I glanced
around Katy's small domain.

She pointed her finger towards the door and the hallway beyond. "He's resting in Lenzen's office. I'm guessing our fearless
leader is reminding our assembly presenter that the school is not
legally liable for any injuries he may have sustained when he was
attacked by a student who thought he was a rooster defending the
coop. Especially since the hypnotist was the one who caused said
student to think he was a rooster."

"We have insurance like that?" Boo asked.

"Oh, yeah," I assured him. "It's in the fine print of the school
policy."

Katy laughed. "I bet you it will be now, if it wasn't before. I
think Lenzen has the school district lawyer on speed dial. Speaking
of which," she added, turning to me. "I heard you found another
body. Are you trying to give Lenzen a heart attack, or what?"

"Ah, I see that Officer Rick has made the rounds," I replied.

I turned to Boo and gave him a look loaded with warning. "Do
not trust our school police officer with anything you don't want to
be made public," I cautioned him. "The man has a mouth the size
of the Mississippi."

Boo was silent for a moment, obviously registering my unspoken message that I was aware of his secret identity.

"Okay," he slowly agreed. "I'll be sure to keep that in mind."

Satisfied that Katy and Boo had the situation under control,
I returned to my office to find the big mouth himself pacing outside
my door. Before I could say a word, though, he grabbed my upper
arm and pulled me into my office, shutting the door quickly behind
us.

"Gina's involved," he blurted out.

"With you, I know," I told him. "I thought that was a good thing."

"Not with me," he said, then shook his head. "No, I mean she is involved with me, but she's involved with the investigation now, too, and that's going to put me in a really awkward position, if not an impossible one."

He raked his fingers over his head. His anxiety rippled through the air.

"Rick, what are you talking about? What's going on?"

"Sonny Delite," he said. "The murder investigation. Gina's involved."

CHAPTER EIGHT

"GINA KNORSEN? OUR CHILD development teacher?"

Rick dropped into my visitor's chair. "Yes, Gina. Our child development teacher. The love of my life."

"The love of your life? Aren't you moving a little fast here, Stud?" I asked him. "Yesterday she was the 'I've got a feeling about her' woman, and today she's the love of your life?"

He gave me a look of pure despair. "Bob, Gina was the last person Sonny Delite called before he died."

I let out a low whistle and dropped into my own chair behind my desk. "Well, that's . . . not good," I finished lamely.

"Not good? We're talking terrible, Bob," Rick corrected me. "I walked back to her classroom with her after the assembly broke up, and when we got there, there was a detective waiting to talk with her. I said he could say whatever he wanted in front of me, but when he told Gina they'd found her phone number on Sonny's cell, and that the call was made at 2:00 a.m. Sunday morning, I excused myself from the conversation."

"Conflict of interest?" I suggested.

"Conflict of everything, I'm afraid," he moaned. "Sonny called her at 2:00 a.m.? I didn't know she even knew Sonny, let alone that she was on his 2 a.m. call list. Gina's not a birder, Bob. Sonny wasn't phoning to give her a birding tip, I'm pretty sure. So why was he calling her?"

"Did you ask her?"

Rick stood back up and paced the few steps to my closed door.

"I will," he assured me. "As soon as the detective is gone. I was at Gina's house on Saturday night and I didn't get home until 3:00

a.m., which means Sonny's call came in while I was there. She must have seen it after I left."

He slapped both of his palms on the door and leaned his head against the wood. "She knows I was at the Arboretum on Sunday. She knows I knew Sonny. She knows I'm a cop and that I have a pipeline to this investigation."

He turned his head to look back at me. "So why didn't she say something to me about that phone call?"

"Because it's none of your business?"

He slapped the door again with his palms, paced back to his chair, and dropped into it again with a sigh of resignation.

"It is my business, Bob. I'm in love with her."

"Then at least give her a chance to explain before you go jumping to the worst possible conclusions," I scolded him. "For all you know, Sonny misdialed."

"If only," he muttered.

"I'm telling you, Rick," I warned him. "If you care about this woman, you better trust her. She trusts you, doesn't she?"

"More than you know," he said.

"Then don't give her a reason to doubt you. Now get back up to her classroom and stand by your woman, Stud."

He stood up and headed for the door.

"And tell me all about it after you find out," I added.

He looked back and smiled grimly. "Not a chance," he told me. "From now on, 'mum' is my middle name."

It took me only a second after Rick left to realize what I'd just done. If Rick was really going to keep his mouth shut, I probably wouldn't be able to get him to confirm that Boo Metternick was the Bonecrusher when we went birding on Thursday to Morris.

Not that it mattered now. After our bonding experience rounding up student chickens, I had no doubt that our physics teacher was a man with a secret in his past—a secret that would stay buried, if Rick's new resolution was as solid as he promised. I hoped it was, because I liked Boo. Boo was a good guy, and I'd hate to see him haunted by his history.

Unlike someone else I could mention, by the name of Sonny Delite.

Sonny's past had done more than just haunt him, however, if his death wasn't the result of mistaken leaf identity, a possibility which, I had to admit, had dimmed more every time I'd considered it in the course of the day. Granted, I knew I wasn't always the brightest-eyed bird in the morning, but even if on automatic morning mode, I couldn't imagine that anyone who knew enough to forage in the forest would pull hemlock instead of ginseng to put in their teapot.

I reached for my cold cup of coffee still sitting on the corner of my desk from this morning and froze in mid-reach.

If Sonny had been drinking poison tea just before he lay down to die, where was the empty cup?

I closed my eyes and tried to visualize exactly what I'd seen when I'd found Sonny on Sunday morning.

Bright sunlight filtering through the orange and yellow leaves still hanging on the trees. A body awkwardly propped against the foot of a big maple, black crows perched above in bared branches. Baggy blue jeans, flannel shirt, beat-up felt hat and heavy work gloves. No straw.

I paused the picture in my head and inspected the ground around the body.

No metal lip of a cup catching a glint from the sun.

No white Styrofoam cup sticking out of the carpet of fallen brown leaves.

No thermos sitting next to Sonny with a big arrow pointing to it, labeled "Hemlock."

I opened my eyes and put my fingers on my laptop's keyboard. I typed in "Hemlock."

Within a second, I had a list of results, and right at the top was the official site . . . of Hemlock, the heavy metal band.

Gosh darn. I got rid of my leather wristbands decades ago. Pass.

I looked at the next result listed.

The Hemlock Tavern. Located in San Francisco.

Unless it was the home of microbrewed poisons shipped overnight anywhere in the United States . . . another pass.

I read the third entry.

Ah, yes. Wikipedia. The best friend of every student who was looking for somewhat reliable information to slip into a poorly written research paper.

I'd learned early on during my tenure at Savage High School that the quickest way to rile any of the teachers on staff was to defend Wikipedia as an acceptable source of research. In fact, I'd instigated so many heated debates in the faculty lunchroom that Katy the Trauma Queen routinely accused me of using the Wikipedia card to raise the blood pressure of certain teachers. I assured her that I was simply doing my part to improve the American educational system by thinning the herd.

Having no objection myself to using the online site, I began to read about hemlock. About two-thirds of the way through the posted information, I found what I was looking for: seizures could begin in fifteen minutes and turn fatal within a few hours of drinking a hemlock-infused concoction. If medical help was immediately available, activated charcoal could be administered to help block the stomach's absorption of the toxin while anticonvulsant drugs might prevent additional seizures which could result in respiratory, kidney, or cardiac failure.

Good to know. The next time I unknowingly drank hemlock, I'd be sure to do it within shouting distance of an emergency room.

But the last paragraph on the page stopped me cold, because it claimed that hemlock had a sharp scent, one that was readily recognizable by people who were knowledgeable about wild plants.

People, I supposed, like Sonny, who knew the forests and fields. Those folks wouldn't mistakenly pick and brew hemlock, because even if the leaf looked like ginseng, it sure didn't smell like it.

Nor would the tea.

Unless you added some real ginseng, or other potent flavor, to the hemlock.

Deliberately.

With full knowledge.

The unavoidable truth hit me like a sledgehammer.

Someone had poisoned Sonny.

I pulled out my cell to call Rick, then remembered he was probably upstairs, either talking to Gina or still waiting for the detective to leave.

Gina.

She'd had a phone call from Sonny just hours before he was poisoned.

A faint alarm went off in my head. For some unexplained reason, Gina and the word 'poison' were connected in my thoughts.

What the heck?

I frantically searched my memory for all the conversations I'd had with Gina during the faculty workshops. We'd talked about her teaching stint in the inner-city. She'd told me about the one year she'd worked at a charter school and how much she loved it. We'd compared notes about our favorite camping spots around Minnesota: I liked Blue Mounds State Park near Luverne, and she preferred Itasca State Park, home to the Mississippi head waters. Clearly, she was very knowledgeable about nature and enjoyed a variety of outdoor activities, but to the best of my memory, she hadn't once brought up the subject of harvesting and brewing hemlock.

I tried to recall what Rick had said about her. She had a fire pit, she knew the constellations of the night sky, and he had a feeling about her.

That probably described half of the women he'd ever dated.

Rick had a thing for fire pits.

He'd also known about the flour babies, because Gina had told him he could be the child protection officer and . . .

Safety.

Child safety.

The ever-truant Sara Schiller had reported that her child development class covered a unit on safety, including a warning about poisonous plants at the playground. On the crazy, highly unlikely, chance that Sara had actually been in class for the entire unit, she would know if Gina Knorsen was familiar with hemlock. For all I knew, Gina gave each of her students a laminated plant identification card to help prepare them for their eventual responsible parenting duties, which included keeping their kids from ingesting marbles, nails, and poisonous substances.

Like hemlock.

And if Gina Knorsen could readily recognize hemlock, who was to say that she couldn't also have picked some on one of her camping trips?

You know . . . just to have on hand in case she needed to provide a visual aid for a class lesson on child safety.

Or to poison someone.

My stomach dropped.

I'd just remembered the name of the charter school where Gina had worked: the Minnesota New Country School.

It was located in Henderson, the same place where Sonny had bitterly fought the utility company over the power line project.

Then I remembered something else Gina had told me during faculty workshops. The same year she'd taught at the charter school, her brother shared her apartment with her while he waited for a construction job that never came through.

A construction job with the local utility company.

Then, at the end of the school year, Gina had given up the job she loved and moved to the Twin Cities so her brother could find work.

Crap.

If Gina knew that Sonny was behind the reason her brother had remained unemployed and the reason she'd decided to leave the New Country School, then she probably wasn't one of Sonny's biggest fans. And given the amount of publicity that had surrounded the whole utility line debate, there was no way Gina wouldn't know about Sonny's role in defeating the project, unless she'd been living in a sealed bubble, which I highly doubted. Minnesota might have some interesting architectural landmarks and structures scattered around the state, but if Henderson had bubble housing, it was news to me.

Another troubling thought followed on the heels of that one: according to what I'd learned from the police the last few times I'd discovered a body, murder was usually personal.

Did a 2:00 a.m. phone call qualify as personal?

Let's be honest here. When someone calls me at two in the morning, I take it very personally. On top of that, I confess that after getting a 2:00 a.m. phone call, murder has crossed my mind a few times, too.

Unless it was a call from a birding buddy who was giving me the heads-up about a rare bird currently appearing in his or her field of vision.

Night vision, that is.

So . . . Sonny had called Gina . . . about an owl?

Yeah, right, Sherlock.

My stomach dropped a little more. Despite my own advice to Rick to trust our new Family and Consumer Science teacher, I suddenly had a very bad feeling that whatever reason Gina Knorsen had for being on Sonny's 2:00 a.m. call list, it wasn't a good one.

CHAPTER NINE

I TURNED OFF MY COMPUTER and checked my office phone for messages before leaving for home. Two birders had left reports of sighting birds that were uncommon for this time of year in different Minnesota counties: a Purple Sandpiper in Swift County and a Red Phalarope in Sibley. If Rick and I were lucky, the sandpiper might stick around another few days, and we could try to see it on our way up to Morris on Thursday. Sibley County, however, was farther off the route we'd be taking, so I'd have to leave the phalarope for another season.

I sighed heavily.

So many birds, so little time.

A knock on my door caught my attention as I turned to grab my jacket from my office coatrack.

"Hey, Boo," I said as the big guy leaned into my doorframe. "Thanks for help with the chickens today."

"No problem," he replied. His eyes fell to the jacket in my hand. "You got a minute?"

"Of course," I said. I put the jacket back on its hook and gave him a smile. "What can I do for you?"

He returned my smile with his own big grin.

"Actually, I'm here to do something for you."

Yes! I mentally pumped my fist. *I knew it!* After our bonding experience today, Boo Metternick had decided to throw caution to the winds and trust me with his secret identity.

He was going to tell me he was the Bonecrusher.

My own smile broadened in anticipation.

"Alan said you were interested in wind energy farms," Boo said.

The fist pump vanished in my head.

"What?"

"Alan said you were interested in wind turbines," Boo repeated.

Yup. That's what I'd heard the first time, all right. I was evidently going to have to find something more trust-inducing than chasing down hypnotized students together to earn the big guy's confidence.

I let out a sigh of acute disappointment.

What did Boo Metternick have to do with wind turbines?

I realized that he was waiting for me to respond while I just stared at him like an idiot.

Luce has told me more than once it's a good look for me, by the way. And not an uncommon one, apparently, either.

"I am interested," I finally said, then immediately wondered what else Alan had told him.

Had my brother-in-law mentioned to Boo that my interest was connected to a homicide?

Or that I made it a habit to find the bodies of dead birders when I went out in the woods?

I was well aware that Rick squealed on me all the time, but I sure hoped that Alan hadn't jumped on the bandwagon. It would be nice to know that at least one of my close friends could keep his mouth shut and refrain from tarnishing my reputation.

"He said you had a bet going on," Boo informed me when I didn't offer any further elaboration. "That you bet him that turbines killed more birds than people every year. I told Alan he lost the bet because thousands of birds are killed every year, but I only knew of twenty people who'd been killed by wind turbines in the last two decades, and three of those cases were highly questionable."

"Questionable?" I repeated, while blood rushed from my head as I tried to keep my overactive imagination from picturing what a person might look like after going through a "questionable" death by a wind turbine.

"You all right?" Boo asked. "You look kind of white."

"Yeah, that's me," I said weakly. "White. Bob White."

I dropped into my chair, and Boo took a seat on the other side of my desk.

"Wait a minute," he said, sudden realization crossing his face. "It's not what you're thinking. I've never heard of anybody getting cut up by a wind turbine. That would definitely be a stomach-turner. I meant they got killed working on them while they were installing them. You know—freak workplace accidents that can happen on any large-scale construction project."

He sat back in his chair. My vision cleared.

"Except for the three questionable fatalities," he added. "In those cases, the guys died of heart attack or stroke, and their families insisted it was because of the turbines. The guys didn't work on the turbines at all—they just lived in the general area and apparently told everyone that the turbines were affecting the normal functioning of their bodies. Something about an overload of vibrations or incessant humming that was interfering with their heart rates and brain waves."

He crossed his arms over his chest.

"There was speculation that the guys might just have been nuts, too."

I looked across the desk at Boo, suddenly aware that he'd spoken more words to me in the last few moments than he had in the last two months.

"No sliced torsos or split guts with intestines hanging out?"

Boo grimaced. "No. Oh, my gosh, no. Believe me, I never would have worked on turbines if I thought I could get caught in one. When I was a kid, I watched a doctor sew my dad's finger back on after an accident with some equipment on the farm, and that was more than enough to convince me I didn't ever want to come close to a spinning blade."

"But didn't you just say you worked on turbines?"

I felt like I was speed-dating. We were barely minutes into our conversation and I had already learned that Boo Metternick not only had a great memory for trivia, but he'd also worked with machines.

At this rate, I was going to have his phone number in less than three minutes.

Boo nodded. "I did. I spent a summer while I was in college working on wind towers in northern Iowa. All we did was put them up, though. I was on the construction crew. I never got anywhere near an operating turbine. My interest now is purely academic. Windmills make great examples of certain physics principles."

"So I win the bet, huh?"

The bet about avian fatalities that I'd never made, that is.

I silently thanked Alan for being circumspect about my 'interest' in wind farms and for not sharing any more details than necessary with our new physics teacher. Becoming known as a corpse finder wasn't my current career objective, nor did I want my weekend discovery to become the topic of the week in the staff lounge. I figured that Boo, with his own Bonecrusher skeleton in the closet, could probably relate to that same appreciation for discretion.

"You do win," Boo assured me. "Although I've got to tell you, wind farms get a bum rap when it comes to bird mortality. Power lines kill birds more than ten thousand times as often as wind turbines—up to 174 million birds a year, according to the U.S. Fish and Wildlife Service. And cats—both domesticated and feral—take out another couple hundred million birds every year. Compared to those numbers, the wind turbines' toll of ten to forty thousand a year looks pretty small."

Geez Louise. The man was a walking statistics report.

"But housecats aren't killing Golden Eagles or Burrowing Owls," I argued.

"Oh, so some birds are more expendable than others? No one's going to miss a couple million robins and sparrows, but a thousand raptors rate special consideration." He blew out a breath of disdain. "Sounds like avian discrimination if you ask me."

I opened my mouth to reply, but nothing came out. Put that way, the case for saving raptors did sound like species discrimination.

"Are you an ethics teacher on the side?" I asked him.

Boo laughed, his somber mood gone as quickly as it had come.

"No," he replied. "I just like to argue. My dad always said I was born to start fights. If he said the sky was blue, I'd say it was green. If you'd said that the bird death count from turbines was inconsequential, I would have made a case for the specific bird populations affected, like the eagles and owls that you just mentioned."

He rolled his shoulders and cricked his neck to either side.

"But here's something else I would have added to the argument," he continued. "Turbines aren't just a problem for birds in the air. Studies for new wind farm locations now focus on the nesting habitat, which is often on the ground and might be disturbed by tower construction. You destroy those breeding sites, and there won't be enough of those birds around to even consider flying near the wind turbines."

He cracked the knuckles in both hands.

"And let's not forget the damage to the bat population," he added. "Those casualties are in the thousands, too. Did you know that some species of bats experience fatal internal bleeding as a result of the air pressure changes caused by spinning turbine blades?"

I studied the big man in my office. For a former seasonal construction worker, he seemed to know an awful lot about the bigger issues around wind energy.

"Who are you really, Boo Metternick?" I asked. "You're teaching physics, you argue ethics, and now you display a keen knowledge of emerging issues in Minnesota conservation. I think you're either campaigning for a position on the school board, or you're an advance man for *Jeopardy!* Which is it?"

Boo laughed again.

"Neither. I'm just a farm kid from western Minnesota," he insisted. "I grew up detasseling corn and riding a tractor on family land."

"And wrestling steers," I reminded him.

My bet with Alan about turbines may have been a convenient fiction, but I still had ten bucks riding on Boo being the Bonecrusher.

"That, too," he said. "Our family has had that land for generations, but times are hard for an awful lot of small farmers, including my dad. These days, farmers have to get inventive with their crops to survive, and wind energy is a booming cash crop if you can get it."

He stood up and smiled. "So it's kind of become my hobby— learning everything I can about the wind energy industry so when my dad finally signs the contract to rent our family's land to the utilities people, I'll be reassured that he's not only guaranteeing his retirement income, but that he's doing the right thing ecologically."

"And are you reassured?" I asked.

He nodded. "I will be, once the deal is done. Our land isn't a bird breeding ground like the big parcel next to it that the energy company has been considering for rent, so that means the company should be knocking on my father's door."

He crossed his arms over his chest and frowned.

"But the energy people have some consultant who keeps insisting that it's our property that has the breeding ground, not the one next door, so my dad's going crazy trying to prove this consultant wrong," Boo continued. "It seems like every time Dad turns around, this consultant has more 'evidence' that the birds— grasshopper sparrows, I think they are—are nesting on our land, even though my dad paid out of his own pocket for ground surveys to show our land isn't being used by the birds. And get this—it turns out that the big parcel where the sparrows *are* breeding belongs to a cousin of this consultant."

"The plot thickens," I commented.

"But it's still transparent," Boo added. "The consultant is biased. He wants the rental income from the new wind farm to go into his cousin's bank account, and he's willing to lie about our land to make that happen."

He placed his palms on my desk and leaned towards me.

"I don't like liars," he said.

I looked at his hands spread out on my desktop. They were the size of boxing gloves. Extra-large boxing gloves.

"Me neither," I agreed.

"You were good with the chickens today, too," Boo said. "You could pass for a farm kid from Spinit yourself."

The name of the town sounded familiar, but I couldn't quite place it. Seeing as I've driven to every corner in the state chasing birds for the last nineteen years, I wasn't completely surprised I couldn't recall its exact location, but I knew it would nag at me until I looked at a map.

"Spinit—isn't that near Buffalo Ridge?"

Buffalo Ridge was a big spread of elevated land that stretched from the edge of South Dakota down through several southwestern counties of Minnesota and into northern Iowa. It was also home to one of the largest wind farms in the United States.

Because I occasionally birded in the area, I was also aware that much of the ridge was privately owned farmland, some of which was rented to the energy companies for turbine tower placement. One farmer I met told me he received an annual royalty payment of $4,000 for each turbine on his land, and that he knew of others who earned up to $8,000 per tower. The bigger spread a farmer had, the more turbines he could accommodate, and the more lease money he could earn.

If Boo's family's land was located on the ridge, I imagined his dad could make a pretty solid bundle of money from royalties.

As long as some consultant didn't block the deal.

"No," Boo corrected me. "Spirit is in the west central part of the state. It's a tiny community in Stevens County, not far from Morris. This is a new wind farm project that my dad wants to get in on. The company wants to place turbines seventy-five acres apart to minimize wind speed loss, and my dad says that would mean seven towers on our land, with a twenty-year agreement. With that kind of annual income, he and my mom could be comfortable for the rest of their lives without having to work the farm."

He stood back up and glanced towards my open doorway, then lowered his voice.

"My dad's a proud man, Bob," he said with affection. "I've offered to help my folks out in their retirement with some money I've got invested from my previous career, but he won't take it. So I told him to let me know if there was anything—anything at all—I could do to make this deal happen for him."

"You're a good man and a good son, Boo," I told him. "I hope it works out for your dad."

"Thanks, Bob."

He gave me a little salute.

The gesture reminded me of my conversation with Red at Millie's Deli on Sunday. She'd saluted me, too.

Poor Red. I hoped she was doing better after her fall down the stairs and that her memory had returned, because I wanted to ask her about Sonny. In particular, I was curious as to why she thought he was opposing the planned wind farm while Alan claimed the opposite was true. What had Sonny said to her the last time he was eating at Millie's? And what exactly was her relationship with his wife, Prudence?

Once again, I found myself wondering about Red and what she might be able to tell me about the Delites. If Red was going to be working on Thursday morning, Rick and I could swing by the deli for an early breakfast on our way north. Then, while Chef Tom scrambled some eggs and fried bacon for me, I could grill Red.

"Hey, Bob?"

Boo had stopped outside my doorway.

"You guys be careful driving to Morris on Thursday. This time of year can be iffy with weather. I can't tell you how many times I've gotten caught in sleet storms out there and almost ended up in the ditch . . . or worse," he warned me.

I tried to remember when I'd mentioned the Morris trip to Boo, but I came up blank. I'd gradually become accustomed to the fact that my wife had an uncanny ability to read my mind, but I didn't especially like the notion that someone I barely knew could pull off the same trick. It made me feel vaguely uneasy.

Threatened, even.

Weird.

I had to ask. "How did you know I'm going to Morris?"

Boo laughed once more.

"A little bird told me." He held up his hand in farewell and walked away.

It didn't take any imagination at all to guess that Rick, Officer Big Mouth, had broadcast our plans to Boo. The two men must have become real buddies since Rick had learned the truth about Boo's past—maybe that shared secret had provided them with a bonding experience, in the same way that the hypnosis-gone-awry incident had apparently made Boo feel more comfortable with me. I'd learned as much about Boo during our brief student round-up as I had in the last two months of working with him.

Heck, if I'd known that talking to chickens was the key to opening up the channels of communication between me and our celebrity faculty member, I would have gladly demonstrated my famous turkey call for him weeks ago.

In fact, the more I thought about it—Boo's reticence, not the turkey call—I realized that the man's reluctance to get close to people was probably no surprise, given his former identity as a wrestling celebrity. During our back-to-school workshops, and even since classes had started in the fall, I'd noticed that Boo avoided casual conversations with the other faculty members. At times, I'd thought his silence had bordered on being spooky, the way he'd watch his colleagues during lunch breaks without saying a word. But now it made perfect sense. The man had lived in the glare of publicity as the masked Bonecrusher, and while he might have enjoyed his ride of fame and his reputation in the ring, he was in a different world now. I expected the last thing he wanted was his showbiz past to follow him into the halls of a high school and his future as a respected faculty member.

Notoriety wasn't always a good thing.

Just ask Sonny Delite.

Actually, I guess you'd have to ask his widow now.

Unless Red had her memory back.

I wondered again if Rick and I would see Red on Thursday morning before we took off for Morris.

I grabbed my jacket off the coatrack and locked my office door behind me. From down the hall, I could hear some kids loitering, slamming lockers and yelling at each other. I shook my head. My day wasn't done yet. Time to be the voice of authority at Savage High School.

But someone beat me to it.

"You. Out," Boo said, his voice carrying back down the hall to me.

Whoosh. Those kids were gone.

Disappeared.

Vanished.

Geez.

I'd thought Boo was spooky because he'd been so quiet around other adults, but that was nothing compared to how spooky he was when dealing with students. Those kids hadn't even stopped to breathe when he told them to leave. When I asked kids to quit loitering, they handed me a pile of excuses about why they were there and who gave them permission, even when I knew they were lying to me. Instead of compliance, I got stories, disrespect, and defiance.

The Bonecrusher got results.

Forget about getting Boo on my lunchroom shift.

I wanted him as my personal valet.

Then again, I now knew that the Bonecrusher didn't like liars, and I had no doubt that even though a lot of students couldn't recognize their own stupidity if it slapped them in the face—sometimes repeatedly—every one of Savage High School's population could clearly hear the take-no-prisoners tone in Boo Metternick's voice. I guessed that wrestling steers on his father's farm in Spirit taught the young Boo a thing or two about asserting himself.

Imagine that—the world-famous Bonecrusher hailed from a dot on the map out in Stevens County.

The same Stevens County where a new wind farm was proposed that would insure Boo's parents' retirement, unless a sketchy consultant lied his way into stopping the deal.

I stopped in my tracks.

Stevens County was the site of the wind farm that Red said Sonny was fighting, and Alan said Sonny was supporting.

So which side had Sonny been on?

A more troubling question pushed that one aside in my head.

Was Sonny a consultant for the energy company?

The consultant that Boo accused of lying?

When I'd heard about Sonny's involvement in the project, I'd assumed he was acting as an environmental advocate, since that was the role he'd always played in the previous projects. To me, that implied that Sonny was against the construction of a wind farm, and Red's comment had seemed to support that.

But Alan's announcement had corrected that misconception: these days, both the opponents and proponents of an energy project called in assistance from environmental experts to support their side of the debate. To meet government guidelines, the development companies had to prepare and submit studies to the public utilities commission of how the proposed project would impact local species, along with plans to manage the natural area responsibly. Those studies were the work of environmental specialists.

Likewise, those groups opposing a project prepared their own studies, also produced by experts in conservation research. Just as in any case where two perspectives are represented, commissions often heard two different stories about the same topic. With any luck, the studies all came to the same conclusion, but often enough, it seemed, the two versions sat squarely on opposite sides of the fence. When that happened, the feathers began to fly, just as they had in the Goodhue County situation, with each side accusing the other of fabricating, or omitting, important information.

If Sonny had joined the payroll of an energy company as its environmental consultant, I wanted to believe that he'd be as committed to conservation as he'd always been as an independent concerned citizen. But if Boo had his facts straight, the consultant in the Stevens County project was deliberately misleading the energy company in the attempt to benefit his relative.

The consultant was a liar and a cheat.

Which, I unhappily recalled, was the very thing that Prudence Delite had said about her husband.

Her *murdered* husband.

Chapter Ten

I DODGED AROUND RICK and launched the ball toward the basket. It hit the rim and bounced back towards me, but Boo jumped up and snagged the ball out of the air. He dribbled it back out beyond the top of the key with Rick hot on his heels. A moment later, Boo had turned and shot the ball in a perfect arc that sent it straight through the basket with barely a swoosh of the netting.

"Pretty," I told Boo. "I bet your high school coach loved seeing you make that shot."

Boo grinned. "Yeah. Every time I did it, he just about cried."

It was early Wednesday morning in the Savage High School gym, and Boo had joined Rick and me once again for our weekly before-school-hours pick-up game.

"So when is that lightweight brother-in-law of yours going to get back in the game with us?" Rick asked, the basketball cradled on his hip. "It's not like he's the one who gave birth. I can't imagine he's not up to playing basketball yet."

"The operative word there is 'up,' Rick," I told him. "Alan takes the midnight shift with Baby Lou most nights so Lily can have a break and get some sleep. Then by the time he gets back to bed, he's only got a few hours before he needs to be in the classroom. Getting up early for basketball isn't rating very high on his list of priorities right now."

"Like I said, he's a lightweight."

"I want to see you say that to him when he does get back on the court, Stud. He will clean your clock."

"He's that good?" Boo asked, a trace of a challenge in his voice.

I looked over at the muscular frame of our new physics teacher. Boo had his hands clasped together on the top of his head, his triceps bulging like thick ropes between his shoulders and his elbows. If you painted him green, he could be the Hulk for Halloween.

Which reminded me that I was still up in the air about a costume for the faculty party.

I'd only had the one idea so far—the buzz saw-carrying hockey-masked serial killer—but with the murder case of an old friend gaping wide open, I just couldn't generate any enthusiasm for it.

"Alan Thunderhawk would give anyone a serious run for the money," I assured our secret celebrity. "He would, that is, when he's on top of his game," I amended. "Fatherhood has made some inroads into that at the moment."

"I'll say," Rick added. "These days, Alan looks more like something the cat dragged in, instead of the hotshot collegiate athlete he used to be."

He turned to Boo. "Where'd you go to college?"

The big guy shrugged. "Out east. I didn't play basketball, though. I was a wrestler."

Well, duh.

With a move so quick I hardly saw it, Boo snatched the basketball from Rick and sent it flying towards the backboard.

It dropped through the hoop in a perfect basket.

"Are you guys going to Stevens County just for the day?" Boo asked.

Rick watched the ball bounce and then roll in his direction.

"Man, you are both fast and accurate," he said to Boo, clearly impressed with the Bonecrusher's court performance. "Remind me to be on your team when Alan gets back and we start playing two-man basketball." Rick turned to me. "We will crush you, Bob."

"Yeah, right," I said. "You and the Bonecrusher."

Rick's eyes darted in Boo's direction, then back to me. He crossed his arms over his chest and smiled. "I didn't say that."

I rolled my eyes. "You didn't have to. I'm not totally without my own resources, you know."

Boo said nothing while he scooped the basketball up from the floor with his big hands.

"That's the plan," I finally answered Boo. "Rick and I want to try to sight a Ferruginous Hawk that's been hanging around up there this week. We're hoping to find it on Thursday, but this particular species of hawk is notorious for being here today, gone tomorrow. It may well be out of the state by now."

He spun the ball on the tip of his finger.

"Could I ride along with you guys? I'd like to get up there to see my dad and find out what's going on with the wind farm plans." He popped the ball up and back into his hands. "If you could just drop me off in Morris, that would be great, if it's not too much trouble for you. I'm sure I can catch a ride out to the farm from there. And then I could be back in town in time to catch you on the way back."

I glanced at Rick, who nodded in agreement.

"Sure," I told Boo. "You direct me to your dad's farm, and we'll drop you off right there. But we need to be back in Savage by six o'clock, since Stud has a big date lined up."

"Let me guess," Boo said. "Gina Knorsen?"

"News travels fast," I observed.

"Not all news," Boo pointed out. "I don't think anyone else on the faculty knows yet that she's being investigated in connection with the murder at the Landscape Arboretum over the weekend."

Rick's face went hard. "What do you know about that?"

"Not much," the Bonecrusher admitted. "I ran into one of your police buddies in the parking lot after school yesterday. He was talking into his cell phone, and he didn't hear me coming up behind him."

"You're joking," Rick said. "No way a police officer wouldn't hear you coming up behind him."

"Just like you saw me coming when I stole the ball from you before my last basket?"

I jabbed a finger into Rick's shoulder.

"Got you there, Stud. Not only is our new physics master silent, but he's invisible, too. He's Boo the Ghost."

Shoot. Another great idea for Boo for the faculty party. I might as well be his costume designer at this rate.

Boo laughed.

Rick didn't.

"You need to not say anything about Gina or this investigation to anyone," he warned Boo, his voice cop-serious. "She doesn't have anything to do with that murder, and she sure doesn't need anyone asking her questions about it."

Boo took a step closer to Rick, his voice softer, but just as serious.

"I know that," he said. "Gina Knorsen wouldn't hurt a fly. She might have picked up a few combat skills from teaching in the rough part of town, but the woman's a sweetheart."

He leveled his gaze at Rick.

"You're not the only one she's impressed, you know."

I felt the testosterone level in the gym suddenly spike.

Great. Our new Family and Consumer Science teacher had clearly caught the eye of more than one male on the staff. If Rick and Boo started circling each other on the gym floor, I was going to have to call security.

How was that going to work?

Rick *was* security.

He was Savage High's very own school police officer. Calling him to break up this fight would be downright awkward, if not physically impossible.

Before I could make that observation, however, Boo held up the basketball in one palm. "Have we got time for another five minutes of play?"

"You bet," Rick said, simultaneously batting the ball from Boo's hand and heading back towards the basket at a run.

Boo took off after him. Just as Rick stopped to shoot, though, the Bonecrusher, unable to stop his forward momentum, plowed into Rick from behind, sending him sprawling face-first across the gym floor. Boo tripped into a heap beside him.

For a moment, neither of them moved.

A groan came from Rick.

Another groan came from Boo.

"I think I just got hit by a semi," Rick said, his voice muffled by the floor. "Am I roadkill?"

I walked over to where he was spread out on the floor.

"You will be if you don't get up," I told him. "The first-period gym class plays volleyball in here. I've seen some of them in action. They're merciless. They don't care who they have to step on . . . or over."

Boo lifted himself up to a sitting position. Blood ran out of his nose and down his chin. He grabbed a handful of his jersey and held it up to his nose to stop the bleeding.

"I am so sorry," he told Rick through the cloth covering his nose and mouth. "I didn't see you'd stopped until I hit you. I'm not very good at stopping once I get going."

Rick rolled over onto his side, squeezed his eyes shut, and let loose with a string of profanity. A grimace of pain accompanied his words.

"That bad, huh?" I asked him. "You want me to just shoot you and put you out of your misery, Stud?"

"Shoot him first," Rick replied, gritting his teeth and nodding toward Boo. "I think he broke my ankle."

"He's probably going to arrest you as soon as we get him vertical," I warned Boo, "though I'm not sure what the charge will be. Hmm, let's see . . . charging? Unnecessary roughness? Sheer stupidity on his part?"

"It's going to be for publicly humiliating me," Rick informed us. He sat up slowly and probed his ankle with his fingers, wincing all the while. "Although stupidity might take precedence. My mind says I'm eighteen, and my body just laughs."

"You really think it's broken?" Boo said, wiping off the last bit of blood from below his nose.

"Nah," Rick told him. "A bad sprain for sure, though. I'm going to have to stop in at the ER and get it wrapped. I'll probably have to stay off of it today and maybe tomorrow. Keep it elevated."

He turned to me. "I don't think I'm going after that hawk tomorrow, Bob. It's all yours."

"I'll take pictures," I assured him.

"You're still going to Stevens County?" Boo asked.

I nodded. "The Ferruginous Hawk waits for no man," I said. "It's tomorrow morning or not at all. You still want a ride?"

"You bet. Unless you happen to get yourself injured before then, too. In which case, I'll pass."

"I'm not planning on it," I told him.

"Like I really planned this," Rick groused from the floor. "Will you guys help me up, or are you going to chitchat all morning?"

Boo and I both reached a hand to Rick and helped him up off the floor. As soon as he touched his left foot to the floor, he choked out a few more choice words. He shifted his weight to his right foot and gingerly drew his left foot up so only the toe of his sneaker tapped the floor for balance. I grabbed his upper left arm to give him more support as he hobbled to the locker room door.

"I guess I won't be taking Gina dancing tomorrow night, either," he complained. "Could I have any lousier timing?"

I looked over at Boo to tell him what time in the morning to expect me, but the words caught on my tongue.

I could have sworn he was trying not to grin.

CHAPTER ELEVEN

THE REST OF THE DAY WAS UNEVENTFUL. I helped three seniors finish completing multiple college applications, referred two juniors to our chemical dependency counselor, advised one sophomore to quit mimicking his math teacher—especially since said math teacher had angrily herded said sophomore into my office after hearing himself being mimicked in the hallway between classes—and found a partridge in a pear tree.

No, wait. Wrong season.

It wasn't a partridge. Or a pear tree, either.

It wasn't Christmas yet. It was almost Halloween.

It was Mr. Lenzen, waiting outside my office at the end of the day.

Trick or treat?

Believe me, it wasn't going to be a treat, I was sure.

"I understand you were involved in a rather gruesome discovery at the Minnesota Landscape Arboretum this past weekend," our assistant principal began, carefully brushing some lint from his immaculate suit jacket sleeves.

"Yes, I was," I admitted.

Since I was clearly busted—thank you, Rick—I decided to make the most of it.

"The blood wasn't even dry yet. And the ripped out guts—have you ever smelled torn flesh and bloated—"

"Mr. White!"

Mr. Lenzen, his face visibly paling, stopped me in mid-sentence. I gave him my most innocent expression.

"What?"

He pulled a pressed handkerchief from his back trouser pocket and delicately blotted away the beads of perspiration that had appeared above his upper lip. "I assure you, I don't need the details."

"I'm sure you don't," I agreed, "especially since I'm also sure that Officer Cook already beat me to it."

"Officer Cook?"

"Officer Cook. You know—our school police officer who gladly rats me out every time I so much as jaywalk."

He gave me a stern stare. "You jaywalk, too?"

I was getting nowhere fast, when all I really wanted was to go home.

"Mr. Lenzen," I said. "Was there something you needed?"

"To be perfectly frank, I think I need some antacid. Between you and Ms. Knorsen, my ulcer is going to land me in the hospital."

"What about Gina?" I asked, not wanting to let him know what I knew before I knew what he knew.

Mr. Lenzen sighed dramatically. "You'll have to ask her, Mr. White. I don't carry tales about our faculty members."

That's right. I'd forgotten. Mr. Lenzen was the president of the Savage Secrets Club.

I expected him to whip out a detention pass at any moment. Instead, he brushed more lint from his sleeve.

"Although I expect you'll have a hard time asking her anything right now," he noted. "She just left the building in the back seat of a patrol car."

"Why would Rick put her in the back seat?" I blurted out. "I thought they were dating."

Mr. Lenzen gave me a smug look.

"It wasn't Officer Cook's squad car," he said. "I believe it was the same police detective who stopped in yesterday."

"Gina's seeing another cop?"

"I wouldn't know anything about that, Mr. White," he primly sniffed, "and, quite frankly, I'd rather not know about it. What Ms.

Knorsen does on her own time is none of my business. Unless it impacts her teaching in the classroom," he qualified, "which is, at this moment, no longer a concern."

He checked his wristwatch. "As of twenty minutes ago, Ms. Knorsen has been suspended from her teaching duties until further notice."

"Because she left in a patrol car?"

And then I realized what Mr. Lenzen was trying to not tell me.

Gina had been arrested.

Rick was going to be a mess.

"Thank goodness we have fall break tomorrow," Mr. Lenzen continued. "Please don't do anything . . . controversial . . . over the weekend, Mr. White. I don't want to have to add a second suspension to our staff."

"Got it," I absently replied, still focused on what Rick's reaction to Gina's arrest might be like. "No bodies and no headlines."

"Exactly." Satisfaction filled Mr. Lenzen's voice. "Now, if you'll excuse me, I need to get back to my office to line up a substitute for Ms. Knorsen for next week. I hate to leave these things till the last minute."

I watched him walk away, wondering how soon I'd hear from Rick.

"Earth to Mr. White."

I blinked and turned my head to the left. Sara Schiller was sitting at one of the tables out in the counseling department reception area. A bag of flour stood on the table in front of her.

"Hey, Sara."

I walked over to the table and checked out the front panel on the flour. "You've still got Robin, I see."

"You can't have him," she was quick to inform me. "You're a cannibal. You ate my last baby."

"It's a bag of flour, Sara. It's only pretending to be your baby."

"Ms. Knorsen said that a lot of times, a woman's maternal feelings don't kick in immediately after birth," she reported. "That sometimes, it takes a while for the mother to bond with the baby because her hormones are all screwed up and she's really worn out. I figure that's why I didn't do so well with my first baby—my hormones are always screwed up, and I was really worn out."

"I don't know about the hormones part, but of course you were worn out," I agreed with her. "You'd just driven to Wisconsin and back."

She gave me a glare.

"Only because a *certain counselor*," she emphasized, "loaded me down with an impossible class schedule that was so bad I had to get away for a day so I wouldn't have a total mental and emotional collapse."

"So it's my fault you ditched school and drove to Wisconsin?"

"That's what I just said."

"Sara, I think we need to work on the concept of personal responsibility a little bit," I suggested. "You ditched school. That was your decision, not mine."

"I know, but—"

"No buts," I cut her off. "No matter what the reason you had for skipping classes, it was your decision to act on those reasons in that particular way. You have to take responsibility, Sara, for both the good and the bad you do. That's what growing up is about."

Sara gathered the bag of flour into her arms and pulled it against her chest.

"I was going to say 'but I talked it over with Ms. Knorsen' before I was so rudely interrupted," she said. "Do you want to hear this or not?"

"Sorry," I apologized, only mildly repentant. "Yes, I want to hear this."

She sat back in her chair, the bag of flour clutched against her body.

"When I told Ms. Knorsen that you had switched my baby because I had left it with you, she said that we all make mistakes—even, sometimes, when we think we're doing the right thing—and it takes a mature person to own up to it and to learn from it. She said, if I wanted, that I could give the assignment another try since it was clear my maternal instincts were just slow in developing the first time."

She slid the flour up to her shoulder and gently patted its back.

"I really don't want an F in the class, Mr. White," Sara explained. "I want to pass all my classes so I can graduate and get out of high school and get on with my life. Ms. Knorsen is the first teacher who's even tried to understand me, and I want to prove to her I can do better. I want to show her I can take responsibility."

I stared at the young woman in the chair. She wanted to pass her classes and graduate? She wanted to be responsible?

Who was she?

"If I'm ever going to have kids of my own," the Sara imposter said, "I'm going to have to set an example for them. And that means being responsible."

Holy cow. Gina Knorsen was a miracle worker with a bag of flour, and Sara Schiller was a born-again student.

I couldn't think of a single thing to say.

"And if I were responsible, then maybe Ms. Knorsen would introduce me to Noah," Sara added.

"Who's Noah?"

Sara slid me a sly grin. "Ms. Knorsen's brother. I saw him talking to her Monday morning before class, and I'm guessing he's like twenty-six, which is sort of old, but I could make an exception for him."

She patted Robin on the back again and sighed dreamily. "I could definitely make an exception for Noah."

Wonderful. Just what I didn't need to know: Sara Schiller had her eye on a twenty-six-year-old who happened to be the brother of a faculty member.

"Although he's kind of a crab from what I could tell," she continued. "He was arguing with Ms. Knorsen about something, and he left all angry, and then she was pretty upset during class."

My eyes drifted to the clock on the wall.

It was after four, and I didn't want to hear anything more about Gina or any other Knorsen, especially one that Sara had a crush on. As far as I was concerned, business hours were over, and I was done for the day. Besides, I had a couple of errands to run before dinner, and then I needed to check the MOU postings on the computer list serve to see if the Ferruginous Hawk had made an appearance in Stevens County today. If it had, there was still a good chance I could find it tomorrow.

"Was there something you wanted to see me about?" I asked Sara, beginning to back up toward my office, already planning my route home.

She bolted upright in her seat, Robin still glued to her chest.

"Yes! I know it was a mistake to ask you last time to watch my baby, and I take full responsibility for that, but could you take Robin—"

"No."

"You don't even know what I'm going to ask!"

"It doesn't matter," I said, turning my back on her and heading into my office to collect my jacket and briefcase. "I'm going out of town," I said over my shoulder, "I'll be up in Morris tomorrow."

I grabbed my jacket and briefcase and then locked my office door. When I turned around, Sara was still in the chair at the table, glaring at me.

"So what's up in Morris that everyone is going there?" she asked.

"What do you mean?"

"That's where Ms. Knorsen's brother said he was going when he stomped off on Monday," she explained. "He said his job was done down here and he was going home, whether she liked it or not. I think he quit his job or something, and that's what they were arguing about."

"You shouldn't be listening to other people's conversations, Sara," I scolded.

"Other people shouldn't be arguing in front of me," she re-torted. "Especially when one of them is as hot as Noah Knorsen."

She stood up and balanced Robin on her hip. "I bet he's got a killer smile to go with those abs. Did I mention that he's ripped, too?"

"Sara—"

"I'm outta here. Have fun in Morris. Tell Noah 'hello' for me if you see him. I hear it's a small town." She grabbed her backpack with her free hand. "I just might have to take a drive up there next week and check it out for myself."

"As long as it's not during school hours," I told her. "Officer Cook will send a posse of state patrolmen after you if you pull that little trick again."

She gave me a pouty look.

"Girls just want to have fun," she said. "Spoilsport."

"Sara, go home."

"All right, I'm leaving already," she snapped, hugging Robin back to her chest. "Why anyone ever thought you would be a good counselor is beyond me. Honestly, you can be so clueless sometimes, Mr. White. Bye."

Clueless?

I shook my head in exasperation as I made my way out of the building towards the staff parking lot behind the gym where I'd left the car this morning before playing basketball. If anyone was clueless, it was my perennial delinquent Sara Schiller who somehow thought she was going to attract a man ten years her senior by her demonstration of responsibility towards a bag of flour.

Man, was I glad the day was over.

Except that it wasn't.

I stood behind my cardinal red SUV and silently ran through the same list of profanities that Rick had used while he was sprawled on the gym floor this morning.

All four of my tires had been slashed.

CHAPTER TWELVE

"**N**EED A RIDE?"

A sleek black car pulled up next to me with Paul Brand leaning out of the driver's window.

"A lift to the Tire Shoppe would be good," I said. "Looks like I need a new set of tires."

"It's on my way home. Hop in," Paul invited me.

I slid around the front of the vehicle, noting the polished chrome and smooth hood.

"Nice car," I told Paul. "It looks new."

"It is," he replied. "It's Honda's new CR-Z hybrid. Today's muscle machine."

I glanced appreciatively around the black leather interior and spotted his art satchel stashed behind his seat. Yup, those were definitely wrestlers on the bag's front panel. I stole a look at Paul's profile as he peeled us out of the faculty parking area.

I tried again to imagine the black mask and leotard on him. Somehow, sitting in his sporty black muscle car, whipping down the road a good ten miles over the speed limit, it wasn't nearly as hard to see Paul Brand in a wrestling ring.

With or without his art satchel.

And now that I really thought about it, what better way to disguise a broken nose than with a full facemask?

"I promised myself I would go hybrid with my next car," Paul said. "I'm already seeing a huge drop in my gas bill."

He hit the brakes and came to a screeching halt at a stop sign.

"Sorry," he apologized. "I like speed."

"No problem," I told him. "I tend to drive a little fast myself."

"Thanks for talking to Sara," Paul said, accelerating into the intersection. "She was in class today."

"She's a good kid," I told him. "She just doesn't think through to the consequences of what she does. She acts first, thinks later. And then, once she realizes she's screwed up, she has no idea how to fix things, so she just plows on ahead, which only digs her deeper into her original mistake."

"Like if she misses one class, she figures she might as well miss the rest."

"Exactly."

Paul pulled a hard right into the Tire Shoppe's parking lot.

"I think we're all slow learners at times, don't you?"

"Probably," I agreed. "We all do stupid things."

"Like painting a bulls-eye on your car with a vanity plate?"

I opened my mouth and nothing came out.

Instead, I immediately thought of all the times my license plate had gotten me into trouble: the extra highway stops by state patrol officers who recognized my BRRDMAN license. The time my brakes were tampered with to discourage me from pursuing a murderer. The flat tires I got when a killer put bullets in them to frame another suspect.

Gee, I guess that meant I wasn't exceptionally quick on the uptake, now was I?

"You're saying you don't think my tires getting slashed was a random early Halloween prank?" I asked Paul.

I'd assumed it was a no-brainer. Halloween was getting close, it was a school parking lot, and students liked to pull pranks—especially the students who had too much time on their hands because they skipped classes to hang out in the parking lot to pull pranks.

He shook his head. "Nobody else in that whole parking lot had slashed tires, Bob. Your car was the only one vandalized in any way. You might want to consider getting rid of the plates."

I opened the door and climbed out of Paul's car.

"Say, Bob," he added, leaning across the now-empty passenger seat to catch my eye. "It's not always a great thing for people to know too much about you. I speak from personal experience."

He grabbed the inside door handle and pulled it shut. With a roar from the engine, he sped out of the Tire Shoppe's lot.

Who would want to slash my tires?

And what kind of personal experience was Paul Brand referring to?

I watched his car careen expertly around a corner. He had quick reflexes, that was obvious. He also didn't offer much in the way of personal information about himself. I tried to remember everything I knew about our new art teacher, and realized much of it was only rumor. From our brief conversation this morning, all I'd learned was that he'd taken worse hits than the one that broke his nose in a high school hockey tournament; where and when he took those hits was a mystery, because he hadn't elaborated.

Just like he hadn't elaborated about his personal experience of it being better to be an enigma than someone who publicized his identity on his license plate.

Good thing I hadn't already spent those ten dollars I bet Alan about the Bonecrusher being Boo Metternick. After spending a little more time in Paul Brand's company, I had to admit that Alan's pick for our secret faculty celebrity wasn't as far-fetched as I'd originally thought. Paul had a penchant for speed, muscle, style, and mystery. He'd been an athlete in high school, and he had a bag with a wrestler on it.

If he showed up at the faculty Halloween party in a black leotard, I was going to be kissing my ten bucks goodbye.

So much for my being a great judge of character. Maybe Sara Schiller was onto something when she said I could be clueless.

Clueless? Me?

Not in a million years.

I had plenty of clues.

I just didn't always come to the right conclusions.

Like why my tires got slashed.

I had to admit, Paul had a point about anonymity. If nothing else, I bet I'd see a real reduction in how often I got pulled over for speeding if I got rid of my vanity license plates. I knew I was somewhat of a celebrity myself among the state highway patrol officers, since over the years, I'd met police in almost every county in the state. Rick had even tried to convince me that there was a BRRDMAN club for everyone who had ever given me a warning or citation.

If that's what I have to deal with as a birder, I couldn't imagine what it would be like to be a world-famous celebrity wrestler. I'd peel off that leotard so fast and try to find the furthest spot I could away from the public eye.

I'd become a teacher in a little high school in Savage, Minnesota.

So now I had to ask myself: what would I be teaching in that little Minnesota high school?

Physics or art?

Only the Crusher knew.

Well, that wasn't completely true.

Rick, scum and now-lame, knew who the Crusher was, too.

I heard a distant crying noise above me and looked up to see a large flock of Red-winged Blackbirds flying south. It reminded me that by this time tomorrow, with any luck, I'd be adding a Ferruginous Hawk to my life list.

But not unless I had four new tires on my SUV first.

I watched the last blackbird disappear into the horizon, walked over to the Tire Shoppe's front door, and pulled it open.

Crap.

Rick wasn't going with me to Morris. That meant he wasn't going to tell me who the Bonecrusher was in exchange for getting the Ferruginous Hawk.

No matter. I was going to find that hawk, anyway.

Just like I was going to figure out which teacher was the Crusher.

I walked into the Tire Shoppe and spied my regular car-care guy at the service desk.

"You got a set of tires I can buy?"

CHAPTER THIRTEEN

TWO HOURS LATER THAN I had originally anticipated, I parked my car—with its brand new tires—in the garage next to Luce's Volvo.

"Honey, I'm home!" I announced as I walked through the door into the house.

"I love it when you call me honey," Rick said, his foot propped up on the coffee table in my living room.

"You're not my wife," I observed.

"Whoa! You're quick," Rick said.

Luce walked in from the kitchen and handed Rick a tall glass of iced tea.

"He called me for a ride when I was leaving work," she said, placing a warm kiss on my cheek. "He told me it was your fault he had a sprained ankle and that I could at least invite him to have dinner with us to make up for it."

"It wasn't my fault. He thought he could outrun Boo Metternick."

"You invited him to play with us," Rick pointed out.

"Well, yeah. I'm not going to tell the Hulk he can't play with us. Are you crazy? The man could squash us like bugs if he wanted to. Besides, he played nicely enough with us last week, didn't he?"

"That was before I found out he has a thing for Gina," he complained.

"Speaking of which," I said, "did you know that they're both from the Morris area? For all we know, they're related. Kissing cousins. Morris is a small town, after all."

"Not that small."

Luce stepped directly in front of me, making a time-out sign with her hands.

"Could we start this conversation over so I know what you two are talking about?"

I grabbed her hands and brought them up to my lips for another kiss. "Your wish is my command."

"Spare me," Rick muttered.

I quickly explained to Luce about the morning basketball game, then gave them both the highlights of my conversation with Sara.

I left out the part about my being clueless, though. Between Luce and Rick, I was pretty sure they would have a field day with that part, and we'd never get the conversation back on track.

"I knew that Gina's brother had a job in the southwest suburbs, but I didn't know what he did," Rick said, "or that he quit on Monday. His employment situation wasn't at the top of my list of questions when Gina and I talked last night about her connection to Sonny Delite and why she'd gotten a 2:00 a.m. phone call from him just hours before you found him at the Arboretum on Sunday morning."

I waited a beat for him to continue, but he didn't.

"Why don't we move this to the dining room and have dinner before it gets even colder?" Luce suggested.

"Sorry," I apologized. "The Tire Shoppe was busier than I expected. I was just happy they had the tires I needed in stock. I'm going to find that hawk tomorrow if it kills me."

Rick pulled himself up and balanced on his crutches. "I'd rather you not put it quite that way, Bob. Too many things are beginning to get weird around here."

I watched him hobble into the dining room.

"What things?" Luce asked me, a note of concern in her voice.

I took her shoulders in my hands and turned her toward the dining room. "I have no idea," I lied.

The truth was that I'd had plenty of time while I'd waited for my new tires to mull over the events of the last few days since I'd found Sonny doing his scarecrow imitation at the Minnesota Landscape Arboretum. Despite being the person who discovered Sonny's dead body, I'd assumed my involvement would end after the police had interviewed me at the scene of the crime on Sunday, since I had no connection to him aside from a casual acquaintance and no idea of what had been going on in his life.

Yet circumstances around me seemed to keep pointing back to Sonny's demise, and, being a naturally curious person, I couldn't help but wonder if I was stumbling across random pieces of information that might eventually lead to solving the mystery of his death.

Not that I was making a list of those pieces, exactly. Like every birder I know, I already had plenty of lists to keep me busy: my birding state list, individual county lists, my life list, my vacation bird list, my backyard list, my birds-seen-while-eating-Luce's-food list, my birds at gas stations list, my . . . you get the idea.

It just seemed like so many incidents or conversations lately were conspiring to keep me thinking about Sonny Delite.

For instance: one of my best friends was involved with a woman who'd received a phone call from the deceased shortly before his death. Why couldn't Rick be dating some nice woman who'd never heard of Sonny Delite, let alone one who had lived in Henderson during Sonny's big media splash and was on his phone list? But no, he had to be falling in love with a possible murder suspect who knew what hemlock looked like and might have blamed Sonny for her brother's unemployment and her own sacrifice of a job she loved.

Second example: My new faculty pal had a direct connection to Sonny's recent project, and not in a good way, either. Boo's dad needed Sonny to support the rental of his land by the energy farm company, and that clearly hadn't happened. Worse, Sonny may have been the consultant who lied in the attempt to get the contract into his own relative's hands, and Boo hated liars. Oh, and did I mention that the man was very possibly a former professional wrestler and big and strong enough to carry three Sonny Delites into the woods if he so chose?

Third example: My tires were slashed in the school parking lot the night before I planned to go to Morris. True, that could have been a total coincidence, but after my discussion with Paul Brand, I wasn't so sure, and the only reason I could think of for someone wanting to ground me was that I was planning to go to Morris the next day. Morris—where Sonny had been involved in a high-stakes energy controversy.

Fourth example: Rick, my birding buddy, who also happened to be a police officer and involved with a possible murder suspect, had to back out of my trip to Morris thanks to a freak accident, leaving me with the possible Bonecrusher as my co-pilot.

The same Bonecrusher who just a day earlier told me to be careful of driving to Morris, but now wanted to go with me.

"Are those homemade biscuits I smell?" Rick asked as he awkwardly slid into his chair at our dining room table.

"They're baby biscuits," Luce told him, removing the cloth napkin that she'd tucked over the basket of biscuits to keep them warm, "made from Sara Schiller's bag of flour."

"You cooked Sara's baby?" Rick made a show of inhaling the mouth-watering scent that floated out of the basket. "I may have to turn you in for child neglect to Gina."

He palmed two of the biscuits and dropped them on his plate. "After dinner, of course."

"I brought Sara's baby home last night since she skipped out after leaving it with me," I explained to Rick, "and Luce thought it was hers to use."

"You have done well," he intoned to my wife. "I will bring you a fatted cow tomorrow."

That was another thing that had bothered me while I waited for the tires to be replaced on the car: even Sara Schiller had inadvertently dropped me another piece of the Sonny story. Gina and her brother—the one who'd been an unemployed construction worker in Henderson when the utility project fell through—were from Morris, which was the same area where Boo Metternick was from. As Sara had noted, Morris was a small town, but the Twin Cities were anything but, so what were the odds that these three people who all had a link—and a negative one, at that—to Sonny Delite would have been in Savage this last weekend, just a half-hour drive from the place where Sonny was poisoned?

Okay. I admit it. Math has never been my strong suit, so I really didn't know what the odds were. I just knew it was odd.

Really odd.

"So what time are you planning to leave in the morning?" Luce asked me as she lifted a delicately browned chicken breast from a heatproof casserole dish and placed it on her plate. It was glazed with a honey mustard sauce.

I loved honey mustard sauce.

"Is this a new recipe?" I asked my wife.

"New to us. I got it from Chef Tom at Millie's on Sunday morning before Sonny's widow showed up and made a scene with Red."

That was another weird event to add to my list: the almost girl fight at Millie's and the odd chemistry between Red and Prudence Delite. Were the women friends or enemies? Prudence had taken a swing at Red, and Red had restrained her, assuring all of us there that Prudence didn't mean anything by it and was just overcome with grief. Yet I'd seen Prudence continue to stare at Red the rest of the time we were there. There wasn't grief in that glare, either. It had been desperation.

And then she'd let everyone know that she blamed Sonny's death on Red because Red had made a big public deal about Sonny's latest advocacy involvement. Prudence claimed that in doing so, Red had thrown Sonny to his enemies . . . enemies who must have been likewise lunching at Millie's.

Pretty darn convenient for the enemies, I'd say.

You get lunch and your intended victim handed to you on a platter.

You want coleslaw or American fries with that murder plot?

But Sonny wasn't killed over lunch, I reminded myself. He died after an early morning cup of tea.

Memo to me: morning tea can be fatal. Especially if it's handed to you by your enemy. What's that old saying?

Oh, yeah.

'When in doubt, throw it out.'

Either that, or get an official taster like those kings in the Middle Ages. I guess they knew what they were doing when they added tasters to their workforce.

"I think someone might try to poison me today," says the king to his taster-employee. "You try it first."

Talk about sub-par job security, but I guess it was a living.

For a while, at least.

Maybe.

If you were lucky.

Geez. And I thought I had lousy job benefits. The coffee in the faculty lounge was bad, but it hadn't poisoned anyone.

That I knew of.

Yet.

"I need to tell you something," said Rick, beginning to drum his fingertips on the table.

"You're drumming," I said, picking up my fork and knife to slice into the succulent chicken breast I'd just laid on my own plate. "This is not going to be good, is it? You always start drumming when you're tense or upset. Nice polo shirt, by the way." I hoped I could distract him. "Is it new?"

"Yes, and that's what I have to tell you."

"You bought a new shirt?"

"No. I mean, yes." His fingers stopped drumming and he looked up at the ceiling, sighing. "I'm out of uniform for a reason, Bob."

"You're off duty?" I guessed.

"I'm on unpaid leave."

"How bad is the sprain?" Luce asked him.

He looked at Luce, his face filled with misery.

"I'm a possible suspect in the murder of Sonny Delite."

Chapter Fourteen

"**Y**OU WANT TO RUN that by me again?" I asked, my silverware poised in the air.

"You're kidding, right?" Luce added.

Rick slowly shook his head slowly in an unmistakable "No."

"I wish I were kidding," he moaned. "This is a nightmare."

"Then you better wake up, Stud, and tell us what's going on, because I don't have a clue how you could be implicated in Sonny's death. You're one of the good guys." I laid my knife and fork back down on the table so I wouldn't be tempted to stab him with either one in order to get the whole story out of him faster.

Then I realized I did have a clue. Several, in fact.

Yes, me, the clueless Mr. White.

"It's because you're involved with Gina," I guessed. "And the phone call came while you were at her home. Somebody on this case thinks you went crazy because some guy called your new girlfriend at two o'clock in the morning, so you tracked him down and killed him?"

I shook my head. "You may have a big mouth, Rick, but you're not a jealous homicidal maniac."

"Tell it to the judge, Bob," he said, then grimly added, "if it comes to that."

"It's not going to," I assured him.

"How can you say that? I don't have an alibi, Bob. No one can testify to my whereabouts from 3:00 a.m. to when I showed up at the Arboretum looking for you."

"So that means you're a suspect?" Luce asked. "Because you were alone on Sunday morning?"

Rick shook his head again. "No. I'm a suspect because I've been telling everyone at work how crazy I am about Gina."

He picked up his own fork and stabbed it into his chicken.

"And because the real reason Gina left Henderson wasn't her brother's lack of employment," he told us. "She said she was forced to leave by the school board there, because she got involved with the utilities fiasco . . . and Sonny Delite."

"Involved?"

Rick looked up from his plate. "She didn't know he was married, and he never bothered to tell her. Henderson is a small town, and people talked. She quit her job, moved to Minneapolis and started over. She didn't even know it was Sonny calling her on Sunday morning until she checked her messages later in the day."

"After he was dead," Luce pointed out.

"But there's no way to prove that," Rick countered. "When the detective questioned her after school yesterday, he had proof from Sonny's phone log that he had called Gina early Sunday, and only Gina's word that she hadn't taken the call. She can't prove with her phone when she actually checked her messages."

His face got even gloomier.

"Gina's honest, Bob. She told the detective I'd been with her that night when the call came in, and she told him all about her past history with Sonny."

He stabbed the chicken again.

"She even told him about the message Sonny left. 'Meet me behind the Arboretum's Learning Center at 6:00 a.m., Gina. It's important.' She'd already deleted it from her phone, or she would have played it for him, but of course that doesn't make her look any better at the moment. She's doing the right thing, being completely upfront about all this. It's the only chance she has to get out of this mess."

But Gina's being upfront was putting Rick right in the line of fire . . . along with his big mouth.

"Come on, Rick," I said. "Your own boss thinks you might be involved in a murder? What kind of working relationship is that?"

Both Rick and Luce stared at me in disbelief.

"Hello? Who worries about his job every time he finds a body in the woods?" Luce pointedly asked me.

"Does the name Mr. Lenzen ring a bell?" Rick added.

I held up my hands in surrender. "Forget I said that. My mistake. Obviously you can have a working relationship with someone who thinks you're capable of murder—I'm living proof of that. Although I wonder sometimes if what I have with Mr. Lenzen is less of a relationship and more a strained tolerance. But you've always had the respect of your captain, Rick. He can't possibly think you're a viable suspect."

"I don't think he really does," Rick agreed, "but he's got to play by the rules. And, of course, it probably doesn't help that I told at least three of the guys that I'd do anything for Gina. Anything at all."

I groaned.

"At the time, I was thinking along the lines of a tattoo, or maybe raking up the leaves in her yard," Rick admitted, a trace of sheepishness in his voice. He fingered the stud in his ear, courtesy of the last girlfriend to whom he was hopelessly devoted . . . for about eighteen months, if I was remembering correctly.

"I guess I'm just a fool for love," he conceded. "What can I say?"

"I think you just said it," I replied, "though I probably wouldn't qualify it with the 'for love' part. 'Just a fool' works for me."

"The police don't have any stronger leads?" Luce asked.

"Not for lack of trying," Rick replied, poking idly at the food on his plate. "So far, they've interviewed half of the attendees at the Arboretum conference, along with the employees of the Arb working at it, plus every customer they could track down who was at Millie's on Saturday afternoon. That's one of the biggest holes in their investigation at the moment—they can only identify those customers who paid by check or credit card. Anyone who paid cash is unaccounted for, and since a lot of Millie's customers pay with cash, the only person who could pick out those diners is Red."

"And she's got memory issues from her fall," I pointed out.

Rick nodded. "Let's face it—I'm an easy pick for a suspect. I could have the motive and the opportunity. Plus, I knew Sonny, and I'm a cop, so why wouldn't he take a cup of tea from me during an early morning bird walk? If I was investigating this case, I'd sure take a close look at me."

"Well, that sucks," I said.

"You bet it does," Rick agreed.

Silence fell around the dinner table, and I concentrated on cutting up the chicken on my plate and putting a forkful into my mouth.

Yet again, Sonny's death was demanding my attention. I was beginning to wonder if this was what it felt like to be haunted—every time I had a conversation with someone, Sonny seemed to have a connection to it.

It wasn't even Halloween yet, and I had a ghost knocking on my door.

Trick or treat, right?

This was a lot worse than Mr. Lenzen showing up in my office, though, and even less of a treat, seeing as one of my best friends was now under suspicion for the death of the ghost in question.

On the plus side, though, I knew just what to suggest to Rick for his costume for the faculty Halloween party: he could come in the orange jail jumpsuit he'd be wearing after his arrest for the murder of Sonny Delite.

"Wait a minute," I said, swallowing my bite of chicken. "I heard that Gina was arrested for Sonny's murder."

"When did you hear that?" Rick asked, curious, but not especially alarmed.

"What, no theatrics?" I asked, surprised by his calm inquiry. "Here I was convinced that you would go postal, or at least be really upset. If this is how you react to your lady love getting arrested, you should definitely rethink the tattoo idea, Stud."

Rick held up a slice of chicken on his fork.

"When did you hear it?" he repeated.

"After school," I answered. "Mr. Lenzen told me that Gina left school in the back of a squad car. Since it wasn't your squad car, I assumed that—"

He shook his head. "No arrest, Bob. One of the guys gave her a ride down to the station at my request. I met her there, and we both signed statements. I drove her home afterward."

"But she's been suspended," I pointed out.

"You drove her home?" Luce asked. "You're on crutches. You asked me to bring you over here so you wouldn't have to get behind the wheel. Why were you driving Gina?"

"Ah, Luce, that's so sweet," Rick told my wife. "You're really worried about me. I know!" he perked up. "How about I stay here tonight, and you can bring me a glass of warm milk when you tuck me into bed? I might need a story, too, you know. And a goodnight kiss. Yeah, I think that would really make me feel much better."

I threw part of a biscuit at him.

"In your dreams, Stud. What about Gina's suspension?"

Rick turned his attention back to me. "That's Lenzen's *modus operandi*," he said. "When in doubt, kick 'em out. At least temporarily."

"So Mr. Lenzen equates suspicion with spoiled food," I observed.

Both Rick and Luce gave me funny looks.

"An earlier train of my thought," I explained. "When you have reason to question, or doubt, what it is you're eating or drinking, you should throw it out. When Mr. Lenzen questions a teacher's integrity, he throws them out of school via suspension."

"And?" Luce motioned for me to continue.

"That's all," I said. "No 'and.' Just commenting."

Although something about what I had said lodged in my head. I had an overwhelming feeling that doubting what you eat or drink was somehow important to figuring out why Sonny had been murdered. Before I could piece the thought together with another, however, Rick started talking again.

"Gina told me that Lenzen tried to assure her that her suspension was for her own good, to keep her out of any uncomfortable situations at school that might arise because of the investigation into Sonny's death. He also told her as soon as the case was resolved, he expected her back at work." He slathered butter on one of his biscuits and popped it in his mouth.

"I think she really thinks he has her best interests at heart," he continued. "She's not crazy about attention, and the embarrassment in Henderson was pretty tough on her."

I could imagine. In a small town, scandals marked you for life, even if you were the unwitting victim. From what I'd seen of Gina, though, I would have guessed that if anyone could survive a reputation blow, it would have been our Family and Consumer Science teacher. Gina was tough, and she believed in taking responsibility so much that she demanded it of her students.

Besides, according to Rick, Gina hadn't known that Sonny was married, so why had she felt she had to take the fall?

Everyone makes mistakes.

But some are more costly than others.

Just ask Sonny Delite's ghost. He'd probably thought that his tea was going to wake him up, not put him to sleep . . . permanently.

"But you and I both know that Mr. Lenzen is really only concerned about Mr. Lenzen's best interests," I argued, giving up on pondering Gina's reaction to scandal.

Rick shrugged.

"As long as Gina still has her job when this is over, I don't care what Lenzen thinks or does," Rick said. "I just want Gina to be happy. She wants to get on with her life, and I'm hoping her life will get on right here."

"With you?" Luce asked.

"Preferably."

"Then you have to stay out of jail, Stud," I reminded him. "Any bright ideas on that score?"

Rick smiled. "Funny you should ask, Bob . . ."

CHAPTER FIFTEEN

I PULLED UP IN FRONT OF BOO METTERNICK'S little house in Shakopee at five-thirty in the morning. Before I could put the car in park, though, Boo came striding out of his front door, a big smile on his face and a backpack slung over his shoulder.

"Nice new tires you got there," he said as he slammed the car door shut and settled into the passenger's seat.

"Who told you?" I asked.

"A little bird," he said, still smiling. "Tweet, tweet.

Again with the little bird bit. If he hadn't been almost twice my size, I would have learned over and smacked the side of Boo's head. Forking over the money for four new tires hadn't exactly lightened my mood yesterday, especially since the only tires the shop had in stock were the most expensive brand. Of course, if I could have waited another day, the shop would have ordered in the more economical tires to save me a bundle—another day I didn't have, unless I wanted to forget about driving to Morris and trying to find the Ferruginous Hawk, which I definitely refused to do. So I sucked it up and got the new tires on last night.

Thank you, American Express. I couldn't have left home without you.

Yeah, I know—I always tell people that birding is a very inexpensive hobby, and all you really need are binoculars and a field guide to enjoy endless hours of birdwatching. And that's true, as long as you can bike or walk wherever you want to bird. When you become a "serious birder" like me, though, and you begin to set your sights on building up your bird lists, your hobby starts to generate more expenses, like gas and vehicle maintenance.

Meals on the road.

Birding group memberships.

Magazine subscriptions.

Festival fees.

More expensive binoculars.

Buying raffle tickets to state patrol fundraisers.

Actually, I'm the only birder I know who does that on a regular basis. I figure it's the least I can do for Minnesota's finest. Plus I keep hoping it will work like insurance, so the next time I get stopped for speeding on county roads, I can tell the patrol officer I already gave to his office. Rick's told me more than once it's probably a better idea than offering donuts to patrolmen who pull me over, though he doubts it will keep me from getting the tickets I deserve.

The vanity plate conversation with Paul Brand popped back into my head, but I pushed it aside.

Instead, I thought about Rick, Boo's informant, aka "a little bird."

"I'd say he's more Mr. Big Mouth than little bird," I corrected Boo. "Seriously, I'm starting to think that you and Rick must be sharing some kind of communication hotline, which seems kind of odd, given that you clearly are sweet on Gina too."

Boo stared straight ahead. "It's that obvious, huh?"

"Well, yeah," I replied. "You practically went green with jealousy when I mentioned that Rick had a date with her yesterday morning when we were playing basketball. And the green went virtually florescent the longer we talked about Gina. I think you laughed when I said you were Boo the Ghost, but you do a better imitation of the Hulk, given the opportunity. Very green."

"Please don't say anything to Gina," Boo said.

I stopped at the intersection at the end of his street and took a look at the man beside me.

He was a blond-haired, blue-eyed Norse giant, with biceps built to impress. His shoulders were broad and his chest muscular.

Even with the additional leg room in my SUV, Boo still looked like he was awkwardly folded into the passenger seat thanks to his extra-large frame.

Two indisputable facts emerged from my assessment of the man: one, if he wasn't the Bonecrusher, no one was; and two, most women would be thrilled to be the apple of those bright-blue eyes of his, whether or not he hid them behind a black wrestling mask.

Except, apparently, Gina Knorsen, who was mysteriously immune to his appeal.

"Does she know?"

The Norse giant nodded miserably. "Since we were in middle school."

Middle school.

Great. Rick's romantic competition for Gina was not only a world-class wrestler, but a world-class wrestler who had been carrying a torch for the lady for about twenty years. Rick was lucky he'd gotten off the court yesterday morning with only a sprained ankle.

If Boo had really wanted to hurt Rick, I had no doubt that our school officer would have been waking up this morning in a portable bed in the intensive care unit at the local hospital. Rick was no slouch when it came to defending himself, but Boo was a professional wrestler, albeit retired, with twenty years of unrequited love simmering just below his cool Scandinavian exterior.

Was a serious rival for Gina the trigger that would blow Boo's cool? Maybe I should start calling him the Savage Volcano. He could stage a comeback on the wrestling circuit with a name like that. Mr. Lenzen would be thrilled, I was sure.

Boo seemed to have his temper and feelings for Gina well under control, however, and clearly hadn't taken out a full measure of his frustration on my poor buddy. No surprise there, if the Crusher had been carrying that torch for as long as he claimed. Perhaps his spooky silence at work was likewise a result of his well-trained restraint, and not so much an attempt to stay off everyone's radar to protect his secret wrestling past as I had supposed. Or maybe he was quiet at work because he was too busy moping over his luckless love life.

Man, was I glad I was married. Love triangles and heartbreak could really take a toll on a guy. Even a bruiser like the Bonecrusher.

"Did you have breakfast?" I asked Boo, smoothly changing the topic to something less risky than his interest in his faculty colleague. "I thought we'd grab a hot breakfast at Millie's in Chanhassen, then head up to Highway 12 west. There are a lot more birding spots along that route than if we take the interstate up through St. Cloud, and I want to make the most of the day if possible."

"Breakfast would be great," he said. "I threw some protein bars in my backpack, but a hot meal sounds a whole lot better."

I crossed the Minnesota River on Highway 101 and wound up through the bluffs to Chanhassen. It was just after six in the morning, and traffic was still light, but I noticed I'd picked up a tailgater right on Seventy-eighth Street two blocks from my turn into Millie's parking lot.

"I hate it when drivers tailgate," I muttered, turning on my left turn signal.

"What did you say?" Boo asked as I braked to make the turn. *Smack!*

I could feel the car shudder slightly as the tailgater hit my rear end. The SUV slid a foot forward into the opposite lane of traffic, but fortunately, no cars were approaching.

"Oof!" Boo sputtered as his body lurched a bit forward in the passenger seat. Out of the corner of my eye, I could see that despite his size, his seat belt kept him safely anchored in place.

"I saw that one coming," I said, glancing in my rear view mirror.

The driver of the car behind me was climbing out. Other than a twinge in my shoulder, I was unhurt. My guess was that the car might have taken a bump on the fender, but I seriously doubted there was any real vehicle damage for either myself or the tailgater. I opened my door and stepped out.

"It is you!" Prudence Delite said. "I was trying to read your license plate when I hit you. That's why I didn't notice your turn signal or brake light. I'm so sorry. Are you all right?"

I looked down at Sonny's widow.

What were the odds that I'd run into her again?

Or rather, that she'd run into me?

Literally.

"My license plate," I nodded, beginning to wonder if someone at the Motor Vehicle Division had recently put a curse on my plate. "It's not the first time it's gotten me into trouble, I have to say. In fact, my brother-in-law says I might as well have a tractor beam on the back end of my car the way my plate attracts accidents and speeding tickets."

"Sonny told me he loved your BRRDMAN plate," Prudence said, a small sniffle sneaking into her sentence. "He wished he'd thought of it first. I wish I'd thought of it and surprised him with it."

She sniffed again, her eyes beginning to blink erratically. "It would have made him so happy. All I ever wanted was to make him happy."

Alarm bells went off in my head.

Female crying jag! Danger! Danger!

"We should get out of the road," I interrupted her, hoping to derail the approaching waterworks. "Let's just pull into Millie's parking lot, and we can take a look at the cars there."

A few moments later, Prudence, Boo, and I each made a careful inspection of the two cars. My SUV showed only a scratch on its rear bumper, while Prudence's front fender seemed a bit higher on one end, and the headlamp on the driver's side was cracked.

"Just cosmetic," she assured me, her voice steady again. "It was my fault. I was just so surprised to see your license plate in front of me. It made me think of Sonny."

She took a deep breath, but no tears appeared. "I always thought of him as my birdman."

I began to pull my wallet out of my pocket to hand her my insurance information.

"Don't bother," she said. "I'm fine, really. Believe me, a bumped fender and a cracked headlight are the least of my worries this week."

I probably could have guessed that one. Between her husband's murder and Red's accident, Prudence Delite must have felt like she was a walking bad luck charm.

"I understand that the police are working hard to figure out what happened to Sonny," I said. "Again, I'm so sorry for your loss, Mrs. Delite."

She nodded vigorously. "Can I buy you breakfast? You and your friend?"

I realized I hadn't yet introduced her to Boo.

"This is one of our teachers at Savage: Boo Metternick," I said. "Boo, this is Prudence Delite."

Boo offered Prudence his hand and they shook.

"You look familiar to me," Prudence told him. "Just now, when we were checking over the cars, I could have sworn I know you from somewhere."

"Are you a wrestling fan?" I asked her, then bit my tongue too late. I deliberately didn't look at Boo. For all my criticism of Rick's inability to keep his mouth shut, I was on my way to coming in a close second.

Prudence gave me a funny look. "No, I'm not. Why do you ask?"

"No reason," I said, and quickly changed the topic. "Actually, we were already planning on breakfast at Millie's. Then we're heading up to Stevens County for some birding. But you don't need to buy us breakfast, Prudence. Don't let us keep you from whatever you've got going on this morning."

"I'm heading to Millie's, too," she said. "I've been checking in on Red every morning, and then I just sort of hang around the deli most of the day. She fell down the stairs on Sunday, you know, and had to go to the emergency room."

"I heard," I told her. I didn't add that I'd also heard she'd been at Red's side when it happened. I wanted to see if she brought it up herself.

She didn't.

Interesting.

"Red's son just moved out," Prudence continued, "or he would be checking in on her. But he just got a job again after being unemployed these last few years, and he had to move to Wisconsin for it. It's really hard on Red, to have him so far away."

She stopped outside the front door to the deli and dropped her voice to a whisper.

"Red dotes on that boy. She was furious when he got laid off from that utilities job, but you never would have known it. She just kept smiling at customers like she always does. She really works at keeping an upbeat attitude. "

Prudence Delite sighed. "Red always knows exactly what to do in a bad situation." Her voice got husky. "She's been such a help to me this week. I don't know how I'd be functioning without her."

Desperate to get her into Millie's before more tears arrived, I pulled open the door to the deli and waved her in.

"Hey, Bob!" Red called to me from behind the deli counter. "Sit wherever you want, and I'll be right over."

To my relief, Red sounded . . . like Red. Boo and I took a small table next to the big front window while Prudence headed back to talk with Red.

"Sorry about the wrestling slip," I said to Boo.

"No problem," he said. "I just would have been surprised if she'd known me from wrestling. That was a long time ago. I mean, we were state champs for two years running, but usually the only people who recognize high school wrestlers are the ones whose own kids were in the sport."

"I thought you said you played basketball in high school," I reminded him.

Boo grinned. "I did . . . my freshman and sophomore years. But then I got so big I was afraid I'd hurt my teammates in practice, so I switched to wrestling as a junior. It worked out pretty well for me, all things considered."

I would say so. According to what Alan and I had dug up on the Internet about the Bonecrusher, the man had become a legend on the professional circuit for the five years he'd headlined matches. Based on the product endorsements he'd done, he'd probably banked a couple million before he mysteriously dropped out of the ring. Knowing what teachers got paid, he'd probably been really glad he'd built up a healthy nest egg before he disappeared to become anonymous.

"So what'll it be this morning?"

Red was standing at the end of our little table, handing us both a menu, her smile as broad and genuine as ever. "Do you guys need a few minutes to look over the menu?"

Since I always ordered the same thing on weekday mornings at Millie's, I glanced at Boo to see if he was ready, but his head was bent as he studied the possibilities.

"Give us a couple minutes, Red," I said, then added, "I'm glad to see you're up and about. I heard about the fall downstairs."

Red rolled her eyes.

"What a klutz! It's not like I haven't gone down those stairs a million times to get supplies. But boy! Did I see stars when I sat up again. I told Prudence I was fine, but she and Chef Tom insisted I get checked over at the ER, then they kept me overnight for observation."

She laughed and winked.

"Between you and me, I think they wanted to observe me making a klutz of myself again."

She pulled out her order pad.

"But you're okay now, right?" I asked her. "You've got your memory back?"

"I never lost it! I don't know why everyone keeps saying that." Red looked me in the eye. "So what'll it be this morning? Do you guys need a few minutes to look over the menu?"

"Yes," I said, getting a distinct feeling of déjà vu as Red repeated the very words she'd said when she'd arrived at our table a minute ago.

"Hokey-dokey," she said and sailed away.

"She just repeated herself, word for word," Boo commented, looking up from his menu. "I got the feeling she didn't realize she'd already asked us."

"I got the same feeling," I told him. "Which makes me wonder: if you lost your memory, how would you know you lost it? Red said everyone keeps telling her she lost her memory, but she says she didn't, but how would she know it if she couldn't remember what she forgot?"

"Is that a rhetorical or literal question?" Boo asked.

"Does it matter?" I replied, still trying to untangle my own twists of logic. "All I really want to know is if Red can remember who she saw here in Millie's on Saturday at lunch, and if any of those folks may have held enough of a grudge to plot Sonny Delite's murder."

"Correct me if I'm wrong, but isn't the local police department handling that investigation?" Boo noted. "Why do you want to get involved?"

Aha! So Boo and Rick's umbilical cord of communication wasn't open 24/7 as I had imagined: Boo didn't know that Rick was a suspect in Sonny's death. As I opened my mouth to fill the Crusher in, though, something stopped me.

Why wouldn't Rick have let Boo know of his predicament? Was it because of Gina? If Rick had to spell out all the reasons he was considered a suspect, he'd have to include the fact that he'd been at Gina's place very early on Sunday morning.

Okay then. I could definitely see Rick might not want to share that with Boo. Not only would he be betraying Gina's privacy, but maybe Rick had decided he didn't need to wave any more red flags in the face of a jealous Norse giant. Rick might have the biggest mouth in the state's law enforcement community, but he wasn't a total idiot.

Nor was I.

Most of the time.

I kept my own mouth shut.

"I thought I recognized you!"

Red had returned to our table to take our order, but she was staring wide-eyed at Boo.

I quickly checked around the restaurant to see who else was within hearing, but only Prudence and another customer were seated in the dining area. Prudence turned to see what Red had to say, but the other customer was engrossed in reading the newspaper. If Boo was finally going to be publicly unmasked as the Bonecrusher, he couldn't have asked for a smaller audience.

Red studied Boo's face as a bright pink flush crept over his cheeks. The man really had an aversion to getting caught in the spotlight. Was that why he'd always been masked? To cover his blushing embarrassment? I supposed that wouldn't have helped his image if his fans had seen their big, tough, no-holds-barred, wrestling idol blushing like a Disney princess.

"You were in here for lunch on Saturday," Red announced. "I never forget a face. And you weren't alone, either. There was somebody with you who got really upset when I was talking to Sonny about his windmills."

She turned towards Prudence. "Where is Sonny, anyway? I got that loose leaf tea he likes so much already brewing."

Red focused her attention back on Boo. "So what'll it be this morning? Do you guys need a few minutes to look over the menu?"

Chapter Sixteen

I STOOD AT THE SIDE OF THE COUNTY ROAD, my binoculars to my eyes, trying to make out the field identification marks of the grayish bird slowly making its way along the far side of the shallow wetlands. Mixed in with a small flock of Sanderlings, the bird in my binos was grayish overall with a white belly, along with orange-yellow coloring at the base of its thin bill. Since it was also in approximately the same location north of Appleton in Swift County where the Purple Sandpiper had been reported earlier in the week, I was fairly confident that's what I was seeing.

The wind had picked up considerably since Boo and I left Millie's, and my car thermometer was showing a rapid drop in temperature as well. Despite signs of incoming inclement weather, though, I figured the twenty-minute detour from our more direct route to Morris would be worth it if I found the sandpiper. More typically found on the East Coast of the United States, the Purple Sandpiper nested farther north than most shorebirds. The only time it'd been found in Minnesota was during migration. Even then, those sightings were all in the northeastern quadrant of the state. To find a Purple Sandpiper this far south was unusual, to say the least, which is one reason the MOU list serve had been buzzing with it earlier in the week.

While Boo stayed in the car, I watched the bird for another minute, enjoying its intense scrutiny of the wetland as it searched for food. I almost envied the sandpiper's simple lifestyle: seek and eat, fly and sleep. No delinquents to counsel, no murders to solve. Birds even knew who their natural enemies were and where to expect danger, which was more than I could say for humans at the moment.

Especially the humans I knew. Sonny had taken poisoned tea from someone he trusted. Rick had sprained an ankle in a freak court collision. Red had tripped down the stairs she climbed every day. My tires had been someone's target, and now I wondered exactly what the man beside me in my SUV might be capable of, besides herding chickens and wrestling steers.

For the last two hours, I'd had that same "down-the-rabbit-hole" sensation I'd previously experienced in the course of being involved in a murder investigation: just when you think you know exactly what's going to happen, something totally different occurs, and you're so disoriented that, for a while, nothing makes sense at all. You don't know who to trust. You don't know what to believe. You're not sure which end is up.

I looked at the Sanderlings around the Purple Sandpiper. Several tipped their heads down into the water to snatch a snack from the wetland, their bills completely submerged.

No mistaking which end is up with shorebirds, that was for sure. Ducks and geese were even easier—they stuck their rear ends clear up above the water line when they feed. Too bad people weren't as transparent. Interpreting human behavior would be a breeze then, although it might be a little awkward . . .

Whoa! See that guy bending over? He's clearly being an a . . .

Anyway, head over heels and vice-versa was kind of the way I'd been feeling since Red insisted that Boo had been a customer on Saturday. I'd been one hundred percent certain she was going to say he was the Bonecrusher. Instead, she said he'd been at Millie's at the same time as Sonny.

Which meant that Boo Metternick knew exactly who Sonny was, along with the fact that my old birding pal had been in town for the sustainable sources conference at the Arboretum. And given that Boo Metternick had known—and loved?—Gina since they were teens, Boo also had to know about the scandal that had resulted in Gina leaving her job in Henderson, which I was sure

131

hadn't endeared Sonny to Boo . . . any more than Sonny's lies about his father's land had put Sonny on Boo's list of favorite people.

The big question was: how really un-favorite did Sonny rank with Boo?

Enough to get himself killed by the Crusher?

I lowered the binos to my chest, but almost immediately raised them back up. One of the Sanderlings swimming in the increasingly choppy water that lined the wetlands didn't look quite right to me. I focused in on the bird, and realized I wasn't looking at another Sanderling, but a Red Phalarope already in its winter plumage. As I watched, it swam into deeper water and began its distinctive spinning motion which helped stir up invertebrates to the surface for feeding.

If it was rare to see a Purple Sandpiper in Minnesota, it was slightly less rare to find a Red Phalarope. Both birds were summer natives to the arctic regions of northern Canada. Had the weather brought them inland?

I hustled back to the car through a stand of drying weeds and grasses, and sent a quick text message to a few birders I knew in the area, letting them know I'd seen a Red Phalarope. With any luck, the bird would still be there when they arrived, and they could confirm my sighting, along with adding it to their own life lists. For my part, I had no doubt I'd seen both a Purple Sandpiper and a Red Phalarope in the wetlands. In any community of birders, though, it never hurt to have a rarity spotted—and identified—by more than one person.

"So these other birders would just drop what they're doing and drive out to see this bird?" Boo asked after I explained to him what I was texting.

"You bet," I told him. "This bird is a real find. And because it's so unusual to see it here, there will inevitably be people who doubt what I saw. Heck, if I'd seen a Red Phalarope sighting posted on the list serve, I'd probably question it myself. If I could, I'd sure try to get out to see it."

"Would a photo help with documentation?"

I tucked my cellphone back into my pocket. "Absolutely, but unfortunately, my camera equipment is back in my townhouse in the front closet. I was so ticked about my car tires last night, I totally forgot to grab it this morning."

I turned in the seat to face him. "You don't happen to have a camera in your backpack, do you, Boo?"

He shook his head. "Sorry, you're out of luck."

"That's all right," I said. "I know what I saw, even if it was totally not what I'd expected."

"You've got to keep an open mind to be a birder, huh?" Boo asked.

I put the key back in the ignition and glanced at my passenger. "Yeah, you do. And since we're on the subject of open minds, would you care to tell my open mind how it happened that you were having lunch at Millie's deli on Saturday at exactly the same time that the late Sonny Delite was having a conversation with Red about windmills outside Morris?"

Boo shrugged. "Total coincidence, I guess. I met an old friend for lunch, and since he was working at the Arboretum, Millie's was close enough for him to get away for his lunch break."

He narrowed his eyes at me. "I never met Sonny Delite, Bob. I'd heard the name, but I never met the man. Just as well, I guess. Based on what I knew about him because of Gina, I can't imagine I would have wanted to be buddies. He just seemed to cause trouble wherever he went."

"What about your dad?"

"What about my dad?"

"Isn't—I mean, wasn't—Sonny the consultant who was ruining your dad's chances to get the contract with the wind energy company?"

Boo blew out a long sigh.

"Yes, he was."

A few snowflakes landed on the windshield in front of me. The storm front was getting closer.

Boo's voice dropped to an ominous whisper in the car. "Are you trying to come up with a motive for me to be Sonny Delite's killer? That would make two motives, then, wouldn't it—my feelings for Gina and my concern for my dad? What would you say if I told you I was at the Arboretum early Sunday morning, Bob? Would that clinch it for you?"

The fine hairs on the back of my neck lifted.

What kind of an idiot was I?

Here I was in a remote spot, alone with a huge guy who could probably crush my throat with one squeeze, and I was baiting him to confess to a murder?

Yep, I'd say that was all kinds of idiot, actually. Especially since I didn't even try to get out of the car or whip my car keys in front of me in a futile defense. The truth was, I was operating on pure instinct: I just couldn't see Boo Metternick killing anyone. He seemed to have iron self-control, and . . . well . . . I really liked him, gosh darn it.

So instead of panicking and imagining that I was going to be dead in the next few seconds, I asked him one last question.

"Can you tell me what kind of plant that is?" I said, pointing to the tall stalk just beyond his passenger door. Snowflakes were already frosting its withered leaves.

Boo turned his head and studied the plant.

"I don't know. Is it ragweed? Yarrow? It's tall and sort of feathery, but I've never been any good at identifying plants." He looked back at me. "Why?"

"You wouldn't have been any good at killing Sonny Delite, either, then," I told him, putting the car in gear and pulling away from the roadside. "That wasn't yarrow, Boo. It was hemlock."

"And?"

I momentarily debated telling him about Sonny's hemlock tea, but since that detail hadn't been released to the media, I decided that the less Boo Metternick knew about Sonny Delite's death, the better. Based on his inability to identify hemlock, I felt moderately assured that Savage High School's new physics instructor hadn't brewed any poison for the deceased.

I did, however, still have a few questions for him.

"Since you brought it up, why were you at the Arb on Sunday morning, Boo? And no, I don't think you killed Sonny Delite. You're . . . too nice." I turned on my windshield wipers to brush away the snow that was beginning to accumulate.

"Really? Too nice? I don't know if that's good or bad. I thought maybe I had you going there for a minute," he confessed. "Life as a physics teacher can get pretty dull, I'm finding. I've been thinking I need to give my image an edge—be the big scary guy, you know?"

"Is that why you don't talk much? To other people, I mean?" I added, realizing that since we'd chased the chickens, Boo had been a regular Chatty Charlie with me. "You're trying to give yourself a make-over?"

Boo peered through the snow piling up on the windshield faster than the wipers could clear it.

"No," he answered. "I don't talk a lot because I usually feel uncomfortable around new people. I always get the feeling that people are intimidated by my size, and I don't know how to make them get over it, so I just listen and watch most of the time."

Which, I knew from my conversations with other faculty members, made them even more uncomfortable. Before I'd gotten to know Boo, I'd thought he was a little creepy that way too. I mean, who likes to see a giant staring at them every time they catch his eye?

"I could always talk to Gina," Boo continued, "but she was the exception. I don't know why it's so easy for me to talk to you, but it is."

I knew why—it's because I have this invisible sign on my forehead that lights up and makes people tell me their life stories, whether

I want to hear it or not. It's a gift. I guess. Or maybe it's a curse. I haven't decided yet. As a counselor, it helps a lot when I'm working with students; when I'm standing in the checkout line at the grocery store and the ice cream is melting in the cart, not so much.

"It's really coming down," Boo commented. "Remember I told you that storms can really blow up suddenly out in this part of the state?"

I slowed the car down to a crawl as visibility approached zero.

"Yeah, I remember," I said, my eyes glued on the white wall in front of the car. "For some reason, I got the feeling you were trying to dissuade me from coming up here today."

"Why would I do that?"

"Beats me. Because you're a closet competitive birder, and you didn't want me to see a Ferruginous Hawk?" I shook my head slightly, still focused on keeping the car on the road. "I don't think so. Because you know Sonny was a friend of mine, and I'd probably snoop around in Morris and dig up some dirt on your father? Maybe."

I felt the SUV's wheels slide, and the slippery ice icon flashed on my dashboard. I slowed even more until I felt the tires grip the road again.

"And then your tires got slashed," Boo commented. "With a license plate like yours, you can't imagine it was random."

"The possibility has been presented to me."

The wall of white receded and the heavy curtain of snow lifted a little.

"But since you didn't call me last night to confirm 'one more time' if we were still going this morning," I explained, "I figured you didn't have anything to do with the slashing. I didn't realize Rick would have tipped you off to the tire replacement, though, so maybe you still should be on my slashing suspect list."

"It's letting up," Boo noted, nodding at the windshield. "I hate these surprise snowstorms. When you grow up out here, you learn how to deal with them, but you never learn to like them."

I sensed him turning toward me in the passenger seat.

"Rick didn't tell me about your tires," he corrected me. "Gina did. I was feeling kind of bad about our little collision during basketball, so I called her to ask how Rick was doing, and she told me about your car. By the way, why do you keep thinking that Rick Cook and I are such great pals? He's dating Gina, you know. I can't say that's making him my favorite school police officer at the moment."

"I figured you two were tight because he knows all about you," I said. "You know—the big secret?"

Boo was silent.

"And it's not that he told me, either," I made sure to add.

Rick was already in enough hot water with the Crusher by dating Gina that I didn't want to add another reason for Boo to be angry with Rick.

A couple of seconds passed by before Boo responded.

"What in the world are you talking about?" he said.

"You! Your former career and secret identity." I glanced at Boo. "I know you're the Bonecrusher."

I only had the chance to register his surprise for a second before I heard the *whump* and the car began a fast spin on what had quickly become a sheet of ice.

CHAPTER SEVENTEEN

"C RAP!" I HISSED AS I STRUGGLED with the steering wheel, trying to stop our slide into the road's snowy shoulder and beyond it, a steep incline down to an ice-crusted ditch.

The car's spin accelerated. Trees on both sides of the road flashed past.

I thought about Luce.

I thought about Baby Lou.

I thought about the money I'd just shelled out for four new tires.

Four new tires that couldn't find a bite of traction on a suddenly icy road.

Last time I go to the Tire Shoppe, I promised myself, then immediately tacked on *for tires. It's the last time for tires.*

Even under duress, I like to be accurate.

Especially when an icy ditch and certain death might be waiting for me.

I turned in the direction of the skid.

Really, I'd like to go to the Tire Shoppe again.

A lot.

Frequently, even.

The speed of our spin decreased.

Yes! I'll even get a customer loyalty card!

"You got it, Bob," Boo congratulated me as the car straightened itself out and came to rest in the opposite direction of the lane I'd been driving. "Nice driving, buddy."

"I try," I said, letting out a long breath I'd been holding as I'd battled the skid. I looked down the road we'd already traveled. "I hit something. I heard the collision, but I don't see anything on the road back there."

"Deer," Boo informed me. "I caught a glimpse of it clipping the front of the car just as it happened." He gazed down the road, too. "Bambi is long gone, it looks like. He'll live to scare the pants off another motorist, I'm sure. It's a common driving hazard in this part of the state: deer dodging."

"It happens everywhere in Minnesota," I told him. "I lost a headlight to a deer a few years ago just driving home from the high school. It's a good thing you can't hunt deer within city limits, or it wouldn't be safe to step outside my townhouse during hunting season. I swear I've got a herd that regularly walks through my backyard. And that doesn't even include all the road kill you see."

I climbed out of the car to take a look at the front end of the car. Snow was still swirling a little in short gusts, but the intense dumping action had stopped. I found a clump of brown deer fur wedged along the fender and the hood of the car, but no blood. The headlights were still working. Boo was right; Bambi would live to terrorize drivers for another day. I got back in the car.

"We're good to go," I said. "Any more weather warnings or driving hazards I should know about between here and Morris?"

"None that I can think of," Boo said. He pointed beyond the windshield. "What's that?"

I followed his line of sight and saw a Merlin perched on the top of a utility pole.

"Good eye," I told Boo. "It's a Merlin, and it's uncommon throughout the state. I won't say it was worth a collision with a deer in order to see it, but it'll go on my list for birds in this county. I hadn't seen one here before."

I gave Boo a suspicious look. "You sure you're not a birder in disguise?"

Boo laughed. "Scout's honor. And I'm not the Bonecrusher, either, by the way."

"Yeah, sure," I said, pulling a U-turn in the road so I could head toward Morris instead of back towards Savage. "Let me rephrase that. I know you are not the Bonecrusher *now*. But you *were*."

"No, I wasn't."

"Yes, you were."

"Wasn't."

The sun was already back out, and the skies were clearing.

I chanced a look in Boo's direction.

No deer attacked the car this time.

"I totally understand that you want your privacy and that you don't need or want your students to get wrapped up in your celebrity wrestling past," I assured him. "But come on, give me a little credit here. Who else on the faculty could be the Bonecrusher? You're the biggest guy on staff, you're around the right age, you wrestled in high school, you don't talk about your past, or much of anything for that matter, as you pointed out. You're a mystery man. And I happen to know you wrestled steers on the farm. If that's not a curriculum vitae for a former wrestling celebrity, I don't know what is."

Boo crossed his big arms over his chest and grinned. "I'm flattered—I think—but you've got the wrong man, Bob. What about Paul Brand, the new art teacher? He's more of a loner than I am, and he played professional hockey for a couple of years. Those hockey players are tough," he reminded me. "I could easily see him head-butting an opponent in a wrestling match."

Well, sure, hockey players were tougher than nails. Everyone in Minnesota knew that. When I'd seriously considered that Paul Brand might be the Bonecrusher, I had taken that for granted, and I could easily see that he had the lean muscle to back it up. But when I mentally compared the two men's physical attributes, Paul was no match for Boo.

Although Boo's nose—straight and unbroken, compared to Paul's crooked one—did give me a moment's pause.

Could a man wrestle for five years without getting his nose broken even once?

My moment of pause stretched out. Was I going to lose this bet yet . . . by a nose?

I swatted the doubt away.

Boo was the Crusher. I wouldn't expect him to own right up to a secret he'd been guarding from everyone at Savage for the last few months. Anyone trying to go incognito would naturally deny it if someone correctly identified him.

But I also knew that Boo hated liars, and my gut instinct told me he'd hold himself to that same standard. Sure, he was a big guy, but he came from a family of Norwegian farmers. And yes, a lot of strong kids wrestled in high school, but that didn't automatically mean they became professional wrestlers. As for being close-mouthed about certain pieces of his past, well, that probably applied to everyone who survived being a teenager.

Myself included.

Stupidity is an equal opportunity employer when it comes to youth.

So now I had to ask myself: Had I let my personal bias color my deductions about Boo's hidden past?

My little doubt buzzed back in and got bigger.

Had I been so sure I was right that I'd neglected to objectively weigh what I thought was the evidence?

Gee, what a novel idea.

Bob White runs with the ball of conjecture and jumps to the conclusion he wants.

He shoots.

Oh! He misses.

He loses ten bucks.

I suddenly remembered that Alan had said almost the same things about Paul Brand when we'd made our bet about the true identity of the Bonecrusher.

With competitive experience on the ice behind him, Alan had maintained that it wouldn't have been much of a leap for Paul into the physical punishment of the wrestling circuit. And that broken nose, which Paul had told me was a souvenir of his senior year in high school, could just as easily have been a reminder of his five years in the ring, or a memento of a rough night on the ice with the big league.

Given how crooked Paul's nose was, it could even have been both of the above.

Not to mention that Paul had a leaner body frame than Boo. Actually, when I'd first looked at photos of the Bonecrusher online, I'd been surprised to see that he wasn't the big hulky guy I'd expected a wrestler to be. In the old shots, the Crusher looked slimmer than Boo did today, but I'd attributed Boo's heavier physique to the inevitable effect of long-term weight-lifting that built bulkier muscles.

Paul, on the other hand, looked more like a runner with his trimmer size. I didn't know if he still hit the rink with a local group, but in my experience, hockey players never stopped playing hockey, even if they just skated alone on neighborhood rinks, slapping the puck against the boards.

That meant he'd still have the lean-muscled shape he'd had while he was wrestling.

And as long as the photos pictured the Crusher in his black mask and leotard, it was almost impossible to get a true read on his size. In fact, now that I thought about it, I realized that in all the photos Alan and I had scrutinized, not once had the Crusher been pictured with anyone else, so there was nothing to use as a scale of comparison.

When you came right down to it, for all the proof you could get from what we'd seen online, the Bonecrusher could have been a ninety-six-pound weakling who just happened to be a genius when it came to posing for the camera and looking big, muscular, and mean.

"Paul Brand, huh?" I asked Boo. "He likes to scrapbook, you know."

"I'm not saying he's the Crusher," Boo equivocated, "but I'm also not saying he's not. He looks like a good candidate though, if you ask me."

"Shoot," I said again. "There goes my ten bucks."

"You had a bet on the Crusher's identity?"

I shrugged. "Yeah, with Alan."

"Do you two guys bet on everything?" Boo asked. "I thought the bet about turbines killing more birds or people was . . . a little unusual . . . but I didn't know this was a regular routine for you two."

That's right. I'd forgotten about Alan's white lie when he asked Boo about his experience with the wind farms. Excellent. Now Alan and I were going to get a reputation as incurable gamblers, when the only real gambling I ever did was driving half-way across the state in hopes of seeing a rare bird.

Like a Ferruginous Hawk.

"Oops," Boo said, pointing across the dashboard. "There's one that took it on the chin. Or maybe the car hood."

Some twenty yards ahead, on the opposite side of the road, I saw the dead deer, or at least what was left of it, laying in the weeds just beyond the blacktop. Perched atop, a murder of crows was enjoying the free meal. "It didn't make the dodge, I guess."

While we watched, the crows abruptly dispersed. A moment later, a large hawk flew low past the carcass and settled on a highway marker overlooking an open stretch of a snow-laced field.

"That's a big hawk," Boo commented.

I slowed the car to give myself a better look. We'd seen quite a few Red-tailed Hawks on the drive west after finishing our breakfast at Millie's, but this hawk's head was noticeably lighter in color. The bird also had a lighter tail compared to what we'd seen earlier, and there was no banding of any kind on it. I'd caught a glimpse of dark legs against white feathers as it had swooped past the deer, but the thing that really impressed me the most was its size.

It really was a big hawk.

So big, it could have been a . . . Ferruginous Hawk.

I blinked.

I was looking at a Ferruginous Hawk.

I immediately pulled over onto the shoulder.

"That's a Ferruginous Hawk," I told Boo. "It's the biggest hawk in North America. That's exactly what I was hoping to see today."

I snagged my binoculars out of the storage compartment between the two front seats and slid out of the SUV. The hawk was still surveying the empty acreage. I focused my binos on his belly. The smooth expanse of his white feathers was lined with only a few fine streaks of gray, and the feathering on his legs was clearly dark. As I watched, he glided off the highway marker and rose a bit in the sky, then paused in a hover over the field. I could see the pale uppersides to his primary and secondary flight feathers contrasting with the darker upperwing coverts.

"Pretty impressive," Boo said from the other side of the car, where he, too, had stepped out to observe the hawk.

"You should start your bird list right now, Boo," I told him, my eyes focused on the hawk as it searched for a meal. "You'd be starting with a bird that other birders would kill for."

An image of Sonny popped into my head. I bit my tongue.

"Forget I said that. That was totally inappropriate given the events of the last few days."

"You think someone killed Sonny Delite over a Ferruginous Hawk?" Boo asked, his voice incredulous. "Birders really get that competitive?"

I looked at Boo.

"Not that competitive," I said.

At least, I didn't think so.

Not to my knowledge.

Geez.

"No," I tried again to explain my comment, "it just wasn't very sensitive of me to make a joke about birders killing each other, especially when one of the best-known birders in the state was found dead days ago of highly suspicious causes."

"And you're the one who found him."

I paused. That wasn't supposed to be public information.

"Gina told me," he answered my unspoken question. "Rick told her. She's concerned about her brother."

I stared at Boo, trying to make sense of his words. "What does Gina's brother have to do with Sonny Delite's murder?"

"Well, for starters," he said, "Gina's brother, Noah, really hated Sonny Delite for two reasons: one—Noah held Sonny responsible for stopping the project in Henderson, which meant Noah lost a good job prospect he was counting on, and two—Noah was furious with Sonny for leading on Gina."

"Okay," I said slowly, "I can understand that, I guess."

"But the part that was really worrying Gina was the fact that Noah was threatening to quit his job because Sonny was going to be at the sustainable sources conference at the Arboretum."

He shook his head. "He just landed that job there last month, and Gina didn't want him to go through the whole unemployment bit again. That's why she wanted me to talk to him. I've known Noah as long as I've known Gina. He was kind of like the little brother I never had, and I know he always looked up to me."

I had a bad feeling I knew where this explanation was going to end up, and I really didn't want to go there. I'd just found my first, and perhaps only, Ferruginous Hawk, and I should be doing my victory dance, not leaning against my car for support while my stomach began to drop.

Noah Knorsen had been working at the Arboretum during the conference.

According to Sara's eavesdropping report, he'd quit his job on Monday, the day after I'd found a dead Sonny near Wood Duck Pond on the Arboretum grounds.

Noah hated Sonny.

"Did you talk to Noah about not quitting?" I asked Boo, not sure I wanted to hear the answer to that. Boo had, after all, admitted to me that he'd been at the Arboretum on Sunday morning.

And though I'd already asked once, he hadn't told me why he was there.

On early Sunday morning.

I looked the Norse giant over once again.

Boo Metternick was easily strong enough to carry Sonny Delite into the woods after Noah Knorsen had offered him a cup of hemlock tea. Maybe Boo hadn't killed Sonny, but maybe he'd helped Noah—the little brother he never had—clean up afterward. It wasn't like Boo had unequivocally stated to me, "Bob, I was in no way involved in the death of Sonny Delite."

Of course, I hadn't specifically asked him if he was, either.

Boo and Noah were close friends. Close friends help each other out.

Hey, best buddy. I just killed this guy for really good reasons. I could sure use your help here so I don't go to prison for murder. I'm thinking we could just prop him up like an old scarecrow in the woods, and no one will ever know. Then maybe we can catch the rest of the football game on TV later. What do you say?

Yikes.

"I talked to him," Boo said. "Saturday. At lunch. At Millie's. Red remembered me correctly this morning, even if she couldn't remember she asked us for our order four times."

"And Sunday morning?" I asked. "You were at the Arboretum . . . with Noah?"

"Not with Noah," he said, shaking his head. "With Gina. After I told her I didn't get anywhere with Noah on Saturday, she insisted on talking with him as soon as he got to work on Sunday. She didn't want him to quit. I offered to drive her to offer moral support. When we got to the Education Center, I stayed in the car, and Gina went in. When she came out a while later, she was really upset, but she wouldn't tell me what had happened. She told me to take her home, so I did. End of story."

For some reason, I didn't think "end of story" was quite accurate.

More like, "dead end of story," I thought.

Sonny's dead end.

CHAPTER EIGHTEEN

I LOOKED BACK OVER MY SHOULDER to where I'd last seen the Ferruginous Hawk, but only empty sky and field was there. The hawk had flown. No surprise.

I climbed back into the car. On the other side of the SUV, Boo did likewise.

"Is Gina afraid that Noah is involved in Sonny's death?" I pointedly asked Boo once we had buckled our seatbelts and I'd gotten us back on the road to Morris.

"A little," he allowed. "Personally, I don't think Noah could kill someone. But I'm sure Gina knows her brother a lot better than I do."

Yeah, that tends to happen with brothers and sisters.

For better or worse.

In my case, I knew my sister really well, and Lily knew what made me tick, too, but we still managed to surprise each other once in a while. Like when she fell in love with Alan, my best friend. I was afraid that was definitely going to end up as one of the "worse" scenarios, but then she married him, and now I have a gorgeous niece, so it turned out to be one of the "better" cases.

If Gina thought her brother was capable of murder, I'd think that was an example of a "worse case" in knowing your sibling well. But if he knocked someone off for her sake, did that make it "better"?

Or did it just make it partners in crime?

Gina had gone to the Arboretum on Sunday morning. With Boo. To talk to her brother who hated Sonny Delite.

That put three people who each had a reason to really dislike Sonny at the scene of the crime.

Was it Noah Knorsen with a cup of tea in the Education Center?

Was it Gina Knorsen with the whole teapot beside Wood Duck Pond?

Was it Boo Metternick with the candlestick in the hallway?

I never was very good at that *Clue* game we played when we were kids. Too many suspects. Too many rooms. I mean, really, did you ever know someone who had a ballroom in their home, let alone a conservatory? I didn't even know what a conservatory was the first time I played it. I thought maybe it was some kind of lab for keeping things preserved. Things like dead bodies, maybe. It was a murder game, after all.

Real murder, though, was definitely not a game.

Even if the dead person did look like part of a scarecrow display.

We drove along in silence until Boo pointed out another hawk flying ahead of us.

"Red-tailed, right?" he said. "I've been paying attention when you've mentioned field marks this morning. I have to admit, I'll probably take a closer look at birds from now on. The challenge of identifying what you see kind of grows on you."

"That's certainly a part of birding," I said. "I know a lot of people have this idea in their heads that birding is really dull, but for people who love the hobby, it's a never-ending source of interest and anticipation. There's always another bird to see somewhere."

We passed a road sign that said Spinit—Boo's hometown— was five miles ahead. Perched on the sign was yet another Red-tailed Hawk.

"I know I'm paying attention to birds this morning, which I don't usually do, but have there always been this many hawks out here?" Boo asked. "I think we've seen one on every fencepost for the last five miles. It's like a plague or something."

I realized I'd registered the same impression: there were more hawks along the highway than I could ever recall seeing in one trip in this area. I'd assumed that the short but intense snowstorm we had passed through had blown in the hawks ahead of it, which could possibly account during a migration season for increased numbers of a species in one area.

"It does seem a little unusual," I told Boo. "Maybe it's the weather fronts."

"Is that why birders have been seeing so many Ferruginous Hawks out this way? Because the weather pattern has been bringing them in?"

I considered Boo's question, but he interrupted my thoughts with another observation.

"What are those platforms out there?"

I looked in the direction he was pointing. Far across the fields to the left of the road were a line of poles that stood about six feet tall. At the top of each pole was a small platform. On several of the platforms were hawks.

The poles and platforms reminded me of something I occasionally encountered when I was out birding in remote places: bird-baiting.

"It's a hawk cafeteria," I said to Boo.

"What?"

"Bird-baiting. Somebody out here likes to watch hawks eat." I nodded towards the line of platforms that extended toward the horizon. "Lots of hawks, too, by the looks of it."

When he still looked confused, I proceeded to explain to Boo about bird-baiting and the sometimes bitter battles it caused among birders in Minnesota.

Sorry. I really wasn't going for a tongue-twister there.

"It's a method of attracting birds," I began, "and it relies on strategically placing something the birds would eat in a spot where an observer can have a clear view of the bird. Some photographers use the method regularly to enable them to "pose" shots with wild birds, or to get photos they might not otherwise be able to take because they can't get close enough to the birds. Basically, they're luring the birds in for a photo op. Other folks bait birds because they feel they're helping the birds out by providing them with a steady diet, especially when climate conditions are severe."

"Isn't that like feeding birds at a birdfeeder?" Boo asked. "Tons of people do that."

"I know," I said. "I have a bunch of feeders on my own back porch, and I don't think that's a bad thing. I get to enjoy the birds, and the birds get to eat. But not everyone agrees. Some opponents of bird-baiting say that by supplying the birds with a contrived food source, you're teaching them to rely on humans, which is, in the natural world . . . well . . . unnatural. Usually, though, when people are debating bird-baiting, they're talking about birders or photographers who deliberately look for a specific species—generally out in the wild—that they want to attract with food."

"So you've got birders who think baiting is okay, and birders who think it's unnatural."

I nodded in agreement. "Not just unnatural, Boo. Many people consider it unethical, and even a harmful way of interacting with wildlife. It's like any ecological issue. Humans need to consider the intricate relationships that make up nature and try to figure out where they should, or shouldn't, intervene."

Of course, there was another category of bird-baiting, but that was the clearly illegal kind. Poachers baited birds for live capture for smuggling sales or to kill them for their feathers. It may not sound like a lucrative business, but the amounts of money involved in the illegal bird trade was unbelievable. For instance, I knew that white Gyrfalcons, which are native to the arctic areas of Russia, are worth upwards of one hundred thousand dollars on the black market to falconers in Arab countries. A perfect tail feather from a Golden Eagle could sell for more than $250. I've heard from more than one Fish & Wildlife Service officer that as recently as a few years ago, smugglers sold tiny songbirds from Vietnam for $400 a bird.

Of course, that was dependent on the smuggler successfully getting the birds to the United States, which didn't always happen. In the last three years alone, airport customs officials had rescued falcons wrapped in towels in luggage, small parrots inside socks taped to a traveler's thighs and chest, and hummingbirds stuffed in underwear.

Oh, and the underwear was on the wearer at the time.

Poor birds.

"Well, I'm sure those platforms weren't out there the last time I drove home on this route," Boo said as we neared the exit to his dad's farm. "This is new."

I felt a tingle of awareness ripple down my spine, as I suddenly remembered there was a fourth reason someone might bait birds.

"How new?" I asked.

Boo pressed himself back in the passenger seat and stretched his arms out in front of him. The movement didn't seem to give him any more room than he already had. The guy really was a giant. If he truly hadn't been the Bonecrusher, he might have missed a promising career option.

"The last time I came this way was back in August," he said. "I came up here to do some aerial surveys for my dad to present to the energy company to prove we didn't have those sparrows colonizing the farm."

"Because Sonny Delite said you did," I added.

"Right."

"So these platforms weren't here? Wait a minute—you did the aerial surveys?"

"Take this next left," Boo directed me. "I've been flying planes since I was sixteen," he added. "I thought I'd launch a cropdusting company at one point, but there weren't enough customers in the county to keep me in business. So I flew jets for the Air Force instead, until I decided I wanted to teach high school."

The SUV rocked a little as the pavement became a hard-packed dirt road.

"You were in New Mexico teaching last year, right?" I asked.

"Yup."

"So you didn't hear about the big showdown in Goodhue County about the proposed wind farm there," I said.

"My dad mentioned it to me once," Boo recalled, "Because of that summer I'd worked on the wind farm, I think he was hoping I'd become a mechanical engineer and make a pile of money. Cash reserves are pretty hard to come by for a lot of farmers, you know."

I remembered our conversation in my office earlier in the week. Boo had said his dad was too proud to take any financial help from his son and was depending on that leasing contract to come through. That was the reason Boo was so angry that Sonny was misleading the energy company with his false reports about nesting birds.

"There was a group of local people fighting the project tooth and claw," Boo continued, "farmers, environmentalists, tax opponents. I think Dad said it was a Texas billionaire pushing to build the wind farm with federal wind subsidy money—a subsidy that Congress was thinking about shutting down, which meant the longer it took to get started on construction of the farm, the less likely it was that the government money would still be around to go into the company's coffers."

"That's right," I told him. "And it's funny you should say 'tooth and claw,' because as it turned out, the presence of Golden Eagles in the area became a huge controversy, with both sides accusing the other of falsifying evidence."

"Eagles," Boo said. "Aren't they protected by federal law?"

"Bingo," I responded. "If you mess with the eagles, you don't get to put up turbines."

Boo pointed out the window to a white-sided farmhouse.

"This is the place," he said. "Metternick Manor."

I pulled the SUV into the long gravel drive leading up to the house and remembered the latest developments I'd read in the news about the Goodhue wind farm proposal.

"But here's the hitch: not even eagles can escape a loophole in the law," I continued. "A lot of people don't know that back in 2009, the federal government came up with a compromise to appease conservationists while still supporting clean energy proponents. Since some birds—including protected species like eagles—will inevitably be killed by the blades of wind turbines, the government devised a permit to allow companies what they call 'incidental take' of wildlife."

"Incidental?" he repeated. "Is that like collateral damage?"

I put the car in park and turned to Boo. "I hadn't thought of it like that, but yeah, I guess it is."

Boo shook his head. "So now the government is saying it's okay to kill eagles."

"No, not really." I tried to make sense of it, too. As usual, the twists and turns of government red tape was a confusing trail to follow.

"No one is accusing wind farm developers of wanting to kill wildlife," I pointed out. "Their intentions are good: to provide clean energy. And engineers are working all the time to make the turbine blades and the placement of wind towers less deadly to birds and those bats you talked about the other day. But there are always costs when population needs and nature collide."

"So someone who opposed the Goodhue wind farm was deliberately baiting eagles to make a case that the 'incidental take' of the birds would exceed any permit limits?" Boo asked.

"Actually, no," I told him. "The state investigators couldn't find any evidence that baiting was happening. But I'm wondering if someone out here took that idea and put it into play—not to defeat the wind farm project, but to manipulate exactly where it was sited . . . and who got the lease with the energy developers."

Boo gathered up his backpack and stepped out of the car.

"All I know for sure is that those feeding platforms weren't in those fields two months ago," he repeated. "I've got the aerial surveys in the house. You can see them for yourself if you want. Come on in."

I debated for only a moment. Since I'd seen the Ferruginous Hawk, my primary birding objective for the day had been accomplished. There were a few areas outside Morris that I still wanted to go check for any late shorebirds, but it wouldn't take long to make those stops, and I wasn't expecting to find anything unusual anyway.

On the other hand, the idea that I might be able to find some leads in Boo's surveys for Sonny's murder investigation was a tempting alternative. During last night's dinner, I had promised Rick that I would keep my ears and eyes open on this trip to Stevens County in case I ran across any information that could help him shake his suspect status.

So far, what I had—Boo's admission that he and Gina and her brother were all at the Arb on Sunday morning—couldn't prove that Rick wasn't involved in Sonny's death, but at least it might provide the police with some other people to consider as serious suspects.

And yes, I would feel awful going to the police and saying "Hey, guys, if you think Rick had a reason to kill Sonny, maybe you should be taking a closer look at Boo Metternick, Gina Knorsen, and her brother, who, I happen to know, were all within walking distance of where Sonny was killed on Sunday morning. Not to mention that they might have had reasons just as good as— if not better than—Rick's supposed reasons to poison Sonny."

Oh, yeah, that was a great way to build new friendships and create loyalty at the workplace. Savage High School—where suspicion and suspects ran rampant. Mr. Lenzen would be so proud.

Not.

But if I could dig up some evidence in the surveys that Sonny's involvement with the wind project might somehow account for a motive for murder, then I'd have a chance at getting Rick off the hot seat.

And if I could get Rick off, then I'd think it would have to help Gina, too.

As for Boo, given his father's high financial stakes in the wind project, he might unfortunately become the best candidate to take the same hot seat that Rick would vacate.

Nice choice for me: help out my old buddy by zinging my new one.

Which was all the more reason I needed to learn everything I could about what had been going on in Stevens County before Sonny Delite turned up as a dead scarecrow in the Minnesota Landscape Arboretum. After my morning drive with Boo Metternick, I was convinced he hadn't killed anyone. Evidence that proved it would be almost as good a find for the day as the Ferruginous Hawk had been.

"Thanks, Boo," I said, stepping out of the car. "I'd like to see those surveys."

I followed him towards the house's front porch and came to a dead stop.

A white-haired fellow was standing on the top step, his eyes squinted at me.

The squinting part didn't bother me at all.

The rocket launcher he had balanced on his shoulder and aimed right at my head, however, did.

CHAPTER NINETEEN

"HEY, DAD," BOO CALLED TO HIS father from the front walk. "Is that a new one?"

He turned to me and winked. "Don't worry. He won't hit you."

I swallowed the lump in my throat. Oh, good. He wouldn't hit me.

Did that mean he was still going to fire it?

Before I could get the question out of my mouth, though, I got the answer.

Boom!

Something streaked over my head and a split-second later, I heard a loud *splat* somewhere behind me.

Splat?

"Just potatoes," Boo explained. "Although sometimes Dad uses zucchini or tomatoes if he's got a surplus from harvesting. He's not picky when it comes to vegetables."

"And he likes to shoot vegetables because . . . ?"

"They don't hurt anyone when they explode. Dad was an ordnance officer in World War II," Boo explained, clapping his hand on my shoulder. "He still likes to fire rockets."

"I was a damn good one, too," Boo's dad called from the porch. He removed the bazooka from his shoulder and leaned it against the house wall, then held his two hands up in the air, ten fingers wiggling.

"I still got 'em all," he announced.

We stepped up onto the porch and Boo made introductions.

"Dad, this is Bob White. He's a counselor at Savage High School. Bob, this is my dad, Vern Metternick."

I clasped the old man's hand in a greeting. His grip was sure and strong.

"So what do you think of my new toy?" he asked us. "I picked it up at a military collectables show last weekend. It's an M1A1 from late 1942. I had to clean it up a bit, but it's working pretty good with the spuds."

"I'd say it was a shortcut to mashed potatoes," I noted. "Maybe you should put together an infomercial and sell reconditioned bazookas as a time-saving kitchen tool. 'It smashes. It mashes. For all your rocket-propelled needs.'"

Mr. Metternick clapped his hand on my shoulder and turned to his son. "I like this guy, Boo. You say he works with you?"

"I'm a counselor at the high school," I said. "I was coming up here to do some birding, and Boo asked if he could get a ride up here to see you. It was nice having the company. It's a long drive."

"Bob wants to see those aerial surveys I took, Dad," Boo told his father. "We just saw all those platforms out in the fields and thought we'd give my surveys another look. I'm sure they weren't there, but maybe the poles were already up, and I just didn't know what I was looking at."

"Be my guest," Mr. Metternick said. "Come on in, and we'll pull them out of the cupboard. Your mother's got a coffee cake in the oven, you know," he informed Boo. "You're going to have to eat it, or I'll be having it all week."

I followed Boo and his dad up the front steps and into the farmhouse. As soon as we got inside, Vern let out a yell.

"Tillie! Boo's brought a friend home." He turned to me in apology. "Sorry for the yelling, but my wife is a little hard of hearing these days. You'd think that I would have been the one to lose my hearing thanks to all those years working with explosives, but I can still hear a pin drop in the next room."

A tiny white-haired woman came from the back of the house, wiping her hands on a dishtowel and smiling broadly. She threw her arms around Boo as he leaned down—way down—to give her a hug, then aimed a big smile at me.

"I'm pleased to meet you," she said. "I'm Tillie. Would you like some crumb cake?"

"We'd love some, Ma," Boo answered for us. "I'll grab the coffee." He gently took his mother's arm and steered her back in the direction from which she'd appeared.

"Tillie's too old to have to take care of this place anymore," Vern confided. "If we can just get that energy outfit to lease our land for their wind farm, I'm moving us into town into a senior housing community. Did Boo tell you about all that?"

I nodded. "He did. That's why I wanted to see his surveys. I'm curious to see why the energy company is hesitant to use your land. I've birded out here for years, and there's never been any significant or threatened population of birds out here that a wind farm might disturb."

"I know that," he agreed with me, "and so do our neighbors."

He walked into the dining room to a heavy antique china cupboard and began to rifle through papers in its top drawer.

"But the energy folks don't," he continued, "and they're going to listen to the environmental consultant they're paying good money to before they listen to me. That's why we did the aerial survey. Pictures speak louder than words, so we thought the aerial surveys would prove we didn't have some plague of rare birds on the farm, and we'd get that lease approved right quick."

From the kitchen, I could hear Boo and his mother laughing, and the sound of coffee cups being set on a tray.

Vern drew a sheaf of papers and photos from the cupboard's drawer.

"But the local utilities commission said our photos weren't worth anything, since you can't see nesting sites at the end of summer," he said. "Now, either the company has to wait for spring and for us to do another survey, or they just go with their consultant's advice and give the lease to my neighbors so they can get started putting up the turbines."

I could easily guess the choice the energy company would make. If they were anything like the development group that had wanted to build in Goodhue County, they wouldn't want to risk any more delay in breaking ground for the new wind farm. Federal subsidies had a bad habit of drying up if you waited too long to grab them.

And that meant that Boo's parents would lose out on the lease and the income they needed to make a change in their living situation.

I took the papers Vern handed me and sat down at the big oak table that nearly filled the room. Boo's mother placed a cup of coffee in front of me, then sat down in the chair beside me. Boo laid a plate full of crumb cake on the far side of the photos I had spread across the table, and I immediately breathed in the warm scent of baked apples and cinnamon.

"Just took it out of the oven," Tillie told me. "It's an old family favorite recipe."

"Those are the best kind," I said, beginning to salivate. I felt like one of Pavlov's dogs, but without the bell. Give me a whiff of something freshly baked and my mouth was watering like a faucet. Since Luce and I had gotten married, I swear my mouth was salivating almost 24/7 thanks to her cooking. I was going to have to start wearing bibs.

"My wife's a chef," I said to Tillie, "and she collects recipes. She says that the new recipes can't compare to the handed-down ones when it comes to pure comfort level."

"I'd agree with that," Vern said, using his fork to lift a square of the cake onto his plate. "Home-made beats store-bought hands down. In fact, that's what I thought was going on when our neighbors put up those poles. I thought maybe they were going to line up rows for a vineyard or some new crop project—try to diversify.

Then when I saw the feeding platforms I wondered what in the heck they thought they were doing, because the hawks around here don't need any help finding food, believe me. We've got plenty of little-bitty field critters for them to pick off."

I swallowed a bite of the cake. I'd thought the same thing. If the owners next door really did put up the platforms to try to lure in birds—like Ferruginous Hawks, for example—they needed to get their avian facts straight. Even if the hawks picked up a few free meals as they passed through the county, it was completely unlikely they'd relocate their nesting grounds because of it. Not to mention that Ferruginous Hawks weren't any kind of protected species.

Sure, it was a thrill for a Minnesota birder to see one, but their presence wasn't going to jeopardize a wind farm site.

So either the neighbors were ignorant or desperate . . . or both . . . to get the lease from the wind farm.

Okay, that much I could believe. If I could earn up to $8,000 a year per tower in leasing payments, I'd want a few towers in my backyard, too.

Accepting that Sonny was advocating for, or advising, these same neighbors, though, that was a stretch I didn't know how to make. Sonny would know—would have known, past tense, I reminded myself—that the idea of trying to bait Ferruginous Hawks, or any other kind of bird, for that matter, in large enough numbers to impact an environmental survey was not only stupid, but doomed to fail. Birds took longer than one season to change nesting habits, and food provision was only a piece of that puzzle.

Yet Boo and his dad maintained that Sonny had been on their neighbor's side of the battle.

Try as I might, however, I just couldn't figure out how Sonny, a respected birding expert in the state, could have given such faulty information and poor advice—not only to the wind farm developers, but to the Metternick's neighbors as well. It was almost like he'd set them all up for failure. Why would Sonny have done that?

"See, there aren't any of those poles or platforms in these photos from my survey," Boo said, smoothing his fingers lightly over the aerial pictures. "Here's our property line. And over here . . ." he paused, his finger coming to rest on a tiny, but bright, pink rectangle a few inches beyond his parents' farm boundary. "Is that Arlene Weebler's pickup truck?"

Vern leaned over to examine the spot on the map.

"I do believe it is, Boo," he said after a moment of scrutiny. "That girl has the only pink truck in the county. Kind of hard to miss, even in an aerial survey."

"So what was Arlene doing out there at 6:00 am in the morning?" Boo asked his dad. He turned to me to explain. "I did the survey at dawn. Arlene is our neighbor's daughter, and she's never been known to be an early riser, much less interested in exploring her dad's fields at the crack of dawn. Arlene is much more the nightlife kind of girl, if you catch my drift."

"I didn't know Morris had a nightlife," I commented.

"It doesn't," Vern answered me. "That's Arlene's problem. She's sort of a grenade waiting to go off, but her dad doesn't have any ordnance training, so it's anybody's guess what she was doing out there or why."

"Is this the neighbor who wants the wind farm lease?" I asked. "The same neighbor who had Sonny Delite running interference with the energy company so they could get the lease?"

"Yes," Tillie said. She was leaning over the map, too, squinting at the pink spot that marked Arlene's truck. "Does that truck bed look funny to you?" she asked.

I looked at it more closely. It seemed like some kind of material was draped over the back end of the truck bed.

"Oh, my stars," Tillie breathed. "I do believe she was entertaining someone in that truck bed. I'd heard a rumor at the beauty parlor, but I don't like carrying tales about my neighbors."

"What did you hear, Ma?" Boo prompted her.

"Well, Clarissa was doing my hair, and she said that if anyone thought the Weeblers were related to that Mr. Delite, who was helping them get the lease, then they were just as bamboozled as the energy company." She sat back down in her chair and looked at each of us, clearly debating how much gossip to share.

"You're saying that Sonny wasn't a cousin to Mr. Weebler?" I clarified.

Tillie picked at her piece of crumb cake with her fork. "That flour I used must be getting too old. This texture just isn't as light as I like it." She returned to my question. "Apparently not, Bob. The reason he was helping the Weeblers was because he had a . . . special friendship . . . with Arlene."

Oh, boy.

"Let me guess," I speculated. "This 'special friendship' included early morning birding sessions in the back of Arlene's pink pickup truck?"

Tillie tried to suppress a smile. She nodded, still focused on ventilating the cake on her plate. I'd heard about letting wine breathe to improve its body, but stabbing crumb cake to make it lighter was a new one on me.

"It seems Arlene finally found a reason to get up in the morning," she offered. "You know what they say about the early bird catching the . . ."

Boo groaned. "Please, don't even go there, Ma."

"Well, she may have caught Mr. Delite, but Arlene sure didn't catch any grasshopper sparrows on our property, I guarantee," Vern said, ignoring his wife's innuendo. "Those birds are over on the other side of the Weebler's farm. I bet once she and Sonny figured out that ruse wasn't going to work, they started putting up those platforms in hopes of attracting some other important birds to our property. They must have heard that Boo's aerial surveys proved that we don't have any big birds nesting out there, so they decided to try to bring some in."

I shook my head. "Sonny would have known better," I insisted. "If he suggested that plan, he knew it wouldn't work from the start, which means he was deliberately sabotaging the Weeblers' plan to get the wind farm lease. The big question is 'why?'"

Tillie cleared her throat. "To get back at Arlene for letting the cat out of the bag about their—ah—birding dates?"

I looked at Tillie. "Is there some other little piece of gossip you want to tell us?"

"I don't think it's technically gossip," she said, "when it's already public knowledge. Sonny Delite was married. He wore a wedding band. But his wife never came with him when he was consulting for the energy company, not that it made any difference to Arlene."

Vern sighed. "That Arlene is a law unto herself, unfortunately for her parents."

Tillie nodded in agreement. "And Stevens County is a long way from the Twin Cities. What's that expression these days? 'What happens in Vegas, stays in Vegas.' Not that Spinit is anything like Vegas, mind you," she assured me. "You can't even buy a lottery ticket in this town. You have to go into Morris for that."

She picked up a piece of crumb cake with her fork.

"I imagine that Mr. Delite must have assumed that what his wife didn't know couldn't hurt her. In other words, he could have his cake and eat it, too."

She popped the bite of food into her mouth for emphasis. After she chewed and swallowed it, she added, "Or rather, he could . . . until Arlene left a message on his home phone message machine to call her."

"Arlene called his wife?" Vern asked. "Arlene may be a loose cannon—and I, of all people, know what a loose cannon can do—but she's not stupid."

"Clarissa said that Arlene told her it was a mistake," Tillie reported. "But I'm not so sure."

She tapped the empty fork on her plate.

"I have a sneaking suspicion that Arlene Weebler knew exactly what she was doing when she left her phone number on Mr. Delite's home message machine," Boo's mother said. "That girl always did have a knack for causing trouble, especially when she was the one who could benefit from it."

"You think she was blackmailing Sonny into helping her family snag the lease," I said, mentally connecting the dots that Tillie had drawn.

"I can't imagine that Mr. Delite would want his wife to know he was keeping company with another woman while he was away from home on a business trip," Tillie pointed out. "That tends to ruin marriages."

Especially if it was the second time it had happened, I silently considered.

Thanks to our own little soap opera at Savage this week, I knew that Sonny hadn't been the model husband. And I wasn't the only one who knew it, either. Between Boo, Gina, Gina's brother Noah, Rick, the Savage police department and probably innumerable students who heard snippets of conversations they shouldn't (Sara Schiller came to mind), Sonny Delite's past infidelity was old news.

And contrary to the old saw that "the wife was the last to know," it was crystal clear to me now that Prudence Delite had known.

Sonny Delite was a liar and a cheat. Prudence's announcement of that at Millie's Deli on the morning of Sonny's death couldn't have been clearer . . . now that I knew what she'd been talking about.

At the time, though, I hadn't known, but I'd learned a lot more about my occasional birding pal's private life than I ever wanted to in the last few days. He may have been an ace birder and outstanding environmental advocate, but his personal life had been going down the drain for a while.

Until it got completely flushed away, that is.

A sudden chill swept down my spine.

Had Prudence pulled the plug on her husband for a repeat offense?

She'd acknowledged that he was dishonest, and she'd mentioned how hard it had been on her when he was away on his environmental crusades, but had she finally decided his extracurricular activities were just too much to overlook?

I replayed the Sunday morning scene at Millie's in my head.

Red had been surprised to see Prudence and moved quickly to contain her friend's violent outburst when she arrived. Then, even though Pru had slapped her, Red had immediately attributed it to grief and begun to virtually smother the bereaved wife with concern.

Now I found myself wondering: was the concern Red showed Pru not so much the key to that scene as the smothering? By restraining her and feeding her ham and eggs, Red had effectively stopped Prudence's behavior from spiraling even further out of control. Our favorite waitress had, after all, told her old buddy to "put a lid on it." At the time, I'd assumed that Red was reminding Pru that her grief was blinding her to Red's superior combat skills, although now it seemed equally possible that she could just as easily have been warning Prudence Delite to put a lid on something else.

Like her mouth.

Or guilt.

Had Red jumped to Pru's defense to keep her from incriminating herself in Sonny Delite's murder?

How close of a friendship did Red and Prudence have? Close enough that Red would be an accomplice to murder?

The smallest snippet of conversation from Sunday morning came roaring back to me.

When Luce came back from the kitchen, she said that Chef Tom needed Red to help with food prep, even though she'd come in to work late.

I knew from countless breakfasts at the deli that Red always came in at 6:00 am.

But not, apparently, on the Sunday morning that Sonny Delite was murdered.

Red had come in late.

True, Red had seemed surprised when she learned from the radio that Sonny Delite had been found dead, but it wasn't like she was overcome with shock, I recalled now, especially given that the dead man was the husband of her dear old friend. Then, when Prudence herself showed up shortly thereafter at the deli with her police escort, Red had visibly paled. I'd gotten the clear impression that Sonny's death hadn't upset our waitress nearly as much as Pru's unexpected appearance did.

I ate another bite of crumb cake while Boo rolled up the aerial surveys, and I remembered another piece of conversation. This time, it was from this morning.

Red's son had lost a job in utilities a few years back, and she'd been furious, Prudence had told me.

And then I could almost hear Alan speculating at Millie's over our brunch. He'd suggested that Sonny's death was the delayed result of the Henderson utilities defeat—that someone had waited two years to exact revenge on Sonny for shutting that project down.

Could Red have been that someone?

Sonny wouldn't have thought twice about taking a cup of tea from Red. He'd probably done that every time he'd eaten at Millie's. Red was someone he knew and trusted.

But how could she have known he was at the Arb early on Sunday? And wouldn't Sonny have thought it odd to run into Red near the Education Center, especially if she was waiting for him there with a hot cup of tea?

I looked at the last bite of cake on my plate and lost my appetite.

They'd done it together. Prudence and Red had joined forces and murdered Sonny.

Yup. Lying and cheating really did tend to ruin marriages, didn't it?

Not to mention lives.

I suddenly tuned back in to the conversation at the table. Tillie was arguing with Vern about Arlene's role in Sonny's demise.

"If Arlene's blackmailing somehow led to Mr. Delite's death, she ought to face some kind of responsibility for her actions," Tillie insisted.

"Well, there's only one way to find out if Arlene was blackmailing Mr. Delite," Vern replied. "Let's ask her."

"Right," Boo said. "You're just going to walk up to Arlene, ask her if she was having an affair with Sonny Delite, and if she was blackmailing him with that information. I don't think so, Dad."

"I don't think so, either, son," Vern grinned. "I'm not asking her anything. You are."

Boo tipped back on his chair, his head shaking a clear refusal. "No, I'm not."

"Just hear me out," his dad told him. "Here's what I'm thinking."

I listened carefully as Vern outlined his plan to extract the truth from Arlene Weebler. It involved his vintage bazooka, surplus tomatoes, and Arlene's pink pickup truck. Boo was going in as point man, and I was playing back-up. As long as we didn't end up in jail for acting like a bunch of high school delinquents, I figured that Vern's plan to get the truth, the whole truth, and nothing but the truth, about Sonny's death was . . . well . . . better than nothing.

"Now we just have to find Arlene and get this show on the road," Vern said.

"If it's Thursday, I know where she is," Tillie announced.

"It's Thursday," Boo, Vern, and I answered in chorus.

Twenty minutes later, Boo and I were back in my car. Behind us, Vern climbed into his truck, loaded for bear.

Well, maybe not bear, exactly. More like a supply run to the local farmers' market.

Our mission: take down Arlene Weebler and convince her to spill her guts.

Our destination: Betty's Beauty Spot and Nails on Third.

Our chance of success: I had no idea, but I was pretty sure it was going to be a lot more fun than cafeteria duty at work.

At least, I sure hoped so.

It was my day off, after all.

CHAPTER TWENTY

THE SKY HAD CLEARED and the sun was out, quickly melting what little bits of snow had accumulated along the country roads. I hit the button to lower my window, and the honking racket of migrating Canada Geese filled the air. A moment later, the big V formation of the flying geese appeared as it passed high above us, heading south for its winter home. Not far behind, a smaller group of bigger birds was following the same direction.

"Tundra swans," I told Boo, pointing to the white bodies. "Big white birds with black bills."

"You don't have to do this, you know," he said. "Take a right at this next road."

I threw him a quick look as I made the turn towards the tiny town of Spinit.

"Identifying birds? It's sort of in my blood, Boo," I replied. "I can't go anywhere without noticing what birds are around and checking them against the lists I have in my head."

"No, I don't mean the birds," he clarified. "I mean Arlene. Dad loves a hare-brained adventure, but that doesn't mean you have to do it with him."

"Are you kidding me?" I shot him another glance. "It's not every day I get the chance to see tomatoes shooting out of a restored bazooka in the effort to secure justice."

Boo laughed.

"Besides," I added, "Sonny was my friend, and I want to know the sequence of events that led someone to kill him."

I didn't share with him my conclusion about Red and Prudence, however. After already admitting to Boo that I'd considered him a suspect, I was afraid he'd think I was paranoid, at best, if I told him I now had zeroed in on a new probable killer.

Or killers, as the case might well turn out to be, if I was right in my speculations about Prudence and Red.

"Not to mention that Rick is my friend, too," I said, "and he's been suspended from the police force as a primary suspect. Whatever Arlene can tell us can only help Rick's situation. I'm the one who dragged you and your dad into this, remember."

"It doesn't take much to drag my dad into anything these days," Boo said. "I think he still misses the action of combat, even after all these years. He must drive my mom crazy with all his war toys."

"Everyone needs a hobby," I reminded him. "I know that birding has saved my sanity more times than I can count."

Like every time I was ready to pull my hair out after spending a few hours spinning my wheels with my problem children at the high school.

Sara Schiller came to mind.

"How long have you been teaching?" I asked Boo.

"Five years," he answered. "Before coming to Savage, I taught for three years at a small school in New Mexico that served a lot of Native American and Hispanic students. My first job teaching was in Redwood Falls, not that far from here."

I did the math in my head. Assuming Boo was somewhere in his late thirties, that still left about ten years of him doing something else, but he had yet to say what that something was.

"I can see you doing the math," he said.

Geez Louise. Was he a mind reader, too? Or was it just that I was the only human on the planet who was incapable of having a private thought?

"I'm leaving out about ten years between college and my first teaching job."

"Yeah, that occurred to me. Any particular reason for that?"

Like the fact that he really was the Bonecrusher, and he'd been lying to me earlier in a last-ditch effort to protect his secret identity?

All right, I admit it: I'm tenacious. I'm a birder, what can I say?

"I don't usually like to talk about it," Boo said. "I figure the past is best left in the past. Take another right, right here."

I spun the wheel and checked my rear-view mirror to see Boo's dad following us into town.

"I spent a decade traveling with the circus," Boo said.

Okay, so that was totally not what I was expecting him to say. I slid a quick look at the man in my passenger seat.

Boo's face was serious.

"I was the Strongest Man Alive," he confessed.

An image of a bare-chested, big-muscled Boo in a side-show booth, lifting weights, popped into my head. I could almost smell the cotton candy and popcorn and hear the calliope music of the merry-go-round.

Boo Metternick, the Strongest Man Alive.

Actually, that worked for me.

"You don't say," I replied. "I can see it, Boo. Really, I can. But I have to admit, I was a little concerned there for a second that you were going to say you were the Bearded Lady."

Boo laughed. "Believe it or not, she was a real fox under that beard."

"I don't want to know," I laughed back.

"You're going to want to park on the left side of the street up there," he said, pointing towards the small shopping area that was coming into view. "Betty's Beauty Spot and Nails is just around the corner, but you don't want to park in front of the salon if Dad's going to be tossing tomatoes anywhere near there."

"Is he sure he isn't going to get arrested for assault, or for damaging property?" I asked Boo.

When his dad had laid out the plan, Vern had assured us he wasn't going to get in trouble with local law enforcement, but I wasn't convinced. Pelting a truck with tomatoes to get a confession from a woman had to be violating some kind of law, even if it was only a law of simple courtesy.

You know what I mean: don't stare, don't eavesdrop, don't kick your sister under the table, don't throw tomatoes at people on Main Street.

"Dad will be fine," Boo said. "He knows the one police officer in town—Maggie Fleming—and her mother is Dad's second cousin. I think I also heard that Arlene was hitting on Maggie's husband a while back, so I can't imagine that Maggie wouldn't conveniently look the other way if Dad got Arlene riled up over a tomato attack on her pickup."

Ah, yes, frontier justice still exists, especially in small towns where almost everyone is related.

I pulled a U-turn at the end of the shopping block and took a parking slot where Boo suggested. Vern, meanwhile, had taken a left turn onto the street that fronted Betty's salon.

"Last chance," Boo offered me. "You can sit this out right here and avoid the ugly stigma of being a participant in a tomato fight."

"No way," I insisted. "This is my big chance. Bigmouth Rick isn't around to see this, and nobody here knows me, so I can, for once, indulge in complete immaturity and not worry about the consequences."

"You don't think I'm going to tell everyone at the high school that you helped plan a tomato fight? Your students would love that."

"So would yours," I reminded him.

"Touche."

We got out of the car and started toward the corner of the block.

"Bob, you won't mention my circus gig to anyone, will you?" Boo asked. "I'd rather it not get around at the high school. I had to put up with a lot of grief at my last school when the kids found out, and I don't want to have to go through that again. It wreaked havoc with classroom discipline for a while."

I looked Boo over. The man was huge. How he could ever have a problem with student discipline was beyond me. He could squish a student under the palm of his hand, for crying out loud. Okay, so maybe he wasn't the Crusher after all, but . . .

"I know," I said. "How about I spread the rumor that you're a famous former wrestler, by the name of the Bonecrusher? I could say you got kicked out of the ring for losing your temper one too many times and maiming your opponents, and the one thing that really ticks you off is when anyone mentions your wrestling past. That should take care of any discipline problems, don't you think?"

Boo smiled. "Yeah, that might do it. As long as the real Bonecrusher doesn't come after me for impersonation, that is. I wouldn't want my wrists—or any other part of me—slapped by the Crusher."

I frowned, trying to imagine our new art teacher Paul Brand throwing Boo to the canvas.

It would be like knocking over a refrigerator.

Paul would have to have some serious muscle, and moves, to do that. I tried to picture it, I really did, but for some reason, I was still having trouble putting that black leotard on Savage's new art teacher.

It seemed that no matter how hard I tried, the only canvas that came to mind when I thought of Paul was one stretched on a frame.

For painting.

Or scrapbooking.

Or whatever the heck it was that they did in Paul's art class.

So unless Boo had a paralyzing fear of glue guns, I had no doubt that Boo could hold his own against Paul Brand any day.

Speaking of guns . . .

We turned the corner just as Vern was loading his first volley of tomatoes into the bazooka. Across the street, a dirty pink pickup truck was parked at a diagonal to the curb in front of Betty's Beauty Spot and Nails. Boo started for the salon's front door. Vern pulled on a helmet and heavy leather gloves. On the back of his windbreaker, the old Looney Tunes character, Wile E. Coyote, grinned knowingly.

It occurred to me that if I'd grown up with Vern for a dad, maybe I would have joined the circus, too.

I sat down on an old iron bench not far from Vern's base of operations.

Let the cartoon begin, I thought.

CHAPTER TWENTY-ONE

"**A**RLENE! I THINK YOU BETTER come out here!" Boo shouted into the beauty salon, holding the door wide open.

I couldn't make out Arlene's response, but since no one appeared in the doorway, I guessed she'd refused.

Boo hollered again.

"I'm giving you fair warning, Arlene! Dad's on the rampage, and I won't be held responsible for him!"

Still no Arlene.

Boo nodded at his dad, and Vern shot off a salvo of tomatoes into the side of Arlene's pickup.

"I gotta talk with you, Arlene!" Vern shouted.

Two white heads of hair poked out of the salon door.

"It's Vern, all right!" an elderly lady in a blue plastic smock cried.

"He's got a weapon!" yelled the other, equally draped in blue. With a squeal, the women ducked back inside Betty's.

"I got a bone to pick with you, Arlene!" Vern shouted, and let loose with another round of tomatoes.

Boo stood back on the sidewalk out of the tomato splash zone. In a tree in front of a store a few doors down from Betty's, I noticed a trio of crows perched in the branches. Could three crows be considered a murder, or was that term only applied to larger groups of the birds?

How about two by the names of Prudence and Red?

Yeah, that could definitely be a murder, I decided.

"Arlene, it's your last chance!" Boo called into the salon.

Vern loaded up the bazooka again.

Even if Arlene had been blackmailing Sonny, I mused, that didn't make her an accessory to his murder. I supposed it provided a possible motive that the police would want to investigate, but generally the person being blackmailed wasn't the one who ended up dead, according to any television show I'd seen. It was the person doing the blackmailing who got knocked off in prime time.

Vern shot more tomatoes at Arlene's pickup.

I watched the juice and pulp run down the side panels of the truck.

Not that this was anything near a prime-time murder mystery, mind you.

This was real life.

Ridiculous maybe, but still real life.

And then Arlene finally came out of the salon's front door.

I assumed it was Arlene. Since I'd never met her, I couldn't recognize her.

Then again, I wondered if either Boo or Vern could recognize the woman underneath the towel headwrap whose face was covered in green foam and whose hands were wrapped in plastic bags.

"You're a crazy old man!" the Thing from Betty's shouted at Vern.

"You're lying about my land!" Vern yelled back. "Admit it!"

"Your father belongs in a nuthouse!" Arlene shouted at Boo.

"Hand me that crate of tomatoes, Bob," Vern pointed at a crate in the back of his truck that he couldn't quite reach from his station with the bazooka.

I got up from the bench and leaned into the truck. When I lifted the case out and turned to hand it to Vern, I almost rammed it into a girl who had suddenly appeared next to me.

"Mr. White?"

"Sara?"

Chapter Twenty-Two

"**A**RE YOU SHOOTING TOMATOES at that truck?" Sara Schiller asked, her eyes wide and a grin spreading over her face. "And here I thought you were such a dud! Wait till I tell everyone back at school!"

"I . . . I . . . no!" I told her, stammering around my surprise. "What are you doing here?"

"What are you doing here?" she asked back. "It looks to me like you're helping this old guy fire tomatoes at a truck. Isn't that, like, illegal or something?"

"Bob! I need more ammunition!"

I set the crate on the ground near Vern's feet, and took Sara's arm to pull her over to the iron bench.

"Sara, you don't know what's going on here. And you don't need to know," I quickly added. "What are you doing in Spinit?"

"I'm on fall break, Mr. White. I don't have to answer to you," she retorted.

Splat! Splat! Splat!

More tomatoes hit the pink pickup.

Arlene screamed at Vern.

Boo crossed his arms over his big chest and leaned back against Betty's big plate window. He said something to Arlene, but I couldn't hear it.

Arlene stopped shouting and glared at Boo. A moment later, her green foam beginning to slide off her face and onto the blue-striped apron that covered her front, she yelled a single word to Vern.

"Yes!"

Vern lowered his bazooka and frowned at me.

"Shoot," he complained, "I still had another crate of tomatoes to get rid of. Tillie's going to throw a fit if she has to can any more tomatoes."

"Is that Mr. Metternick over there?" Sara asked, looking across the street. "Wow. I didn't know he had abs like that. You can't tell with those dress shirts and ties he wears at school."

She stared at Boo another minute.

"Wow," she said again, then turned to me. "Is it too late to transfer into one of his classes this term?"

"Sara," I said, "Why are you here?"

She shrugged. "I felt like taking a drive."

"To downtown Spinit?"

"I've already been to Wisconsin," she reminded me.

I opened my mouth to tell her to go home, when she suddenly became very focused on what was going on across the street. I followed her glance and saw another man speaking with Boo and Arlene. He was almost as tall as Boo and just as muscular. I could practically feel the rush of hormone waves rolling off Sara.

"Let me guess," I said. "That's Noah Knorsen, isn't it?"

"Yes," she breathed, completely mesmerized by Noah's presence. "Isn't he wonderful?"

I waved my hand in front of her eyes, but she didn't even blink.

"At the count of three, you will act like a chicken," I intoned.

Sara cocked her head at me. "What are you talking about?"

"Just wondering," I told her. "I wanted to see if I could be the Amazing Mr. Wist. The hypnotist who came to school the other day."

Sara gave me another odd look. "I skipped school during the assembly. You are so weird, Mr. White."

"Gee, Sara, thanks," I said. "That means a lot coming from a high school student who's a habitual delinquent and happens to be stalking a man twice her age."

"He is not twice my age," she insisted. She threw another glance of longing at Noah, who appeared to be helping Boo calm Arlene down. A note of disillusionment crept into her voice. "Is he?"

"He's old enough to be your father, Sara."

Okay, that might have been a lie, but the math could work. If Noah was in his early thirties as I guessed him to be, he was chronologically old enough to have fathered a child who would now be sixteen. Heck, I was old enough to be Sara's dad, for that matter.

That was a terrifying thought.

"For all you know, maybe he drinks Metamucil every morning," I threw in for good measure.

Sara was silent for a moment, apparently considering what I'd said.

"Eeuw," she decided. She gave Noah one last stare, then sighed. "Okay, I'm going home now. I can probably find something better to do in Savage than look at old guys."

I was about to agree when I noticed something about Noah Knorsen that had me staring at him with almost the same intensity Sara had exhibited.

Except I wasn't admiring his abs.

I was studying the sweatshirt he was wearing. It was dark green, and it had the logo for the Minnesota Landscape Arboretum on it.

My brain flashed back to Sunday morning at the Arb.

Just before we found Sonny Delite's body, Luce and I had encountered a man on the path. He'd been going in the opposite direction, away from where Sonny was doing his dead scarecrow imitation. The guy had been big, I remembered, and he was wearing the same Arb sweatshirt as Noah Knorsen had on now.

And he'd had red hair. A whole headful of it.

My eyes jumped to Noah's hair.

Red. Bushy.

And then I recalled one more detail about the man Luce and I had passed on the trail.

He carried a thermos of coffee.

At least, I had assumed it was coffee.

But maybe it had been tea instead . . . hemlock tea.

Gee, I bet someone who worked in the Education Center at the Minnesota Landscape Arboretum would be able to recognize lots of plants.

Someone like Noah Knorsen, who was very recently employed at that very same Education Center until he decided to quit because Sonny Delite, whom he despised, was going to be speaking at the sustainable sources conference on Sunday.

My, my, what a lot of coincidences: Noah quitting his job at the Arb, Sonny's death at the Arb, Gina being upset at the Arb after seeing Noah the same morning I found Sonny dead, me running into Noah on the same path at the Arb where I found Sonny dead, and Noah having two really good reasons to make Sonny dead . . . at the Arb.

Call me crazy, but that seemed to suggest one of two things: either the Arb was giving off a lot of really bad vibes these days, or Noah had killed Sonny . . . at the Arb.

And just when I thought I'd had Sonny's murder all solved.

Maybe I was just a high school counselor.

"Yeah, Sara, that's probably a good idea to go home," I said, still watching Boo and Noah as they talked with Arlene across the street.

Actually, I wanted to go home, too. I needed to let Rick and the police know that I could place Noah Knorsen on the trail—literally—that led to a dead man. That should gain a reprieve for Rick as a murder suspect, though it would probably make the situation a lot worse for Gina, not to mention for her brother. Before I even did that, though, I felt obligated out of respect for Boo to share my conclusions with him about the longtime friend he regarded as a little brother.

"So, Boo, I'm going to head on back early, but before I go, I wanted to tell you that Noah's a cold-blooded killer. Enjoy the rest of our fall break."

Geez. Could today get any worse?

"Hey, Mr. White! Watch this!"

I turned around just in time to see Sara, with Vern's help, sighting along the top of his refurbished bazooka.

A volley of tomatoes burst forth from the end of the barrel, landing just in front of Boo, Noah, and Arlene. Tomato juice gushed up at their clothes, Arlene yelled a few choice words at Sara, and Boo and Noah just shook their heads.

Vern clapped Sara on the shoulder with pride. "You've got an eagle eye, girl," he told her. "That was a fine shot for your first try. You ever think about going into ordnance operations as a career?"

"What's ordnance?" Sara asked.

"Weapons," Vern said. "Ammunition, bombs, explosive devices. You come on out to my place, and I'll show you what I've got. I'll even let you try out a few, if you want."

I watched Sara's eyes study Vern, clearly trying to gauge the old man's sincerity. A moment later, a slow smile spread across her face.

"Okay," she accepted. "I think I'd like that."

Well, that sure answered my question.

Yes, today could get worse.

Sara Schiller was going to get armed.

CHAPTER TWENTY-THREE

WE MADE A PARADE BACK to the Metternick homestead.

Sara followed Vern's truck in her Ford Escort, and Boo and I followed Sara. Noah had taken Arlene's keys to run the pickup through the sole carwash in town and had promised to meet us all back at the farm within the hour.

"So what did Arlene say to you about Sonny?" I asked Boo as soon as we were on the road back to his parents' place.

Boo shrugged. "What we had suspected. She was trying to blackmail Sonny into fixing the wind turbine deal for her parents. Apparently, he'd been leading her along—just like he did with Gina during the Henderson utility fight—and when Arlene found out, she decided he could make up for his lying to her by guaranteeing her parents got the energy lease."

"But he couldn't do that," I reminded him. "They had no proof your land was critical for birds, whereas it sounds like everyone out here knew the Weebler's property had nesting colonies on it."

Boo nodded. "Right. So to keep Arlene quiet, Sonny kept devising 'plans' to disqualify our land, but none of the plans panned out, which finally tipped Arlene off to the fact that Sonny wasn't going to fix the deal for her folks."

"So she figured, worst case, she could blackmail him with their affair," I filled in.

"Right again," Boo said. "But when she heard that Sonny was killed, she wasn't about to share any of that with the police because she was afraid she'd be arrested for blackmail, if not as a murder suspect herself."

"You got all that out of Arlene just because she didn't want your dad to coat her pickup in tomato juice?"

"No," Boo confessed. "Although she did tell me that she just got the truck back yesterday after it was in the repair shop for the last week."

"So she wasn't in Chanhassen, at the Arboretum, last Sunday morning, then," I surmised.

"No, I guess not," he agreed. "But that's no surprise. Arlene may be a blackmailer, but I don't think she's capable of planning a murder, let alone committing one. That woman can hardly plan her way out of a paper bag, and even if she did, she wouldn't be able to keep her mouth shut about it. Case in point: Arlene told Clarissa about the phone call to Sonny's place."

"And Clarissa told your mom."

"And probably every other woman in Spinit," Boo speculated. "There are no secrets in a small town, Bob."

"So how did you get her to confess to the blackmail?"

Boo cleared his throat. "I told her that I had some aerial photos of her truck out on the property early in the morning, and it was amazing the kind of detail you could get these days with good camera equipment. Some lenses can see right through the tarps you use over your truck bed."

He slid me a sly smile. "And then I said it sure would be embarrassing to have everyone and his mother looking at what was going on in the back of your truck on YouTube."

I let out a low whistle. "You are heartless, Boo Metternick. I never would have thought that of you. Murder, maybe," I added, reminding us both of my earlier, terribly misplaced, suspicions, "but complete humiliation? Never."

"I'm also a liar," he admitted. "Those aerial shots I have of her truck don't show a thing, and besides, I wouldn't dream of making Arlene Weebler a YouTube sensation. She's obnoxious enough already."

"I thought you hated liars," I said.

He'd certainly impressed me with that trait the other day in my office. When he'd leaned over my desk, I'd been tempted to whip out some pepper spray in defense, just in case he decided to literally pound that little detail into me.

"I do," he said. "But sometimes, you've got to think—and act—like a liar to catch one."

"And what about a murderer?" The words popped out of my mouth before I could stop them.

"What about a murderer?" Boo asked.

I followed Sara's car through the last turn towards the Metternick farm.

How was I going to tell Boo that I had recognized his good friend Noah as the man I saw on the Arboretum trail just minutes before stumbling over Sonny's body? Granted, that fact alone didn't prove anything, but it did provide a very good reason for a close examination of Noah Knorsen as a possible murderer.

"I know you said you don't think Noah is—responsible—for Sonny's death, but what if there was evidence that he was involved? You said yourself that Gina was concerned about Noah being possibly involved, and that she was really upset after seeing him on Sunday morning."

I put the car in park in front of Boo's home. Sara and Vern were already out of their vehicles, heading towards a small barn that sat a little way back from the house. From what I could see, the two were carrying on an animated conversation. I wondered if Sara had ever shown that much interest in any classroom at Savage. We obviously weren't offering the right subjects to our students. Instead of Art and Family Science, we should have been thinking Nuclear Devices and Vegetable Weaponry.

Boo sat in the car and crossed his arms over his chest.

"Gina wasn't upset about something that Noah had done, Bob," he explained. "She was upset about something he wanted to do, which was quitting his job. She told him she'd walked away from her past mistakes and that he needed to move on, too. He told her to mind her own business. Gina took it real hard, and I took her home. Noah didn't kill Sonny, Bob."

"So what was he doing on the path at the Arb on Sunday morning," I blurted out, "less than five minutes away from Sonny Delite's body? I saw him, Boo. I was there, and so was he."

Silence filled the car.

And lingered.

I swear I could practically see the gears turning in his head as he processed what I'd told him. Then, his blue eyes slowly went icy, and his face filled with dark anger.

For a split-second, I debated who he looked more like: a furious Hulk on the verge of turning green, or a fair-haired Thor getting ready to rumble.

Either way, I didn't think it was going to be good.

Seconds passed, and then a still-human and very angry Boo was out of the car and storming up the front porch steps.

I stepped out my side of the car and called after him.

"Was it something I said?"

Tillie appeared on the porch a moment later.

"Are you going to be joining us for a nice lunch, Bob? Boo says that Noah's coming over, and I could heat up some ham. It wouldn't be any trouble," she added.

Easy for her to say.

After Boo's implosion in my car, I wasn't sure who he was angrier at—me for suggesting that Noah was a murderer, or Noah for possibly committing a murder. Regardless, the idea of sitting down at the table with both of them sure sounded like trouble to me.

"Thanks, but I don't know that Boo wants my company right now," I excused myself. "I think he's got a bone to pick with Noah."

"Oh, he's just in a little snit," she said, dismissing her son's anger with a wave of her hand. "He gets like that sometimes. He'll be fine once he has some lunch in him. He and Noah have their own way of working out their differences."

For some reason, that didn't give me a lot of confidence. I really doubted that Boo just needed a slice of ham to calm his fury. When he'd slammed out of my car, he looked like he was ready to kill someone.

And I'd really rather it wasn't me.

Especially on my day off.

On the other hand, if it was Noah that Boo wanted to murder, I should probably stick around as a witness. For once in my life, I wouldn't have to figure out who the murderer was.

"That sounds great, Tillie," I accepted. "I'd love to have lunch."

Boo's mother smiled happily and then pointed at the small barn where Vern and Sara had disappeared.

"And what about that young lady I saw my husband take into his museum? Would you go ask her if she'd like some lunch, too? That is, if she can stand to be around Vern any longer after getting the tour of his collection," she added. "Those war relics are his passion, but I'm afraid they put our visitors to sleep, nine times out of ten."

I looked in the direction of the small structure beyond the house. As an avid birder, I was familiar with the passion that could transform a hobby into a life-long love affair. I'd been birding for three decades, and I still got just as excited—maybe even more—about seeing a new bird as I had back when I was six years old. If birding—my passion—made me feel like that now, I could only imagine how Vern must have felt every time he stepped into that little barn and surrounded himself with his collection.

I bet it felt like heaven.

"It's a museum?" I asked Tillie.

She nodded. "All the memorabilia you'd ever want to see," she said. "I told Vern that as long as he keeps it out of the house, he could collect as much as he wanted. At the rate he finds things, though, I think he's going to have to expand that museum of his pretty soon. He's got all kinds of stuff in there."

"Does he, by chance, have any body armor?" I asked.

Not that I expected to take any blows myself during the confrontation I was sure was coming, but considering how big Boo and Noah were, and how small the dining room would feel with both of them in it, I decided it wouldn't be a bad idea to dress a bit more pro-actively for lunch.

It never hurt to be prepared, right?

"I don't know what all he's got," Tillie said. "He might have a couple of those spiked helmets. Just be sure you yell out before you walk into the museum so he knows you're coming, or you might get hit with an antique grenade."

Grenade?

Tillie caught my look of concern and laughed. "They're all duds, Bob."

I breathed a sigh of relief and headed for the barn.

Tillie's voice followed me. "So far, that is."

CHAPTER TWENTY-FOUR

HEEDING TILLIE'S INSTRUCTIONS, I loudly announced myself before I opened the door to Vern's private museum.

Not getting any answer, I took my life in my hands, grabbed the door handle and pulled it wide.

"I'm a friend!" I yelled, bracing for any impending impact.

Vern and Sara looked up from a glass display case in the middle of the room.

"Tillie told you I had grenades, didn't she?" Vern asked.

I nodded sheepishly. "Yes, she did."

"That woman is such a tease," he said. He nudged Sara with his elbow and winked at her. "It's why I married her, you know. She was quite the catch."

Sara smiled back at the old man. "I bet you were, too. Women love fireworks," she said with just the right hint of flirtatious innuendo.

They both burst into laughter.

I stood rooted to the spot.

Sara Schiller had a sense of humor?

When had that happened?

Not only that, but it was clear she was enjoying Vern's company. I didn't know if I should be glad . . . or worry. Sara could only benefit from having the influence of a good man in her life, but if she started skipping school to drive to Spinit to spend time around Vern, I was going to have more than her teachers waiting by my office door.

I would have the pleasure of Sara attending—sort of—Savage High School for more than four years.

Perish the thought.

"You've got to look at this stuff, Mr. White," Sara said, tapping her finger on the glass case. "They're pictures of the decoy tanks and airfields that England used in World War II to fool German bombers and keep them away from their real targets. They painted big pieces of canvas to look like hangars, and then laid them down on the ground, so it would look like a real airfield from the air. Sometimes they put old jeeps, and fake fuel stores, and dummy aircraft around it, too."

I walked over to the display while Sara continued to enthusiastically report on the case's contents.

"Vern's even got a rubber tube that was used to hold up a dummy tank. Look at this!"

I peered down into the case that stretched a good eight feet across the top of a sturdy wooden stand. Inside it were black-and-white photos of fake bunkers and aircraft mockups, along with uniformed men posing beside the structures. A piece of aged painted canvas sat next to a wooden slat that had been part of a "tank" made of wood. Beside a photo of what looked like a Sherman tank was a rubber tube that had been a section of the inflatable dummy tank's skeleton. Leaning against the fake tank were two very dashing soldiers dressed in World War II battle fatigues. The big grins on their faces made it plain that they were tickled by the successful results of their campaign of deception.

"And get this, Mr. White," Sara said. "A lot of the guys who designed and built these decoys were actually from a film studio in England. They knew how to make fake stuff look real with lights and props for movies, so the government asked them to make decoys as part of their war strategy to trick the enemy into bombing the wrong things. They even faked burning buildings and explosions! These guys started out making movies, and ended up saving people's lives because of the decoys."

She paused to take a breath, and I glanced at Vern, who was grinning ear-to-ear. He'd clearly found a great audience in Sara, not to mention someone who shared his enthusiasm for explosives. My problem child virtually glowed with joy.

Funny, my grad school instructors never mentioned ordnance training as an effective approach to dealing with truants.

"Having trouble with keeping kids in class? Give 'em grenades, and you'll be thrilled with the results."

Oh, well. The good news was that I'd know who to start looking for if anything blew up at the high school next week.

"So these film guys were really good at using decoys, Mr. White!" She glanced at Vern to make sure she was getting her facts right.

"In fact, you could say they were," she paused for effect, "masters of deception."

She tapped her chest with her two index fingers.

"I could do that! You're always saying I'm your Mistress of Deception, so I would be really good at this stuff," Sara insisted. "I could make fake explosions for movies, or do it for real in the army!"

"You sure could," Vern jumped in before I could pick my jaw up off the floor.

A terrifying picture formed in my head: Sara Schiller, demolitions expert. I had the sinking feeling I'd just discovered the one thing that could frighten me more than creepy scarecrows at Halloween.

Where was my kindergarten teacher when I really needed her?

"Of course, you have to do well in your classes at high school," Vern advised Sara, "A good ordnance officer has to take responsibility and be accountable. No whining or crying when things don't go your way."

"And no driving to Wisconsin, either," I tossed in.

Sara threw me a dirty look, but I could tell she was sucking up Vern's every word. In fact, from where I stood, I would have banked on the persuasiveness of Boo's dad over the hypnotic talents of even the ill-fated Amazing Mr. Wist any day. Vern's hold on Sara's attention—and imagination—was nothing short of miraculous.

"And it might be a really good idea to take some basic physics classes," Vern finished lecturing her, "because it doesn't hurt to understand some of the principles behind weaponry. You ever shoot off a bottle rocket in class?"

Sara shook her head.

"You need to take a class from my son, young lady. He's an ace rocket-launcher."

Sara's eyes lit up, but I wasn't sure if the source of her excitement was the idea of bottle rockets or the prospect of sitting in a class staring at Boo's biceps for a semester. Her newfound interest in explosions seemed genuine, but knowing the tenacity of teenage female hormones, I doubted that Sara's interest in males had suddenly vanished.

Memo to me: remind Boo to keep wearing those loose-fitting dress shirts to work and leave the snug tee-shirts at home.

"I'm sure if you set your mind to it, Sara, you could be a whiz-bang explosives expert," Vern encouraged her. "Pardon my pun," he added for my benefit.

"You think so?" Sara asked Vern, her voice filled with hope.

"Absolutely," he assured her. "You just take all that fire and passion inside you, and put it to work, young lady. You'll be amazed at what you can do."

Sara smiled again, and Vern threw me a wink.

I gave him a little salute in gratitude.

Vern Metternick was one heck of a motivator, I had to admit, and not too shabby at off-the-cuff counseling, either. I had a graduate degree and years of experience in a high school student services office, but I'd gotten nowhere with Sara Schiller for the last few years. Given less than an hour, though, this World War II veteran and ordnance officer had clearly succeeded where I had repeatedly failed: Vern had made an impression on Sara.

No wonder he and his cronies were honored as the Greatest Generation.

They got the job done.

"Mission accomplished," I said to Vern.

"What mission?" Sara asked, her eyes shifting from Vern to me and then back again to Vern.

"Lunch time," I brightly announced to Sara. "Mrs. Metternick is setting a place at the table for you."

She turned to Vern. "You guys eat at the table? At our house, we usually just eat at the kitchen counter. And we never eat at the same time, either."

I noticed Vern wince, even as he quickly covered it with a big smile.

"Then you're in for a treat," he promised her. "Lunch at the Metternicks' place is a real event."

Vern got that right, although I doubted he knew just how much of an event it might turn out to be today, with his son and Noah facing off across Tillie's fine china and her hot ham platter. For an awful second, I imagined food flying along with accusations. I made a mental note to myself to be sure I got enough to eat the first time the dishes were passed around.

Shoot.

I might have to break up a food fight, and I wasn't even at work.

I followed Vern and Sara out the door of the museum just in time to see a freshly-washed pink pickup truck pull up in front of the Metternick home.

Noah hopped out of the driver's side and came around the car to open the passenger door. Arlene Weebler—missing the green facial mask and ugly salon apron—stepped out.

"Arlene," Vern called to her. "Your folks know you're out here consorting with the enemy?"

Arlene put her hands on her hips and shot him an insolent glare.

"As a matter of fact, I have come out here to bury the hatchet, Vern," she informed him. "The wind farm development group told my parents just this morning that they are putting a hold on the whole project until they have a proper site evaluation completed by a survey team from the university in Morris."

"Well, hallelujah," Vern replied. "It's about time they figured out they ought to call in the experts who are specially trained to make those kinds of decisions. My tax dollars have been funding that wind turbine operating at the Morris campus for how many years now? Those professors and researchers ought to have this wind energy thing boiled down to an exact science by now."

"It'll never be by-the-numbers, Vern," Noah answered. "Every site for a wind farm is different. The developers need to match the particular landscape with a system's array design based on meteorological factors, for one."

"What is he talking about?" Sara asked me. "You can't farm wind."

"Yes, you can," Arlene corrected, turning her evil eye on Sara. "Who are you?"

Vern threw his arm around Sara's shoulders. "She's a friend of mine, Arlene. I'm going to teach her to defuse a bomb with her eyes closed."

Arlene laughed. "Yeah, right."

"Really?" Sara's eyes were fixed on Vern's face.

"You bet," he said. "You've got to work up to it, of course, but when you're ready, I'm going to teach you. If you want to learn how, that is."

"How do you know about wind farms?" I asked Noah. "I'm Bob White, by the way. I work with Boo at Savage High School."

And I'm the poor sap who found Sonny Delite dead at the Arb, I wanted to add. *Does the name ring a bell?*

"Pleased to meet you," Noah replied, extending his hand to shake mine. "I'm Noah Knorsen. You must know my sister."

I was acutely aware of Sara Schiller standing next to me. Feeling obligated as her counselor to set a good example for her, I reluctantly shook the man's hand. How to handle an introduction to a murderer in polite society wasn't something I'd covered with her yet. Come to think of it, no one had covered that with me yet, either.

That was me, all right—Bob White, flying by the seat of his pants.

As usual.

"I worked a summer on the construction of a wind farm. Boo and I did," Noah explained. "Putting up a wind farm involves a lot more than just assembling turbines. You've got to do feasibility studies and assess weather conditions before you can even begin to think about actual project installation." He turned to Vern. "The wind industry is changing just about as fast as the wind does."

"Excuse me for interrupting," Arlene huffed, her words blatantly unapologetic, "but I'm really pressed for time here, thanks to the tomato rinse you gave my car, Vern."

"I got it cleaned off for you," Noah reminded her.

She ignored his comment, along with the rest of us.

"Anyway," she said to Vern, "the wind people told my mom and dad that there's a good chance they might want to use parts of both of our properties, and so we'd all get a piece of the leasing pie, after all."

Hallelujah, indeed. With enough lease money, Vern and Tillie could move into town, and Boo could stop worrying about his parents' financial future. Who knew? Guaranteed a solid income, maybe even the apparently incorrigible Arlene Weebler would clean up her act.

"Anyway," she said again, "Momma and Poppa want you and Tillie to come over for dinner tonight, Vern. They really miss playing cards with you two every Thursday night since the wind farm people came to town."

She glided her left hand up Noah's arm and looked up at him through her thickly mascaraed eyelashes.

"Momma says we should all just be friends again," her voice low and husky. "What do you think, Noah?"

"I think he's a lying piece of dirt," Boo announced from the house porch steps, just before he launched himself across the front path to tackle Noah to the ground.

CHAPTER TWENTY-FIVE

ARLENE GOT KNOCKED AWAY FROM Noah's side and landed on her rump in the gravel next to her truck's right front wheel. Boo and Noah rolled in the opposite direction, both men pummeling away at each other's heads and bodies. Muffled grunts and the scrambling sound of sliding gravel filled the air.

"So, Arlene," I said to the woman on the ground. "How's that 'let's all be friends' thing working for you at the moment?"

She gave me a sour look and stood up, brushing dust and dried grass from her jean-clad legs and backside. Without a word, she moved around the front of her pickup to the driver's door, climbed up into the cab, and with hardly a glance to the rear, put the truck into first gear and spun off in the direction of the nearest county road.

The wrestlers, in the meantime, had moved their contest onto the grass lawn that wrapped around the side of the house. Vern followed the writhing bodies at a safe distance, Sara slightly behind him. The sound of fists hitting flesh was hard to miss.

"Do something, Mr. White!" Sara cried back to me.

I caught up to her and Vern and took stock of the situation.

Boo and Noah rolled over each other, muscles straining as each tried to pull the other down. Their grunts and muffled yells sounded like a soundtrack for a street brawl. I heard the rip of clothing.

I turned to Boo's dad. "Are you going to break it up?" I asked.

He shook his head. "I may have my crazy moments, but I've still got some brain cells working," he told me.

Sara threw me a look of despair. I could hear Mr. Lenzen's voice in my head from our back-to-school faculty meeting: "Never allow a student to witness a teacher beating someone to a pulp."

Okay, that probably wasn't exactly what he said, but I admit I was only semi-conscious at that point in the meeting. It had been a long, warm August day in the Savage High School cafeteria, and not even Mr. Lenzen's stern instructions about appropriate faculty behavior could keep me alert.

Let me reword that: Mr. Lenzen was putting me to sleep.

"Mr. White!" Sara pleaded.

"Those two boys were state wrestling champs back in high school," Vern noted, nodding at the two grown men grappling on the grass. "You'd have to be nuts to want to get in the middle of that."

I took another look at Sara's distraught face.

"That would be me, then," I muttered.

I took two steps forward and reached out for Noah's flailing arm.

"Hey, you two! Knock it off," I yelled in my cafeteria duty voice.

And man, did they knock it off.

Unfortunately, the "it" they knocked off was my arm, followed by the rest of my body.

I landed with a jarring thud on my rump in the grass. The next thing I knew, Boo and Noah were locked together, hurtling my way. Since I've never wondered what it would feel like to be hit by a moving wall—make that two moving walls—of muscle, I dove to the side and narrowly missed becoming the very flat Mr. White.

I decided that the counselor voice wasn't going to do the trick here.

I called to Vern. "Have you got any stun guns in that collection of yours?"

"None charged up," he responded. "You're on your own on this one, Bob."

That was so not what I wanted to hear.

I took a quick look in Sara's direction to make sure she was clear of the wrestling match and learned a very important safety lesson about watching two big wrestlers having a free-for-all within arm's reach.

Do not look away, even for a second.

"Oof!"

I hit the grass again. Boo had backed into me, sending me sprawling once more, just as he tried to put a headlock on Noah. I scrambled out of the reach of Noah's swinging arms and came to the conclusion that Vern knew what he was talking about.

You'd have to be certifiably crazy to try to break up this fight, and since the only certification I had was my state counseling license, I was sitting this one out.

Thankfully, though, the two former champions were beginning to lose some of their steam. They gripped each other's biceps and spun in a circle, dropped to their knees and then, covered in dust and dirt, Noah finally let loose a colorful curse as Boo immediately flipped his opponent over on his stomach and pinned him motionless to the ground.

"Get off of me!" Noah shouted at Boo, his cheek pressed to the dirt. "What in the world are you trying to prove, you idiot!"

Boo didn't move a muscle, keeping Noah caged beneath him.

"What am I trying to prove?" Boo hissed back at his old buddy. "What are you trying to prove? I'm not the one who killed Sonny Delite after you swore to Gina you wouldn't do anything stupid!"

"What are you talking about?" Noah yelled, spitting grit out of his mouth.

"Don't lie to me, Noah. Bob is the one who found Sonny's body at the Arboretum, and he saw you there." Boo tightened his grip on the back of Noah's neck. "Gina told me how you said you'd kill him if he ever came anywhere near her again."

"I would have!" Noah yelled. "The man was a predator! But I didn't, Boo. I didn't kill him!"

"And why should I believe you?"

"Because, you moron, I love Gina as much as you do, and as much as I would have loved to wring his neck, I refuse to cause my sister any more grief on account of him. She's had more than enough. I gave her my word, Boo, and I keep my promises. You, of all people, should know that."

Sara turned to look at me, her eyes wide in surprise. "Mr. Metternick is in love with Ms. Knorsen?"

I gave her a noncommittal shrug and kept my mouth shut. An ache traveled up my arm where I'd hit the ground.

"Too much information," she said. "Teachers aren't supposed to . . . you know . . ."

"Date?" I supplied for her.

Sara cleared her throat. "Yeah. Right. They're not supposed to . . . date."

"That's none of your business," I cautioned her. "But if I were you, I'd make sure not to say anything to anyone about Mr. Metternick's private life, especially if you want to take a class from him. He might be . . . sensitive . . . about that sort of thing, Sara, if you catch my drift."

She looked over at Boo, who had rolled off Noah and then stood up. His shirt was torn, he was breathing hard, and he was covered in grass, but he was still as impressively sized as ever. To be perfectly honest, the last thing he looked was "sensitive," but I wasn't going to point that out to Sara.

"What happens in Spinit, stays in Spinit," Vern suggested. "Discretion is the better part of valor, Sara."

She gave him a blank look.

"I'll explain it over lunch," he told her, offering his arm to lead her into the house. "Shall we?"

They went up the steps and into the house, leaving me with a pair of big, dirty wrestlers, both of whom stared at me with distrust.

"You said you saw him, Bob, right?" Boo questioned me. "You saw Noah near Sonny's body."

"Making me guilty until proven innocent?" Noah asked, a distinct tone of menace in his voice. "Isn't that backwards?"

"Yes," I agreed, standing my ground, literally. "Yes, it is."

I studied the man in front of me.

Up close, Noah Knorsen was even bigger than Boo Metternick. Not only that, but he exuded a tough, "don't mess with me" attitude that would have most people crossing to the other side of the street when they saw him coming. I didn't know what Noah had been teaching at the Arb's Education Center, but if anyone ever asked me for a great Intimidation 101 instructor, I now knew who to recommend. As far as I was concerned, Gina's brother was downright scary.

"You're right," I told Noah, hoping that honesty truly was the best policy, and not the quickest route to a black eye in this situation. "It is backwards, and I was wrong."

I was also injured. I rubbed the growing ache in my arm where I'd landed on it after my first attempt at peacemaking failed. I'd totally forgotten to ask Vern for body armor.

"But in my defense," I continued, "I only told Boo the truth— you were the man my wife and I passed on the trail just before I found Sonny's body. And you were carrying a thermos."

Noah swiped a clump of grass off his shirt. "I walked that trail twenty times a day when I worked at the Education Center—that was part of my job. I was a program interpreter. I always carry a thermos at work. The coffee at work's lousy. I always bring my own."

"You drink coffee," I said.

Noah tilted his head to the side and frowned. "Yes. Is that a problem?" he asked, his voice thick with sarcasm.

"It is if you work at Savage High School," Boo noted. "The coffee in the teacher's lounge will kill you."

Boo froze as he realized where I was going with my comment.

"Sonny Delite was poisoned, wasn't he?" he asked me. "The news stories never mentioned how he died, and you were asking me if I could identify hemlock on our way up here."

He crossed his arms over his chest. "Somebody gave Sonny Delite poisoned coffee to drink."

I shook my head. "Not coffee. Tea."

"He was poisoned? With tea?" Noah echoed. "That should prove to you I didn't kill Sonny right there, Boo. I would have strangled the man. And you know I won't touch tea."

"Look, Noah, I'm sorry," I apologized, knowing full well that my excuse was going to sound totally inadequate. "One of my best friends is suspected of killing Sonny, so I'm trying to run down any leads that might help him out by pointing to the real murderer. I did see you at the Arb really close to where I found Sonny, and when I remembered you'd had a thermos, too, I jumped to the wrong conclusion. I found a straw in you and I grasped at it for Rick's sake."

Noah gave me a long look and finally nodded.

"I understand about wanting to help your friend."

He turned to Boo and punched him in the arm. "What's your excuse?"

"Don't have one," he admitted, rubbing the spot that Noah had just hit.

I suspected it wouldn't be the only place he'd be bruised tonight. He and Noah hadn't seemed too concerned about pulling their punches during their wrestling match.

"Yes, you do," Noah corrected him. "You're still so crazy about my sister that you're hell-bent on being her champion, even if she doesn't want you. You'd do anything for her, including turning in her own brother for murder if he was guilty. If she asked you to take a bullet for her, you'd do that, too."

He wiped away a thin trickle of blood dripping from his nose.

"Read my lips, Boo," he said. "Move on."

Boo studied his friend's face, which was already beginning to show signs of swelling in a few places.

"And then what?" he reluctantly asked Noah.

Gina's brother grinned. "Then you find some other sweet woman to put Gina's hold on."

His hand shot out like a whip and grabbed Boo's neck with the same tight grip Boo had used on Noah when he'd been on the ground.

"It worked for Gina on the circuit, Boo," Noah said. "She never lost a match. Not that any woman is going to want to walk away from you, but if they do, you know how to pin 'em down."

Noah gave Boo's neck a quick squeeze and then slapped him on the back of his head. "Move on, buddy," he repeated. "Now let's go get some lunch. I've been craving a fresh tomato ever since your dad lobbed that first volley at Arlene's truck."

I grabbed Noah's arm as he started to walk by me.

It was rock-hard.

"Gina wrestled?" I asked incredulously. "On a circuit?

"No, Bob, you didn't hear that right," Boo interrupted before Noah could answer. "He meant that—"

"Yeah, she wrestled," Noah said. "Didn't you know that about her? She was the first female on a high school wrestling team in the state. She taught both Boo and me her best moves when we joined the team at the university. She didn't wrestle in college, though. The division wouldn't allow it."

I vaguely recalled the story. I'd been in college at the time, but with my best friend and future brother-in-law Alan Thunderhawk as my athletics-obsessed roommate, I got to hear all the state sports news on a daily basis. Professional, amateur, high school, college, Little League—you name it, if someone in Minnesota was playing a sport, Alan followed it and repeated it all to me.

This particular story was about a female high school student out in a rural district who had fought the state athletics association for the right to compete on her school's wrestling team. Back then, wrestling teams were still boys only, but because she attended a small high school, and her dad brought in a big city lawyer to pressure the school board, the girl got on the team.

When the family tried the same tactic with her college, though, they were unable to swing the same result.

"So Gina hung up her headgear," I guessed, "and went into teaching."

"She did," Noah confirmed. "She loves teaching. She says it brings out all the nurturing instincts she suppressed when she was kicking boys' butts in high school."

Boo pushed Noah towards the house.

"Lunch," he ordered. "Enough about Gina."

I fell into step beside Noah as we crossed the yard to the front porch.

"You're going to think this is really funny, then," I told Gina's brother. "For just a split-second there, when you said Gina wrestled on a circuit, I thought that maybe she was this former celebrity pro wrestler that our assistant principal hired this year, but no one knows who he is yet. I was sure it was Boo, but he denies it, and now he's just about got me convinced that it's our new art teacher. But when you said that about Gina, it occurred to me that I'd only considered the new male hires, which was pretty sexist of me . . ."

I let my words trail off, figuring I'd embarrassed myself more than enough for one day.

Did I need a keeper or what? I readily accused innocent men of murder and pictured female faculty members as cross-dressing wrestlers.

"No kidding?" Noah grinned again. "You thought Gina was a pro wrestler? Imagine that. I'll have to tell her. She'll get a real kick out of it, especially the part about Boo convincing you that the Bonecrusher is this other teacher."

"Noah."

Boo's voice was barely audible from where he walked on the other side of Noah.

"I didn't say anything!" Noah defended himself. "Gina will think it's hilarious that you're pointing the finger at another teacher. Like I reminded you earlier, I keep my promises, Boo, and you know it."

My eyes skipped from one big man to the other.

Noah looked pleased.

Boo looked distressed.

Everything I'd ever learned about body language was screaming at me that these guys were hiding something.

I ran Noah's remarks through my head again and could come up with only one reason why Gina Knorsen would find it funny that her old friend Boo Metternick had suggested someone else was the Bonecrusher.

Because Boo was doing exactly what those former film studio workers in England had done in World War II: he was setting up a decoy. By insisting that Paul Brand was the logical choice for the former celebrity wrestler, Boo was running his own campaign of deception to distract anyone from finding out the real identity of the Bonecrusher.

Boo absolutely knew who the real Bonecrusher was, despite his protest of innocence.

And now, so did I.

CHAPTER TWENTY-SIX

I SETTLED INTO MY SEAT FOR THE DRIVE back home, still mulling over the events—and revelations—of the day in Spinit.

Boo had decided to stay over at his folks' place for the night, so I was flying solo in my cardinal-red SUV. Since his dad and mom had made a date to take Sara to a World War II memorabilia show in the Twin Cities on Saturday, Boo would catch a ride back to Savage with them. Sara, after Vern's urging and a few phone calls, was able to get into an Open House overnight dorm session at the University of Minnesota in Morris nearby. Fired by the old veteran's enthusiasm and his confidence in her future, Sara wanted to explore the history major that was offered at the campus.

Like I already said, Vern Metternick was proving to be a much better college motivator than our Amazing Mr. Wist, our guest hypnotist.

And we didn't even have to convince Sara she was a chicken, either.

As for Noah Knorsen—after he got cleaned up from his brawl with Boo and joined the rest of us at the dining table—I discovered that he and I had a lot in common when it came to older sisters. Like my own big sister, Lily, Noah's big sister, Gina, had always assumed it was her job to keep him in line.

"Tell him about the time she tied you up and tossed you in the bathtub," Boo had said between bites of his hot ham and cheese sandwich.

"And you," he added sternly, pointing at Sara, seated next to his dad on the other side of the table, "have to promise you won't tell her you know this story."

Sara, wide-eyed, crossed her heart. "She tied him up?"

"With duct tape," Noah said. "My dad had an evening meeting to go to, and as soon as he left, she tied me up and threw me in the tub so I wouldn't bug her while she talked with some boyfriend on the phone. She said it was the only way she knew I wouldn't get into any trouble."

Boo's parents snickered.

"But she thought she was being protective of you, right?" I said.

"That's what she says now," he replied. "She wanted to be sure I didn't stick a fork into an electric socket or something while she wasn't looking, but I think it was a good excuse to make sure she knew exactly where I was and what I was doing."

He tried not to grin, but failed. "I had a habit of listening to her phone calls on the extension in the other room and then making comments during her conversations."

"Shame on you," said Tillie, passing him a bowl of potato chips.

"What's an extension?" Sara asked Vern.

"I'll explain it later," Vern said.

"The truth," Noah continued, "is that Gina and I can fight like cats and dogs, but she'd do anything to help me out when I really needed it."

I thought of my sister, Lily. People who didn't know us well always said we got along about as well as oil and water, but that was only on the surface of our relationship. Once you got past the sibling rivalry piece, Lily and I were very fond of each other . . . in a resentful sort of way.

Just kidding.

The truth for us was similar to Gina and Noah's relationship: when the chips were down, we were there for each other, no matter what.

I almost swerved off the road.

No matter what.

A terrible scenario was forming in my head.

How far would Gina really go for her little brother?

She'd housed him in Henderson while he waited for the utility job that never materialized. She'd given up the job that she loved to move to the Twin Cities, just to provide him with better job opportunities. If he'd threated to kill Sonny Delite, would she commit murder herself to protect her brother from his own plan of revenge? Could she have listened to that message on her phone after Rick left her Saturday night and gone to meet Sonny after all, with the intention of poisoning him and removing him from her and Noah's lives for good? Was that why she'd been so upset after talking with Noah at the Education Center on Sunday morning—because she'd killed Sonny, only to find Noah determined to leave the job he'd finally landed because of Sonny's scheduled appearance there?

No.

No to all of the above, in fact.

Not because I absolutely, completely, totally, indisputably, knew for sure that none of that was true, but because I wasn't going to accuse another person of murder today. I'd already done that once, and look where it had got me. My sore arm was already showing a bruise.

More to the point, I still didn't have a clear lead on who killed Sonny Delite. I could think of plenty of motives, and it seemed like everyone who could possibly be a suspect would have had the opportunity, but I was no closer to identifying Sonny's murderer than when I had gotten up this morning and stumbled into the kitchen to start my morning coffee.

Boo, I was sure, was blameless when it came to Sonny's death. Yes, he had a temper, and yes, he was strong enough to drag a dead body halfway across the Arb if need be, but if he'd gone to harvest hemlock with his pathetic knowledge of plants, he was just as likely to have picked any of a hundred weeds that grow along Minnesota ditches. As for a motive, Boo would have to have been a total idiot if he thought that killing the man who had wronged Gina would steer her into his arms. From what I had seen of Boo both in and outside of Savage High, "idiot" was not a description that fit him.

Secretive, yes.

Deceptive, yes.

Strongest Man Alive?

Apparently.

But idiot?

Not a chance.

Noah, too, had appeared to have a strong motive, as well as the perfect opportunity, but his insistence of innocence had rung true when he'd told Boo that he'd never cause Gina grief over Sonny. Not only that, but after I had the chance to spend a little time with him over lunch, every counselor instinct I had agreed that Noah was not killer material. As for running into him at the Arb on Sunday morning so close to the scene of the crime, my best guess was that he was simply in the wrong place at the wrong time.

It happens.

I should know—I'm the one birder in the state of Minnesota who could start a list of the birds I found near dead bodies.

And then there was Arlene and her plan to guarantee herself a lifetime income of hefty wind farm leasing payments. Without a doubt, the timing of Arlene's attempt to blackmail Sonny seemed too coincidental to have nothing to do with his death, but I couldn't find a connection that made any sense. Killing Sonny, or having him killed—she was in Spirit over the weekend, grounded by her truck repair—just didn't make any sense at all. If he was going to be her goose that laid the golden nest egg, she sure wouldn't have poisoned him before the nest egg got laid.

I couldn't claim any kind of familiarity with Arlene Weebler after my brief interaction with her at the Metternick farm, but even that short introduction to the woman had me agreeing with

Vern's assessment of her as a loose cannon. For all anyone knew, maybe Arlene decided that if she couldn't get the leasing payments, she'd at least get revenge on the man who'd made a fool of her; from what I'd seen of Arlene, I wouldn't put it past her to round up some long-distance accomplices to help her get what she wanted.

So, while I knew she herself hadn't poured the poisoned tea for my old friend, until Sonny's murderer was identified and arrested, I wasn't going to eliminate Arlene Weebler from my personal list of suspects.

And I hadn't even gotten around to Red and Prudence Delite, yet.

I shook my head in disgust.

I needed distraction.

I needed to clear my mind.

I needed to do some more birding.

I looked out my windshield and saw a large flock of crows heading towards the west.

"Works for me," I said, following their lead at the next intersection of county roads.

I called up my mental map of Stevens County and got my bearings—no GPS required, thanks to the years I'd spent driving the back roads of Minnesota in search of birds. In another ten minutes, I'd be at the Alberta Marsh State Wildlife Management Area, home of Gorder Lake, or Frog Lake, as it was known in the 1964 *Birding Almanac of Stevens County*. Because the area was filled with wetlands, ponds and old farm ditches, the lake was one of the best spots in the state for certain water birds like Western Grebes. With a little luck, maybe I'd be able to add another rarity to my day's count.

"Eat your heart out, Rick," I added, thinking of my laid-up buddy back in Savage. He'd been disappointed enough that he had to miss his chance at a Ferruginous Hawk for another year, but if I came home with a second score in the same day—make that a third, since I'd seen the Purple Sandpiper, too—he'd probably pull out his department-issued gun and shoot me.

Like he wasn't already in enough trouble with his boss for being a suspect in Sonny's murder.

I shook off the lingering frustration I felt after coming up to Spinit and finding nothing solid to help Rick out of his lousy situation. Gorder Lake was ahead of me, and it was time to focus on birds, not murder.

Although I hadn't seen it mentioned on the MOU list serve in the last week, the Alberta Marsh State WMA had become almost legendary over the years for the unusual birds that were sighted there, including Cinnamon Teal and Burrowing Owl. The most famous rare find in the area that I knew about, though, was the first Minnesota record of a Ruff. Almost fifty years ago, two birders from Duluth came to the spring meeting of the MOU at the university in Morris and went out birding, only to find the Ruff—it was originally called the Eurasian Ruff—in a slough on US 28 near Alberta. At the time, it was not only rare to see this international visitor inland, since it's typically only found on the U.S. coast, but the sighting was a national record for so far north inland.

Since then, Ruffs had made a few more random appearances in the state, but my chances of seeing one in October in Stevens County were about as good as the probability of Elvis making a comeback tour to Minneapolis, if you know what I mean: it wasn't going to happen in my lifetime.

Beyond that, I wouldn't know.

Geez, I'd never thought of that before. Do you get to go birding in heaven?

I'd have to start a new list.

I turned onto the road leading to Gorder Lake just as a Killdeer flew past the car. If it had had a brood this year it would have fledged months ago, so I wouldn't be seeing its classic decoy behavior if I surprised one in the field. According to a friend of mine who worked at a wildlife rehab center, Killdeers showed up in the center on a fairly regular basis, not because they're actually injured, but because they're such great actors. To protect its young from an approaching predator, an adult Killdeer flopped around as if it has a broken wing, attempting to draw the danger away from the nest. Unfortunately, the adult was so convincing, that people who saw the bird but don't know about its decoy act assumed the Killdeer needed help and captured it to bring it into a rehab center.

Of course, that left the babies in the nest alone and defenseless, which was exactly what the Killdeer didn't want. At some point in their future evolution, I assumed that Killdeers were going to have to rethink their deception/protection strategy, thanks to us kind-hearted, but ignorant, humans.

I parked the car and paused.

Thinking about the Killdeer had jostled an idea loose in my head.

The Killdeer acted as a decoy, and it deliberately attempted to draw attention away from its nest to keep its young hidden and undetected.

Just like Boo Metternick had attempted to divert attention away from himself and his past history as a circus performer, along with the question of the Bonecrusher's real identity.

Boo had fooled me on both counts. I never would have imagined him touring the country as the Strongest Man Alive, and he'd just about had me convinced that Savage's new art teacher Paul Brand was the Crusher. The ten dollars I bet Alan had already begun to sprout wings to fly right into his billfold.

Distraction and deception worked, and not just for the former film studio artists of the Allied forces during World War II.

So now I needed to ask myself: Was Sonny's killer using a similar strategy of misdirection to keep himself—or herself—safe from a murder rap?

I groaned.

Using that approach, I might as well start from scratch, since every person even remotely connected to Sonny's murder seemed to be pointing the finger at someone else for something. I figured Gina had picked the hemlock for the poisoned tea; Gina thought her brother Noah might be capable of murder; Noah said that Boo, "of all people" should know that he, Noah, could keep a secret (which secret, I still didn't know); Boo accused Noah of lying; and Vern and Tillie Metternick blamed Arlene Weebler for trying to dishonestly lock up a wind farm land lease by seducing Sonny Delite in the bed of her pink pickup.

If I thought back to Sunday morning at Millie's, I could name even more people blaming others: Alan noted that Sonny had made plenty of enemies in the utilities community; Prudence claimed that Red had painted a virtual target on Sonny; Rick's police buddies admitted he'd told them to arrest me; and Rick himself fingered Mr. Lenzen as the one who let the cat out of the bag about the new celebrity wrestler incognito on the Savage High School faculty.

I'd even gotten in on the name-blaming game, too: I blamed Rick for squealing on me to Mr. Lenzen every time I was involved in a murder case.

Obviously, we were all guilty of something.

Which also made it obvious that I needed more to distract myself from a certain birder's mysterious death than a short hour or so of looking for shorebirds at Gorder Lake.

What I needed was for someone to put a name to Sonny's killer, and the sooner that happened, the better.

Determined to shut it all out of my head, I grabbed my binoculars from under my seat and hopped out of the car. The sun was bright, the air clear, the water calm. In the distance, the prairie rolled west, studded with small groves of trees and more wetlands.

In front of me, the surface of the lake was dotted with ducks and geese. Northern Shovelers and Mallards dabbled along the shallows, while a handful of Redheads and a raft of Ruddy Ducks floated out in the deeper parts of the lake where they could dive for food. A large flock of Snow Geese dominated one side of the lake, and it was there that I trained my binos to see if I could pick out a Ross's Goose among them.

Not that a Ross's Goose would be a real find, since they're rare but regular in Minnesota, showing up sporadically in specific types of habitat, and often with a flock of Snow Geese. I just liked finding them since it was a test of my identification skills. To the untrained eye, a Ross's Goose looks almost exactly like a Snow Goose, except that the Ross's is slightly smaller. The real key to differentiating between the two is the bill: the larger goose's is a bit heavier and longer than the Ross's, and it sports a distinctive dark "grin" patch. Without that tell-tale clue, the Ross's Goose can easily pass for a Snow Goose, especially at a distance. I focused my binos and looked at the individual geese on the outer edges of the floating flock.

Bingo.

Dipping its slightly smaller head into the water with exactly the same motion of its larger companions, a Ross's Goose was idly paddling between two Snow Geese, its dull pink, stubby bill lacking a grin patch, a clear verification of what I suspected from its size. As I dropped my binos back to my chest, I caught a sparkling glint of reflection from back in the trees to my left.

I wasn't alone at Gorder Lake.

Chapter Twenty-Seven

I FROZE FOR ONLY A MOMENT BEFORE I felt a sharp pain in my right shoulder. Spinning around, I came face-to-face with . . .

"White."

Scary Stan, my birding archrival and barely articulate sometimes-friend.

"What did you shoot at my shoulder?" I asked him.

Stan had been a covert government agent in his earlier years, and now, along with his day job as an accountant, he occasionally field-tested hunting equipment. My sister, Lily, once referred to him as a grown man playing at being Robin Hood.

Maybe I would have called him that, too, if he wasn't holding a small tube in his fingers that looked very much like a dart launcher. I immediately clapped my hand over my shoulder where I'd felt the momentary sting.

"You are going to tell me it wasn't a poison dart, aren't you?"

"If you say so," he replied in his usual limited conversational mode.

"I'll take that as a 'yes,' but if I go into convulsions and die," I tried to think of the worst possible thing I could threaten him with, "you're going to have to answer to Lily."

Stan blanched. He'd had a very short-lived relationship with my sister before she was married, but it had been long enough for him to learn that nobody crossed Lily White and survived—intact—to tell the tale.

"You won't die," he said. "Yet."

"Thank you very much, Stan. I appreciate the clarification." I pointed to the gadget in his hand. "What is that?"

"If I tell you—"

"I know, I know," I interrupted him. "You'll have to kill me. Got it. Now tell me what it is."

Stan's mouth twitched. That was his smile. As usual, his eyes were masked by dark reflective sunglasses, so I had to gauge his emotional responses from the millimeter movement of the corner of his upper lip. He was a laugh a minute at parties, I had no doubt.

"Dart gun," Stan informed me. "Uses shellfish toxin. Lethal."

"This is for hunting?" I asked in disbelief. "Hunting for what? Rabid squirrels?"

I realized he'd said "lethal" and totally forgot what I was saying.

Stan's upper lip twitched again. "Bigger game, White. Animal control for parks. And I didn't shoot you, either. Threw a little rock. Catch your attention."

I glared into his sunglasses and changed the subject. "You saw the Ross's Goose, didn't you?"

He nodded.

"I got a Ferruginous Hawk and a Purple Sandpiper today, too," I casually noted.

He inclined his head a fraction of an inch. I could tell he was massively impressed.

My eyes traveled to the dart gun in his hand. "Shellfish toxin?"

"Yes."

"Lethal."

"Yes."

I suddenly wondered how much Stan knew about poisons.

"Would hemlock tea give someone convulsions?" I asked him.

"You're talking about Sonny," he said. "I birded with him, too, White."

"Stan, how quickly would hemlock tea give someone convulsions?"

He stood silently, motionless.

"Fifteen minutes," he answered.

"So Sonny could have walked into the woods by himself before he knew anything was wrong."

Stan nodded.

"And that means his killer didn't have to carry him there," I pointed out.

I paused a few seconds while I tried to put together a sequence of events. In the distance, a flock of Canada Geese flew in formation.

"He could have taken the poisoned tea from his killer, tossed the cup after drinking it, and walked for fifteen minutes before he had his first seizure."

"Possible."

"He would have stumbled off the path, convulsed, lost consciousness."

I glanced at Stan, but he made no response.

"He'd lay where he fell, his limbs contorted from the seizure," I said.

I looked back at the shining lake, but my eyes were seeing a dead Sonny Delite sprawled against a tree amidst a pile of russet leaves, with a murder of crows perched above him. "He'd look like a scarecrow set against a tree."

"Where'd he get the tea?" Stan asked, his monotone sounding grimmer than usual.

My gaze sought out the Ross's Goose, and I lifted my binos to my eyes to catch it in the lens. Like Sonny's killer, the small goose practiced deception as a survival strategy: slip into the crowd and no one could single you out. You'd be safe as long as you acted like everyone else.

So who, among the cast of my own suspects, had most faded into the background?

Certainly not Noah or Boo—their size alone precluded them from ever becoming anybody's wallpaper. You've have to be blindfolded to not notice them in a crowd. Besides, they were both so attached to Gina, I couldn't see either one of them jeopardizing that relationship with a murder rap.

Arlene Weebler, on the other hand, didn't seem to give a rip about what anyone thought of her. Judging from her behavior today, she could give in-your-face lessons to my most talented discipline problem students back at Savage. Now that I thought about it, I also couldn't imagine she would forego the chance to mercilessly harass Sonny with blackmail by hiring some thugs to do the deed for her. Even a loose cannon needs a target.

Which left Gina and Red and Prudence.

Could I share Rick's trust in Gina, or was there a lot more to his new girlfriend than even he realized?

Can you say "duct tape"?

As for Red and Prudence, I tried again to recall every detail from Sunday morning in Millie's Deli. Red had been extremely protective of Prudence, and told me that her friend didn't handle stress well. She'd reminded Sonny's widow to take one step at a time to get through the crisis, and I'd thought that Red would have made a good counselor.

Crisis.

Red sounded like she was doing crisis counseling.

And the reason for that would be . . .

"I think I have an idea," I finally answered Stan, "But I've got one last question I need answered, and I know just who to ask."

I lowered my binos. "I've got to get back to Savage."

"Wait."

I looked back at Stan, but he was pointing toward the lake.

I followed the direction of his finger and spotted a stocky duck with an especially sloped profile. I captured it in my binoculars and studied it carefully. Its bill tapered into a hard shield that stretched almost up to its eyes, and its black cap contrasted starkly with its white back.

"Common Eider?" Stan asked.

I blinked a few times to be sure I was really seeing what I thought I saw. To my knowledge, only four of the sea ducks had ever been recorded in Minnesota, and three of those were in the northern third of the state. A native of Arctic waters, the Common Eider preferred the company of its own kind, and hardly ever traveled alone inland from the frozen coasts of Alaska or the northeastern edges of North America.

A Common Eider didn't belong in the Alberta Marsh.

But there it was.

"Yes, Stan," I finally confirmed. "It is, indeed."

I watched the eider for a few more moments as it floated along with the other ducks and geese in the lake, occasionally diving and coming up shortly thereafter.

"Poor thing," I commiserated. "You probably thought you knew exactly where you were headed, but something went wrong, a fluke of nature, and here you are, swimming in uncharted waters."

And just like that, I knew for sure who had killed Sonny Delite . . . and why.

"Holy crap," I breathed.

"Post it," Stan said.

"What?" I looked at him in confusion, the story behind Sonny's murder finally coming together in my head.

"The bird," he said, pulling my attention back to the eider.

"Oh, right." I fumbled in my jacket pocket for my phone.

"No one is going to believe that you and I were birding together," I said, beginning to text a message to the MOU list serve, "let alone that we found a Common Eider."

I turned to Stan, but he had already vanished.

As usual.

I finished sending the post and walked back to the car. A Killdeer skittered across the parking area and out into the prairie beyond.

"Can't fool me," I told the bird. "I'm on to you."

I pulled out of Alberta Marsh and headed home, reviewing my finds for the day. I'd made positive IDs of a Purple Sandpiper, a Ferruginous Hawk, a Common Eider . . . and a killer.

Not bad for a day off from work.

Before I made my turn onto Highway 12 east, I stopped on the road shoulder and called Rick.

"I need to talk to Gina," I told him. "Can you give me her phone number?"

"She's right here," he replied. "You want to speak with her?"

"Not right now," I said. Over the phone was not the way I wanted to do this. I needed to see her reaction when we talked. I now knew that Gina could avoid the truth, but I doubted that her body language was capable of it.

"How about I just stop at your place when I get back to Savage?" I asked.

"Sounds great, Bob," Rick said. "We'll be waiting. Hey, did you get the hawk?"

"I did," I said.

But I didn't tell him what else I'd discovered.

He would be finding out soon enough.

CHAPTER TWENTY-EIGHT

THE SMELL OF BURGERS ON THE GRILL wafted over me as soon as I stepped out of my SUV in Rick's driveway. I walked up to the door through a mat of wind-blown leaves that crunched under my feet with each step. Posed on a wooden chair beside the door was a life-size plastic skeleton, with one bony hand wrapped around an empty beer can and a sign looped over its ribcage that read "Let the Party Begin."

Shoot. I'd been so absorbed by puzzling out Sonny's death that I still hadn't settled on a costume for the faculty party next weekend.

Thankfully, that particular preoccupation was about to come to a screeching end, though, which meant I could apply my problem-solving skills to something much more enjoyable than contemplating motives for murder.

I reached for the door buzzer, and the perfect costume idea popped into my head.

At the same moment, Rick's front door opened, and I looked down into the pretty face of Gina Knorsen.

"I know what you did," I told her.

Her eyes narrowed. "Really. Who told you?"

"No one," I assured her. "I figured it out myself. Can I come in?"

She stepped aside and Rick's voice carried into the house from his back porch.

"All right, Bob. Get out here and tell me what I missed today in Morris."

"You have no idea," I muttered to myself.

I motioned for Gina to precede me through the house out to where Rick was sitting on an outdoor lounger, his ankle wrapped in a blue cloth brace and propped up on the foot of the lounger. Four hamburgers sizzled on his gas grill, and laid out on the small patio table were an assortment of condiments, hamburger buns, a bowl of potato salad, and a pan of homemade brownies.

"Let me guess," I greeted him, eyeing the picnic spread. "Instead of sucking it up and dragging your bum leg along with me for the six-hour round trip drive to Stevens, you spent the day being miserable, but pampered, by . . ." I shot an accusatory stare at Gina, "Savage High's very own Family and Consumer Science instructor."

"Absolutely not," Rick insisted. "Believe me, I was not miserable for even a second. And I did help stir the brownies, I'll have you know."

Gina offered me a cold can of beer from the cooler on the porch, but I turned it down.

"I'm not going to be here that long," I told her. "Luce is waiting for me."

"So tell me what you found," Rick said, taking a drink from his own beer can.

Gina perched on the edge of the lounger near Rick's foot.

"Wait a minute," I said, the word "perch" triggering another realization in my head. I looked at Gina. "You're the one who told Boo that Rick and I were going to Morris. He said a little bird had told him, and I'd assumed it was Rick, since they were such good buddies."

Gina looked at Rick, then back at me.

"Rick told me about the birding trip when he asked me to go dancing. Was I not supposed to tell anyone?" Gina asked, confusion in her voice. "Boo said he was thinking of going home to see his dad, and I mentioned that I knew that Rick and you were planning to go up there birding."

"No," I replied. "It wasn't any big secret or anything. I just realized it was one more wrong assumption I made in the last few days."

"Like the one that Boo and I were such good buddies?" Rick asked.

He turned to Gina.

"Boo's a great guy, really," he said. "I'm just not that comfortable around him, now. You know—since we've started seeing each other."

"But we've been over this, Rick," Gina gently reminded him. "I'm not in love with him. I was a high school senior when he asked me to marry him, and I said 'no.' Noah is the only other person who knows about it. Boo's just overprotective of me, that's all. We practically grew up together."

Whoa. News to me, that was for sure.

When Boo had admitted his feelings for Gina on the way to Spinit, he'd neglected to include that little detail. No wonder he tackled Noah as soon as he saw him. Not only did Boo hate liars, but he thought Noah had killed Sonny and lied to the woman he loved about it.

Thanks to me, that is.

What was that—wrong assumption #24 of the week? Something like that, I was sure.

But it also reminded me of the real reason I'd stopped at Rick's place. I needed to ask Gina a rather personal question.

"Speaking of being overprotective," I eased into the conversation, "I met your brother Noah today, Gina."

Fine lines of tension formed around her mouth, and I saw the pupils in her eyes dilate.

She shifted slightly on the lounger, and I noticed her fingers curling into fists in her lap.

Ah, yes. Good old body language. Where would a counselor be without it?

Especially when you wanted the truth . . . for a change.

"He kind of reminded me of me," I continued. "I think we have the same opinions of our big sisters."

"How so?" Rick asked. "I've known Lily almost as long as I've known you, Bob, and she adores you. She may not always show it," he added, "but underneath all that bossiness and your bruised shins, all she wants is for you to be happy."

He turned to Gina.

"Do you kick your brother's shins?" he asked her.

"She wants her brother to be happy," I answered for her. "So much so, that sometimes Noah feels a little stifled by her protectiveness." I looked at Gina. "He's a big boy, Gina. You need to give him some space. That's really why he went back to Spinit, isn't it?"

Gina's smile was tight. "He's my only sibling. My mom died when we were kids. I've always felt that Noah was my responsibility, and I needed to be there for him."

I remembered Sara Schiller's complaint about Gina's class unit on nurturing families and responsibility.

"But did you feel his happiness was so much your responsibility that you would leave the job you loved just to get him relocated to another town for better job opportunities?"

I could see the awareness growing in Gina's eyes as she figured out where I was going with this.

I wanted the truth about her time in Henderson.

About her time with Sonny, and what happened afterwards.

"What are you driving at, Bob?" Rick asked, suspicion mounting in his own voice. "Gina didn't have a choice if she wanted to help Noah. Henderson is tiny. They had to move where he could find work."

"They had to move," I informed him, "because Gina couldn't face teaching about the importance of family relationships in a small town where she'd been involved with a married man—albeit unknowingly—and whose wife then tried to kill herself when she found out about it."

Rick's mouth opened and closed.

Twice.

He hadn't known, just as I hadn't. It had taken me all week to remember the comment that Rick's policeman friend had made about being concerned about Prudence hurting herself.

Prudence was suicidal. Red had known it, too—that was why she was so concerned for Prudence on Sunday morning.

"I felt so awful," Gina said softly. "I felt bad enough, believe me, when I found out that Sonny was married, but when I heard about his wife . . ."

She covered her face with her hands and took some deep breaths. After a moment, she put her hands back in her lap and looked at me.

"I couldn't teach there anymore. I needed a fresh start, so I moved us here, which really was better for Noah, employment-wise." She turned to Rick. "Noah and Boo were the only ones I ever told about the guilt I felt—and still feel—for Mrs. Delite's attempt at suicide. I didn't think you needed to know about it, yet," she confessed.

Rick reached over and covered one of her hands with his own. "I'm so sorry, Gina."

He looked up at me, a touch of anger beginning to color his cheeks. "And the reason you're bringing this up?" he asked.

"Because now we know who killed Sonny," I said. "Nobody. He made a fatal mistake. Sonny took—and drank—the wrong cup of tea."

Rick gave me a blank look, but Gina gasped, her hand covering her lips in bleak certainty.

"She did it again," she whispered. "She tried to kill herself. With poisoned tea."

I nodded. "She found out that Sonny was having another affair. My guess is that she'd planned her suicide for the last day of the Arboretum's conference, so that Sonny wouldn't have to miss any of it because of her."

Gina's eyes went wide. "She didn't want to inconvenience the man who'd cheated on her?"

I shrugged. "I could give you a library of literature to read on the psychology of addiction, unhealthy dependence behaviors, and suicide, but let's just say she has some very serious issues, and leave it at that."

"But how did he get the hemlock?"

I looked at Rick, who had pulled out his cell phone.

"You going to call the detective in charge?" I asked.

"Yeah," he said. "He needs to hear this. So how did Sonny get the tea?" he asked again.

"This is all guesswork, Stud, don't forget," I cautioned him, fully aware that I'd already made one wrong accusation today.

Make that "painfully" aware. The ache in my arm where I'd landed in Boo's front yard was spreading into my shoulder.

"So guess away," Rick instructed me.

"I think Prudence had the hemlock with her to do the deed as she had planned, and was making their usual morning tea one last time in their hotel room. Sonny said he had to go early to fit in some birding, and he took the wrong cup with him."

"He was hoping to meet Gina," Rick surmised. "He was hoping she got the phone message and would show up at Duck Lake Pond."

I shrugged again. "Whatever the reason, Sonny left the hotel with his wife's poisoned tea. It's just a five-minute drive to the Arb from where they were staying, so the poison wouldn't kick in until after he'd parked and started walking."

Rick tapped in a number and talked with someone on the other end of the connection.

Gina looked pale.

"It's not your fault, Gina," I said. "It was a series of terrible mistakes, all made by Sonny."

She took another deep breath. "If you're right, why hasn't Prudence Delite come forward and confessed to the police? It's the right thing to do, Bob."

"Of course it is," I agreed. "But like I said, Prudence has issues. I'm not sure she can function on her own, to be honest with you. When I saw her earlier today at Millie's Deli, it was like she's attached herself to Red, as if she was incapable of making any decisions for herself. My guess is that she hasn't told Red yet, because she's waiting for her memory lapses to clear before she can ask her what to do. Or maybe Prudence did tell Red about it when they were finally alone on Sunday, going down the stairs at Millie's, and it caught Red so much by surprise, she tripped and fell down the stairs. Who knows?"

The smell of cooked burgers grew suddenly stronger, and I pointed to the grill on the porch. "You two better eat before all that's left is charcoal."

Gina got up and moved the burgers to a platter on the table, while Rick finished his call and returned his phone to his pocket.

"They're going to bring Prudence Delite in for some serious conversation," he reported. He stuck his hand out and smiled. "Thanks, buddy. This should go a long way to getting me off the suspect list. I owe you one."

I shook his hand and nodded.

"Take care of the ankle," I told him. "Are you going to be out of that brace in time for the big Halloween party?"

"I hope so," he said. "I owe Gina some dancing."

"You could be Fred Astaire," I suggested. I looked at Gina, who had returned to her perch near Rick.

"And you could be Ginger Rogers," I winked at her. "I bet you know all about fancy footwork, don't you . . . Crusher?"

CHAPTER TWENTY-NINE

I STUCK THE UNLIT PIPE BACK into my mouth and sat back on the leather sectional that stretched across Alan and Lily's living room. From the kitchen, I could hear laughter and the voices of several faculty members as they helped themselves to the Halloween party buffet set out on the kitchen island. Beside me, Luce held Baby Lou, dressed in an Incredibles sleeper, on her lap, alternately raising and lowering her own costume's English bowler hat over her eyes, playing peek-a-boo with our niece.

"Ah, you're teaching her to solve mysteries already, my dear Watson," I told my wife in my worst English accent. I gave Baby Lou's tummy a nudge with my pipe. Her little eyes went wide with surprise.

"Sherlock!" Rick said, calling to me from the front door, where he and Gina had just arrived.

"Old chap!" I called back, waving my pipe in the air.

I whistled as they approached. Rick's slicked-back hair and black tux made a perfect contrast with Gina's—or should I say Ginger's?—ball gown of ruffled layers of yellow chiffon as they practically glided over to us.

"You two could have stepped right out of *Top Hat*," Luce said. "I love the dress, Gina. It's gorgeous."

Gina laughed. "I feel like a fire hazard with all this material floating around me. I hope there's no fondue on the buffet—I might spontaneously combust if I get too close to a flame. I assume Alan and Lily have a fire extinguisher in their kitchen."

Rick dropped a light kiss on Gina's temple. "She's already made me replace my smoke alarm batteries," he told us. "I'm beginning to think she has a future as a fire marshal."

"Just being safety-conscious," she pointed out and smiled at Baby Lou.

"She does teach our child development class," I reminded Rick, "and she's doing a fantastic job of it, by the way. Even Sara Schiller said so this week."

"She is really coming around, Bob," Gina said, looping her hand through Rick's elbow. "She didn't miss a single class this week, and she told me all about the war memorabilia show she attended with Mr. and Mrs. Metternick last Saturday. I'm beginning to think she just needed a strong mentor in her life to turn her behavior around."

I was rapidly coming to the same conclusion about my favorite truant, or, as of this week at least, my favorite former truant. In the ten days since she'd met Vern Metternick and learned to shoot off a bazooka, Sara had cleaned up both her class-skipping and bad attitude act. She still wasn't crazy about her art class, but at least she was showing up for it.

"Speaking of behavior," Rick said, "it looks like Prudence Delight is cooperating fully with the police, now. She's got a lawyer and a mental health counselor working with her. I think they'll work out some kind of plea bargain for her since it really was an accident."

"I heard on the news that the police finally located a witness at a gas station where Sonny stopped for gas before heading to the Arboretum that morning," Luce said, bouncing Baby Lou on her lap.

Rick nodded, straightening the white carnation in his tux's lapel. "It was the cashier at the gas station," he reported. "While he was ringing up Sonny's gas purchase, he saw Sonny take a sip from a paper cup with a hotel logo on it. The reason he remembered was because he saw Sonny make a face like he'd just burned his mouth on whatever it was he was drinking."

I reached over and took Baby Lou from Luce, tucking her warm weight against my chest. I looked at the capital letter "I" emblazoned on her little sleeper. Alan had done well in choosing his daughter's first Halloween costume: she really was incredible.

And now that she was a part of our lives, I couldn't imagine life without her.

"I'll take her."

I looked up to see my brother-in-law in a red leotard with the same "I" on his chest as the one on Baby Lou's.

"It's somebody's bedtime," he said, lifting my niece up and against his shoulder. He turned to greet the new arrivals. "Hey, Gina, you look great. What are you doing with Savage's worst?"

Rick clasped his hand around Gina's and tugged slightly on his white bow tie.

"Since I am too much of a gentleman tonight to respond to that insult in the company of these lovely ladies," Rick announced, "I will instead see you on the basketball court, very soon, and I will repay you for your words then."

"I will crush you," Alan promised him.

"In your dreams, Mr. Incredible." Rick nodded at Alan's shoulder. "There's drool on your suit, big guy. And, by the way," he said, turning back to me. "I think we identified your tire slasher, Bob. We finally got a good image from the security camera in the high school parking lot. Does the name Greg Bernson ring a bell?"

I groaned. Greg Bernson was already my number one pick for delinquent of the year, with more hours logged sitting in my office this fall than even Sara Schiller, prior to her turn-around, that is. Less than six days into the new school year, Rick had predicted that Greg wasn't going to make it three weeks before he became a regular in detention hall, and unless my memory failed me, I'd just renewed Greg's detention pass the day before my tires were slashed.

"Can you spell 'suspension'?" Rick asked me.

A chorus of laughter rang out from the front hallway.

"Who's here?" Alan asked, rubbing his daughter's back, her eyes already closing.

A lean, muscular man, clad in a head-to-toe leotard, stepped into the living room. He struck a wrestling pose I recognized from the internet photos Alan and I had looked at weeks ago.

"Hey, Alan! What do you think?" Paul Brand's voice carried across the room.

"I knew it!" Alan said, throwing me a grin. "You owe me ten, White-man."

"Do I?" I asked, pointing at another party-goer who had followed Paul into the room.

It was another, slightly larger, Bonecrusher.

"I'm the man," Boo said as he peeled his mask off.

Though he still looked huge, I had to admit that the black was slimming on him. From a distance, the two men could almost be identical.

I looked at Alan's face for his reaction. His eyes jumped from one Crusher to the other and back again. Paul pulled off his face mask, and he and Boo circled each other while other faculty members cheered them on.

"It's not either one of them, is it?" Alan asked me. "If the Bonecrusher wants to keep his secret identity secret, he's sure not going to show up at a Halloween party in his old work clothes."

"You wouldn't think so," I agreed, putting my arm around my wife and pulling her close. "What do you think, Dr. Watson?" I asked her.

Luce threw a smile at Rick and Gina. "I think the mystery remains a mystery, Sherlock."

"So much for your skill with clues, White-man," Alan groused. "I think you better stick to birding."

I grinned and tipped my Sherlock Holmes hat.

"With pleasure, old boy. With pleasure."

Bob White's
A Murder of Crows
Bird List

Canada Goose
Wild Turkey
Green Heron
American Crow
American Goldfinch
Red-winged Blackbirds
Downy Woodpecker
Bluejays
Sanderling
Purple Sandpiper
Red Phalarope
Merlin
Red-tailed Hawk
Ferruginous Hawk
Tundra Swan
Killdeer
Northern Shoveler
Mallard
Redhead
Ruddy Duck
Snow Goose
Common Eider

ACKNOWLEDGEMENTS

As ALWAYS, I AM GRATEFUL to many people for their kind assistance in helping me out with the details that make my stories real. My brother-in-law took time out of his busy schedule to track down some facts and figures for me regarding wind farm leases, and Dean Beck of the Minnesota Department of Natural Resources verified that the Frog Lake named in the 1964 Birding Almanac of Stevens County is today's Gorder Lake. The controversy about the power line project through the LeSeur/Henderson Recovery Zone is well documented and was my initial inspiration for this story; I want to thank Delores Hagen for her enduring commitment to the birds of the Minnesota River Valley. Once again, I am indebted to my son Bob, who continues to have enormous patience with his mother's requests for his birding expertise, and to my husband Tom and daughter Colleen for their endless support and witty repartee that makes me think they should be writing the Birder Murders, and not me.

My enjoyment of the Minnesota Landscape Arboretum has spanned decades, and even though I think the annual scarecrow display is pretty creepy, I couldn't resist using it as the setting for a murder. Finally, I want to salute the real Chef Tom, Red, and everyone at Millie's Deli for the wonderful meals my family enjoyed there over the years. You are sorely missed!